WE BELONG TOGETHER

ERIKA KELLY

WE BELONG TOGETHER
Erika Kelly

ISBN-13: 9781677316656

Cover designed by Novak Illustration

Formatting by Serendipity Formatting

This book is dedicated to the incredibly supportive and generous romance writing community, a finer group of people I've never met.

Praise for The Calamity Falls series

KEEP ON LOVING YOU

"I adored this book! It is exactly what I love in a second-chance romance. The characters are so vibrant and real, I was rooting for them with every page." —*USA Today* Bestseller Devney Perry

"*KEEP ON LOVING YOU* is such a fun and sexy second-chance romance that I didn't want it to end. Their connection is a swoony blend of tender first love and sizzling heat, and Erika Kelly delivers a highly entertaining and sigh-worthy romance that shouldn't be missed."
—Mary Dube, USA Today

WE BELONG TOGETHER

"I loved every sweet, heart-wrenching, crazy, mixed-up minute of this book. It was an emotional journey from the first chapter to the last. This is Erika Kelly at her best, and this is a not-to-be-missed book!" —Sharon Slick Reads, Guilty Pleasures Book Reviews

"Erika Kelly damn near pulled my heart from my chest with Delilah and Will's story. It's so well-written that you feel everything. My heart got tugged so hard! I honestly cried at a few moments in the book. I fell all the way in love with "Wooby." It's hard not to, really." —Ree Cee's Books

THE VERY THOUGHT OF YOU

"Wow, THE VERY THOUGHT OF YOU was simply OUTSTANDING! This second chance, friends to lovers romance is enchanting and entertaining." —Spellbound Stories

"I just finished this story, and I want to start all over again. Or maybe at the start of series. To once again feel the events, the emotions, that brought these amazing characters together. To hear the banter and the arguments, the sorrow, the loss and the happiness that brought a family together and closer." —Nerdy, Dirty, and Flirty

JUST THE WAY YOU ARE

"An alpha cowboy and a smart, sassy princess collide in JUST THE WAY YOU ARE in Erika Kelly's latest, and it was fabulous! I was cheering for Brodie and Rosalina with every page. If you love stories with heart, steam, and plenty of swoon, don't miss this one!" —USA Today Bestselling Author J.H. Croix

"With the Calamity Falls series, Kelly doesn't shy away from charming. She captivates with delectable characters that wrap themselves around a heart. From the first hello to the final goodbye, Rosalina and Brodie are a match made out of the unpredictable, but the sweetest kind of heaven. JUST THE WAY YOU ARE is the perfect example of why I am hooked on this series. SWOONWORTHY READ!" —Hopeless Romantic Book Reviews

IT WAS ALWAYS YOU

"This book was full of every emotion you could ever feel. Gigi and Cassian proved you can conquer anything with true love." —Cat's Guilty Pleasure

"I could not put this book down! Erika Kelly always delivers a great love story and never disappoints! I recommend this book for romance lovers looking to get lost in a great love story." —Reading in Pajamas

CAN'T HELP FALLING IN LOVE

"I love everything about this emotional and sexy, second chance story. Erika Kelly writes a story that makes me feel like I'm right there with the two main characters, Beckett and Coco. It is a slow burn, passionate story with lots of underlying tension. I not only enjoyed this story, but I found it impossible to put down." —Cocktails and Books

"I loved everything about this book. I loved all the characters, from Beckett, 'I don't believe in love,' to single mom, small business-owning, closed-off Coco, to a fairy-believing five-year-old who will steal your heart! I cannot gush enough about how spectacular I thought this book was." – Bookcase and Coffee

WHOLE LOTTA LOVE

"BRILLIANT! This book was incredible, I could not put this book down, that is how good Lu and Xander's story was. I fell in love with these two characters instantly." – Harlequin Junkie

"Whole Lotta Love was absolutely perfect! You will instantly love this couple and their journey to find happiness!" – Just Love Books

YOU'RE STILL THE ONE

"Griffin and Stella really are soulmates. They bring out the best of each other, and when they're together, everything is better. Their world is better with the love they feel for each other. And I think they made my world better a bit, too." – Jersey Girl's Bookshelf

"WOW! WOW! WOW! Welcome to all the feels! I ADORED Stella and Griffin's story. I was completely lost in this book and didn't want to put it down. I FELT everything, and I can't tell you how much I loved it." – Books According to Abby

Titles by Erika Kelly

The Calamity Falls series

KEEP ON LOVING YOU

WE BELONG TOGETHER

THE VERY THOUGHT OF YOU

JUST THE WAY YOU ARE

IT WAS ALWAYS YOU

CAN'T HELP FALLING IN LOVE

COME AWAY WITH ME

WHOLE LOTTA LOVE

YOU'RE STILL THE ONE

THE DEEPER I FALL

LOVE ME LIKE YOU DO

Rock Star Romance series

YOU REALLY GOT ME

I WANT YOU TO WANT ME

TAKE ME HOME TONIGHT

MORE THAN A FEELING

Wild Love series

MINE FOR NOW

MINE FOR THE WEEK

Sign up for my newsletter to read the EXCLUSIVE novella for my readers only! You'll get two chapters a month of this super sexy, fun romance! #rockstarromance #teenidolturnedboyfriend Also, get PLANES, TRAINS, AND HEAD OVER HEELS for FREE! I hope you'll come hang out with me on Facebook, Twitter, Instagram, Goodreads, and Pinterest or in my private reader group.

Acknowledgments

- To Superman, the best man I know.
- To Olivia, for taking that first, awful look every single time—and still coming back for more.
- To KP, my guiding light.
- To Sharon, for your friendship and endless support.
- To Kristy DeBoer: one simple conversation swerved this book in the right direction. Thank you for being there right when I needed you.
- To Abbi Nyberg and Brock Butterfield: your help on this series is invaluable. Any mistakes are either creative license or my bad.
- It takes a village, and here's mine: Jamie Beck, Stephanie Wayman, KP Simmons, Amy DeLuca, Carrie Padgett, and Sharon Pochron. Thank you for making my blurb!
- To Erica, for your patience and generosity. You were there for me when I needed you on this one.
- To the romance writing community: I couldn't do this without the bloggers and reviewers like TotallyBooked Blog, Obsessed with Romance, Krista's Dust Jacket, Guilty Pleasures Book Reviews, About That Story, Reading in

Pajamas, Zoe Forward, Shirin's Book Blog and Reviews, Reads and Reviews, Rabid Readers, and Isha Coleman—to name just a few; and my friends in writer groups like the Dreamweavers, The DND Authors, and CTRWA.

Chapter One

Under the bright blue umbrella on the patio table, the little girl bounced a huge stuffed chicken in her lap. Her tumble of brown curls fluttered in the soft June breeze. Beside her, Marcella, their long-time house manager, read something on the screen of her laptop while talking on her cell phone…

…ordering a *stroller.*

Will Bowie couldn't wrap his head around it. That kid? That two-year-old? She might be theirs.

She *was* theirs. *Look at her.* A shaft of sunlight gleamed on her hair, revealing bronze and gold strands tangled among the brown—exactly like Will and his brothers. And those blue eyes?

They're mine.

But she wasn't his. He knew that for sure. So, whose was she?

In a few minutes, their lawyer would walk in the door with the birth certificate they'd subpoenaed from the hospital. But it wouldn't matter what name was on that document—all their lives would change.

Because they'd handle it as a family. The four of them would raise her together.

"It's not complicated." From her throne on the leather club chair, his mom sounded exasperated. "Which one of you slept with Christy Leigh?"

Their mother had flown out to Calamity for the opening of his brother's resort. As luck would have it, she'd also gotten hit with the whammy of finding out she was a grandmother. *Maybe.*

Probably.

Had it been a boy, she wouldn't have cared. She'd only kept popping out babies in the hopes of scoring a girl. She'd washed her hands of the whole mess after the fourth son.

She wouldn't stay involved, though. The type of mother who could walk out on her own children—ages six, seven, nine, and eleven—wouldn't hang around to raise this feisty little girl. He'd give his mom a week before she hightailed it back to Manhattan.

"Well, it obviously wasn't me." His youngest brother, Fin, had only ever been with one woman—his childhood sweetheart.

"Obviously." Brodie laughed.

"But, seriously, man," Gray said. "You've never been the least bit curious what it'd be like with someone else?"

"No." Fin's response was so immediate, so frank, that everyone stared at him.

Anyway, that left the three of them.

Two. Will had never slept with Christy Leigh.

"Well, I don't even know who she is," Gray said.

"You say that like it eliminates you." Brodie, the brother closest in age to Will, grinned.

Gray seemed the most likely to have fathered a kid he

didn't know about. He led a nomadic life, chasing the biggest waves and fiercest snow storms. With his easy-going nature, he found fun everywhere he landed.

"You make an excellent point." Gray gave him a lazy look. "Nevertheless, the kid's twenty-seven months, which means she was conceived exactly three years ago. I'm in Bali every June, big brother. I couldn't have knocked Christy up."

The attention turned to the last remaining brother.

"Don't look at me." Brodie raised both hands. "I live in Utah."

All three brothers gave him a look that said, *So?* Brodie spent more time at home in Wyoming than in his office. In fact, he'd spent the past year turning the ghost town on their property into a high-end resort that opened to the public next week. So, yeah, he'd spent a lot of time in Calamity.

"She doesn't have to be one of ours." Fin pointed out the obvious. "The baby book says she's a Bowie, but there are other Bowies out there."

"In Calamity, there's only us and Uncle Lachlan." Brodie shook his head. "And there's no way Ruby's mom slept with an old man rocking a pompadour."

Two days ago, right in the middle of Fin's twenty-fourth birthday party, a woman had shown up at the house with Ruby Leigh in tow. Apparently, the little girl's mom had left her with a babysitter for a long weekend in Big Sky and never come home.

Brutal car accident on the Gallatin Road. *Damn.*

Thanks to Wyoming's Kinship Placement program, they'd allowed Ruby to stay with the only babysitter she'd ever known until they found a forever home for her. But when the sitter had gone to Ruby's house to pick up some clothes and toys, she'd found a baby book.

So, they knew everything about her firsts—first smile, first time she'd rolled over, and the first time she'd walked —and they knew a Bowie had fathered her.

They just didn't know which one.

In a rustle of fabric, their mom shot off the chair. "Stop playing around." She looked like she was waiting for them to feel chastised. When it didn't happen, she clamped her lips together and tipped her head back. "This stupid sense of loyalty your father drummed into you." She let out a frustrated breath and said, "You know she's Will's." She flicked a hand in the vicinity of the backyard. "She's a carbon copy of him."

The way she looked at him—with such disdain—sliced the skin of an old scar. But trying to prove himself to her was a waste of time, so he focused on his brothers. "We're not going to know anything until we get the birth certificate." Which would happen any minute. "So there's no point in speculating. The only thing we do know is, if she's one of ours, we're going to take care of her. As a family. So the important conversation is *how* we're going to do it."

"Her *father* will be responsible for her." Her gaze bore into him with a message that demanded he meet his responsibilities.

Jesus, would she ever see him as anything other than the reckless kid she'd left behind? "I know that. My point is, whoever's her father, we're all going to help. We're her family."

"Dude." Gray held out his arm. All four brothers reached in and bumped fists.

"I think that's a lovely sentiment, and exactly what

your father would expect of you, but someone's got to be the voice of reason here. And the fact is none of you has any idea what it's like to raise a child."

To his brothers' credit, no one said the obvious, *And you do?* Because she wasn't the point. "We'll learn."

"On the fly," Brodie said. "Like every other parent."

Their mom folded her arms across her stomach. "Most parents don't have your lifestyles, which in no way suit raising a child."

"Our lifestyles will change," Fin said.

"Don't get me wrong," their mom said. "I think it's lovely that you want to take care of her, but she's not even two and a half. She's young enough that she won't remember her mother. She can assimilate quite seamlessly into a new family. Maybe the best choice is to give her that. A mother, a father, siblings. She needs the kind of dedication and care that four single men simply can't give her."

His mom had never been good at reading body language, so she probably didn't notice how all the men's postures went rigid, their features hard. Will spoke for all of them. "I'm going to pretend you didn't suggest we give our niece up for adoption."

"I'm sorry." But, of course, she sounded more belligerent than apologetic. She pointed to Gray. "Aren't you heading off to Bali for a surfing competition that will lead you to God knows what adventure next? You probably won't even be home until September." She lifted a chin toward Brodie. "You're missing the opening of your own resort to spend the summer in Asia."

She made it sound like Brodie was screwing off, but he'd finally realized his dream of making the Olympic terrain park design team at his firm, and construction for next Winter Games began this summer. He couldn't miss that opportunity.

Her hand flicked toward Fin. "And he's heading off to Europe for the summer with his girlfriend."

"Fiancée," Fin said.

"And while *you* might be home this summer…" Will's mom looked at him like he was a registered sex offender. "You've just come back from six months of competitions all over the world. None of you is in any position to raise that little girl." Still not reading their body language, she said, "None of you is ready to be a *father*."

It struck him how different this conversation would be going if their dad had been alive.

Not a day went by—a little more than two years since his death—that something didn't trigger a memory, giving Will a slam of grief that buckled his knees and knocked the air out of his lungs.

And the idea that Mack Bowie wouldn't meet his granddaughter—*dammit.* He turned away, sorrow crashing over him. That little girl would miss out on getting to know her grandpa, and that was a damn shame. Their dad was the best man Will had ever known. He'd know just how to raise this kid.

If she's ours.

Is she?

But his dad *wasn't* here, so Will had to handle it. He turned back to his mom. "I'm going to say this one more time, and that'll be the last we ever speak of it. If the paternity test shows she's our blood, we're going to raise her. If you can't handle that, then you'll need to leave, because there will be no discussion whatsoever of adoption or sending her away."

Remembering the ultimatum she'd given his dad, *You*

either send Will to boarding school, or I'm leaving, Will's determination doubled down. "That little girl will never be exposed to any idea other than the fact that she's one of us and we love her. You get me?"

"Oh, don't make me out to be the cold-blooded mother who left her family. You all could have stayed in the city with me—"

Except me. You didn't take me.

You took my brothers—but left me behind. No, Will didn't value her opinion much at all. "I'm going to need an answer."

She held his gaze with a defiant expression, but she had to know he'd follow through. He wouldn't let his mom anywhere near this child if she held even a sliver of belief that Ruby belonged with another family.

"I get you." Each word had the texture of hard candy stuck in her teeth.

"The only thing that matters is finding out whether she's a Bowie." He glanced out the window again. The chicken's big yellow legs flopped every time Ruby lowered it to the table.

His mom let out a bitter laugh. "Oh, she's a Bowie all right." Her gaze held accusation.

Will led a simple life. Sure, from an outsider's perspective he lived on a three-hundred-thousand-acre legacy ranch in the Tetons. He'd won the World Games Freestyle Halfpipe a good number of times. But he lived a clean life. He didn't lie, steal, cheat. So, the idea that his mom would think he'd deny sleeping with Christy…knowing the paternity results would show up in the next day or so….

It tells me exactly what kind of man she thinks I am.

Her opinion doesn't matter. "The point is—"

"Hang on a sec," Gray said. "I want to make sure I've

got this right. Basically, you're saying the kid's Will's, but he's such a hooligan you'd rather see his daughter—your *granddaughter*—put up for adoption? Do I have that right?"

His mom narrowed her eyes. "That fine sense of loyalty your father instilled in you might just be blinding you to what's in her best interests."

"It didn't come from Dad." The words tumbled out of Will's mouth without forethought, but he didn't back down. "A mother walking out on her kids teaches a hard lesson on family loyalty."

"Excuse me?"

But Brodie rolled right over the flare-up. "You get that Will just won the World Games for the *seventh* time, right? That means for seven years in a row he's outperformed every other freestyle skier in the world. That's unprecedented."

He wouldn't let them defend him to her. "I've already got a list of nanny agencies—"

"No, hang on." Gray, normally unflappable, stepped closer to their mom. "What he's accomplished? Winning *seven* times? It comes from pure dedication, determination. It comes from—"

"Stop." Will couldn't take another second of it. "Any minute now we're going to find out who her father is and, as soon as we do, I'm getting on the phone and starting the interview process." Their house manager was taking care of the nursery, and Callie, Fin's fiancée, was at the grocery store getting kid food. "Fin, you go to Europe with Callie on her buying trip. You two…" He tipped his chin to Brodie and Gray. "Depending on the results, you can do your thing. I'm here this summer anyhow, so I'll get everything set up, hire the nanny—"

"It's not going to be easy to find someone who'll move out here," Brodie said.

"That's for sure." Their mom, who'd moved to New York City seventeen years ago and never looked back, gave a bitter laugh.

"Unless they're local," Fin said.

"We don't want seasonal help," Brodie said.

"We don't?" Gray said with a smile.

An historical western town at the foot of the Tetons, Calamity's population swelled during tourist seasons. The resorts and restaurants had their pick of ski lovers and hikers who wanted to live in mountain paradise for a few months.

"We need someone who'll stay," Will said. "We're not having nannies in and out of her life."

The doorbell rang. Everyone jerked toward the sound.

For most of his life, he'd had his dad to count on. In all the worst situations, Mack Bowie had taken control. He was the kind of man who faced his fears—walked right through them.

So that's what I'll do.

He broke away from the pack and headed to the door. Sensation ripped across his skin as he turned the handle. But, instead of seeing their lawyer, his dark hair, pressed khakis and button-down shirt, he found the babysitter—the same woman who'd delivered the kid to their house the day before yesterday.

"Hi." She gave him a tentative smile. "I hope it's okay if I stopped by."

"Of course." He stepped back to let her in.

"I found something when I went back to get the rest of Ruby's things." She lifted a white plastic garbage bag, the contents weighing the bottom down.

That's all this kid has in the world, what's in that bag.

No matter what name they found on the birth certificate, he would make sure Ruby had everything she needed. He'd take her into town that afternoon, let her pick out some books, puzzles, blocks…whatever she wanted.

"This was in Christy's desk drawer." She held up a file folder, turning it around so it faced Will.

Death file.

"It's got all her bank account and insurance information, passwords, stuff like that." She pulled out a piece of plain white paper. "And a will. Not an official one, but she says what she wants in the event of her death. And she names the father."

His brothers crowded around, as Will took the sheet of paper.

The woman gave an apologetic smile. "At least we know for sure she's yours." And then she looked beyond him to their mother. "I'm sorry."

Why would she apologize to their mom?

"Well, come on. What's it say?" Brodie leaned over to read the paper. "Holy shit."

Will skimmed until he got to a name.

"Who's the father?" Fin asked.

It was the babysitter who answered. "Mack Bowie." She looked right into Will's eyes. "Your dad."

Chapter Two

"More cake?" Delilah Lua's sister gathered the wrapping paper and ribbons and shoved them into a big, black garbage bag

"You guys." As the youngest of seven kids, Delilah was used to being teased, but tonight they were *killing* her. "I love you, but can I please open my present?" She'd waited her whole life for her twenty-sixth birthday—for the gift every Lua kid got on this special day.

"Well, hang on. There's one more." Her sister gestured to the rectangular package resting against the wall.

Come on, *already*. Her siblings had only gotten *one* present on this birthday. A plain white envelope that held a fat sheath of papers: the lease contract for the next Da Nonna's family restaurant.

Today, Delilah would get the eighth and final franchise. She wished—God, did she wish—her parents could be here for this milestone. They'd died eight years ago, just weeks shy of her high school graduation. But, at least, with the restaurant, she'd always have a part of them.

"This one's from Callie." Her sister brought the package to the table.

Delilah had to push back her chair to fit it on her lap. Callie Bell—her closest friend since freshman year at NYU—had postponed her trip to Europe by a day to share this momentous occasion with her, so of course she'd happily open her present. She slung an arm around her friend's shoulder and tugged her in close. "Thank you so much for coming to my birthday party."

"Are you kidding?" Callie clasped her hand. "I wouldn't have missed it."

Actually, she almost *had* missed it. When Delilah's siblings heard she'd invited two friends to the party they'd said no. *Can you imagine?* The Lua home was party central. People came and went all day long. *So, why would they say no tonight?*

Of course Delilah wanted her closest friends here. She and Callie had gone through everything together the last seven years, and her boyfriend, Marco, would be the pastry chef at her new restaurant. They'd been working on their plans since they'd first met four months ago in the flagship restaurant's kitchen, where he worked to put himself through school.

Da Nonna's didn't have a pastry chef. Her family ordered from a fantastic bakery in Brooklyn. But, for Delilah's franchise, she wanted her boyfriend to create his mouth-watering delights. *You bet I want him here when I open that envelope.*

Delilah slid a finger under the taped edge and ripped off the paper.

"Oh, my God, Delilah," her sister said. "That wrapping paper's so pretty, and you're manhandling it."

"Yeah, save the manhandling for me." Marco was the

only one to laugh at his comment. Her family had long since stopped attaching to the guys she brought home. If she didn't take them seriously, they weren't about to.

"Pretty sure you know how impatient she is to get to the real present." Callie gave a warm smile to Delilah's four brothers and two sisters.

She'd expected that glint in their eyes, the joy they felt in bestowing this fabulous gift on behalf of their parents. Instead, she got…anger?

Were they really that pissed she'd invited her friends? Good thing Callie's fiancé hadn't come. He'd stayed in the hotel to get some work done before they left for Europe in the morning. Imagine a third guest at the table. *Oh, the horror.* She had no idea why it was such a big deal.

Tearing off the paper revealed a gorgeous mixed media depiction of an old Wild West town. "This is beautiful." But it was more than that. It was evocative. She could feel the warm, dusty air, imagine women with full skirts and bonnets walking on the boardwalks, the heels of their boots clacking on the wood. "You're so damn talented."

Her friend had grown up in Calamity, Wyoming, a ski resort at the foot of the Tetons, but they'd only known each other in New York City. Impulsively, she hurled herself into her friend's arms. "I love you. Thank you so much." She pulled away. "I always pictured cowboy boots and bolo ties when I thought of your hometown, but you make it look magical."

"You have to come visit. When I get back from my buying trip at the end of summer."

"Oh, I'll be a little bit busy then." She flashed a mischievous grin to her sister who held the white envelope.

Either her sister had to go to the bathroom really badly

or she'd eaten a bad clam. *What the hell?* Delilah shot a look to her other siblings and their significant others. Something wasn't right. "What's going on? Why're you all acting so weird?" She didn't miss the silent exchange between her oldest brother and sister.

Her sister's expression said, *Do I have to?*

Her brother's said, *Do it.*

"Just give it to me already." She was dying here. Under the table she reached for Marco and Callie's hands and gave them a quick squeeze—*this is it*—before claiming the envelope her sister offered. Her excitement was marred only by the way her family watched her, like she might find a horse head in it. "What?"

Her sister looked away. Her brother's chin tipped up.

She tore open the envelope to reveal a single sheet of paper.

A tear sheet.

A review? The moment she read the by-line a whole bag of Pop Rocks went off in her stomach. She closed her eyes to let it all sink in. Harry Morgenstern had reviewed Da Nonna's flagship restaurant.

Is this happening? The top food critic in New York City had eaten her food and liked it enough to review it for *The New York Daily Times.*

Are you kidding me?

Second best birthday present ever.

Except when she looked up to share the moment with her family—expecting to see huge, proud smiles—she was shocked to see trepidation and…disgust.

Uh oh. She read it.

Our robust city has twenty-four thousand eating establishments. With an eighty-percent failure rate, it seems incredible—yet nonetheless true—that new ones open each day. Certainly, it's my expectation they'll do something special to stand out. An innovative theme, a wildly creative presentation, the chef's unique take on an old standard. Most nights, my taste buds welcome the surprise. I am, after all, a food critic.

But sometimes I just want something familiar. A perfectly seasoned steak, alongside a steaming baked potato topped with a dollop of sour cream and a handful of chives. A Caesar salad with crisp iceberg lettuce, the particular tang of anchovy in the dressing.

Or the kind of borscht I got in Moscow that summer of 1968.

Last night I wanted pasta e fagioli. I wanted manicotti. I wanted tiramisu.

Old school. Just the way Nonna Abelli made it.

Da Nonna's has been the gold standard in Italian food since 1923 and, by God, I knew I could count on that basil-flecked marinara. The cognac-soaked Ladyfingers of their classic, sweet, and creamy tiramisu.

Or so I thought. Twenty-five-year-old up-and-coming chef Delilah Lua, daughter of tragically deceased owners Elsa and Ike Lua, dolled up the marinara sauce with andouille sausage and peppers. She added escarole to the pasta e fagioli. The dessert—mislabeled tiramisu—had raspberry and Meyer lemon curd.

Now, I grudgingly concede every bite was magnificent, every flavor lingered so lovingly on my tongue that I didn't want to move onto the next course.

But it was most definitely not Da Nonna's.

Thus, the next time I crave old school Italian food, I will go to Isle of Capri.

Today we mourn the loss of one of the best and most authentic Italian restaurants in the city.

The thin piece of paper trembling in her hands, she quickly set it down.

Impoverished, her parents had come to New York City for a better life. Her dad, from Hawaii, had started out at Da Nonna's as a dishwasher. Her mom, from Sweden, worked as the hostess. For all the turn-over in the restaurant industry, her parents had stayed loyal and true to Nonna Abelli—and were rewarded ownership when the matriarch passed.

Every single morning when her parents had awakened, they'd glanced to the ceiling to make sure they still had a roof over their heads. Every day they waited for their luck to run out. For their brand to go out of style.

They'd passed that concern onto their children.

This review was her family's worst nightmare. Only, they'd certainly never considered their own sister would issue the death knell.

When she could no longer take the silence in the room, she reluctantly looked up to face the music.

Color flushed her sister's cheeks, and her brother's jaw was set in a rigid line. The others looked like they wanted to be anywhere but at that table witnessing this horrific car crash.

Crawling out from under that last, devastating line —*Today we mourn the loss of one of the best and most authentic Italian restaurants in the* city—she rallied. "He really liked my food."

The continued silence made her stomach hurt. But she faced kitchen crises every day of the week, so she'd fix this. "Fortunately, the majority of our customers don't read reviews."

"Harry Morgenstern's the top food critic in this city," her brother said. "If he tells his readers to eat at Isle of Capri, that's what they'll do."

That was painfully accurate, but she could spin it right around. "Yes, but he's also just brought in new customers who'll want to try my 'magnificent' cuisine."

"Delilah." The brother sitting across from her shook his head. *Stop.*

"The only reason any of us makes a living is because of Da Nonna's reputation. *You* don't get to destroy it." Her oldest brother slammed his palm down on the table, rattling the wine glasses. "This is our livelihood."

"I'm not destroying anything. I'm making it better." *Every bite was magnificent, every flavor lingered so lovingly on my tongue that I didn't want to move onto the next course.*

Unlike her siblings who'd gotten business degrees, Delilah had gone to culinary school. She'd apprenticed with some of the greatest chefs in the world. She'd won awards, for goodness' sake. She knew how to transform the hundred-year-old recipes into something better, brighter, sharper.

If her siblings would just trust her, her dishes would bring people in.

"Our patrons don't come for something better or different," her brother said. "If they want that, they have thousands of restaurants in the city to choose from. They come to ours for old school Italian food and, if we don't meet their expectations, they'll stop coming, and we'll go out of business."

She heard the unspoken fear, *And then what will we do?* They'd all been raised to work in the family business. This question, she could answer. "I get what you're saying, but I see it differently. I think if we don't change, our brand will go stale. We'll get boring. Using the same sauce for a hundred years? Come on. Shaking things up is good. Change is happening whether we want it or not. I mean, there's hardly anything left of Little Italy."

"There's Da Nonna's," her sister said.

"And it's my job to make sure there will always be a Da Nonna's," her brother said.

She wasn't going to win this argument. "Okay, well, the good news is that once I open my franchise, the flagship goes back to serving old school Italian." And she could do whatever she wanted with her own restaurant.

"It won't work," her brother said.

"What won't work?" Fear had her looking for the second envelope. The fat one. The one with the lease agreement. But there wasn't one. The gift pile was empty. "Are you saying I don't get my restaurant?" The foundation beneath her turned into a sinkhole, and she scrambled for traction. "Because it's in the will. I get one on my twenty-sixth birthday, just like all of you."

"And I'm the executor of the estate," her brother said. "It's my job to make sure everything our parents built doesn't disappear."

"It's my restaurant. How is that destroying the other seven? Nothing changes for you guys or the flagship."

"It's our money, Delilah. We're the ones investing in it."

The world spun like it did on a playground Merry Go Round. Her brothers, her sisters…they didn't believe in her. "It's not your call to make. Mom and Dad wanted me to have the eighth franchise."

"Mom and Dad wanted us each to have a *Da Nonna's*. That's not what you're going to do."

"Fine. Okay? You win. I'll make the signature dishes." *Way to play hardball, guys.* "Jesus." What a crappy way to send a message. *On my birthday.*

"Maybe in the beginning you might." Her brother's tone softened. "But, over time, you won't be able to help yourself. You're going to experiment. Put your own spin on the dishes. And, before long, it won't be Da Nonna's."

"You can't help yourself," her sister said. "It's who you are. You're inventive and playful and—"

"You don't want this, keiki," the brother closest in age to her said quietly. "You don't want to churn out the same menu night after night."

Tears blurred her vision, but she wouldn't let them fall. "Yes, I do. I want it more than anything." They were threatening her entire future, and it wasn't right.

Besides, she'd earned it. She was the only one who'd gone to the Cordon Bleu, who'd apprenticed with great chefs in Tokyo, London, and Florence. She was the only one who even cared about cooking.

But she guessed that was their point, wasn't it? The only way to run a franchise of the family restaurant was to make the exact same food every night—never deviate from the "signature dishes."

Dammit, she'd waited her whole life for this gift, and she had to fight for it. "Even more than I want to try lemon curd in the tiramisu, I want to be part of this family's legacy. Mom and Dad wanted *all* of us to share it, so I'm asking you not to shut me out. Don't make me the only one who doesn't get a restaurant." Why were they staring at her like that? "I've worked in the kitchen since I was twelve. I can make those dishes in my sleep. I won't let you down."

"But you'll let yourself down," her brother said. "You have so much potential as a chef. You'll never realize it at Da Nonna's."

More dirt gave way beneath her feet. "I don't have anything else. If you take this away from me, what do I have?"

"You have talent." Her brother reached for her, but those sturdy arms that had picked her off the floor when she'd had food poisoning, that had jerked her when she'd stepped off the curb in front of a cab, offered no comfort. "Now, you just have to find the best way to use it."

Why hadn't she listened to him? Just last week, she'd added three different cheeses to the *pasta e fagioli*, and her brother had steamed over to her, shaking the bowl so hard the soup sloshed over the sides. *"This isn't pasta e fagioli."*

She'd ignored him, confident she'd knocked the dish out of the park. It had happened too many times to count, and she'd never listened.

"Starting tomorrow, I swear on my life I'll run the kitchen exactly how Dad taught me." She watched her siblings carefully, waiting for even one of them to soften. They had to. They would. "Come *on*."

Her sister looked sad but resolute.

"You guys?" This is not happening. They wouldn't take this from her. "*Please.*"

"I'm sorry," her brother said. "You won't be getting a franchise."

Chapter Three

IN HER CHILDHOOD BEDROOM, DELILAH STARED OUT the window into the darkness. The top corner of a brownstone in Greenwich Village, it afforded a view of the little gated park across the street. Clusters of teenagers hung out at the fountain, mostly obscured by trees, and late-night dog walkers hurried by.

She was in freefall.

What am I going to do?

"You okay?" Callie sat behind her on the blue velvet chaise longue.

Pressing closer to the cool window pane so she didn't have to see her reflection, Delilah stared at the patch of light pooling around the street lamp. "I'm…" *Lost.* Totally and completely lost. "I don't know how to fix this."

"You've got two choices," Marco said. "You either get a job in another kitchen—which won't be hard to do—or you go out on your own. Start your own restaurant."

"I don't have any money." Her mind raced ahead. "I need a job." Because in that moment she knew she couldn't go back to her brother's kitchen. "I'll start making calls in the morning. My friends from the New School, the Culinary Institute, NYU…someone will have a lead."

"Well." Callie got up. "There's a third option."

Delilah waited, tense with hope.

"Go to Calamity."

Okay, *so* not what she'd expected. "You want me to go to *Wyoming?*"

Marco chuckled. "That'd be hilarious. Delilah in shitkickers and a cowboy hat." He tipped his head back and laughed. "Delilah on a fuckin' horse."

"Calamity's much more than that," Callie said. "Though, at its heart, it *is* a ranch town, it's also—thanks to Yellowstone and the Tetons—a vacation destination. We've got a huge artist population. Which means we've got great restaurants and shops."

"I'm not…I can't…" She loved her friend, but she really didn't need to hear about her hometown right now. "I have to get my life on track."

"Listen to me." She tugged on the hem of Delilah's blouse. "That networking you need to do? You're not going to find better than what's happening in Calamity this summer. You know how competitive the Bowie brothers are, right? So, instead of just hiring a chef for the spa restaurant, they're having a competition. They've flown out five of the best chefs in the world, given each one a cottage for the summer and a stipend for expenses. It's a big deal."

"Why would a world-famous chef want to run a restaurant in Calamity, Wyoming?" Marco asked.

"They might not. The point for the chefs is the free PR. The judges are all food critics and travel writers, so there's going to be lots of press around. But, also, they get to interact with other world-renown chefs and enjoy all Jackson Hole has to offer. It's a vacation from their usual routine. Besides, the prize isn't running the spa restaurant—that's for the board of directors to decide. But, come on, how fun would that be? Hanging out with those chefs? And, you never know, you might hit it off with one of them—"

"Hey, now," Marco said.

"I meant professionally," Callie said. "I know for a fact that one of them runs a Michelin-starred restaurant in Italy. If you hit it off with her, who knows, she might offer you a job. What do you have to lose? Go to Calamity, hang out with the chefs for a couple of weeks, and make some new and interesting connections. If nothing else, you'll have tried new cuisine and gotten some time away from here. Why not?"

"Because I need a job. I won't be able to think about anything else until that happens." But, even as she said the words, she thought of going downstairs and seeing her family. Of interacting with them tomorrow and the next day. She wasn't going to sulk, but what was she supposed to do? Act happy? Pretend they hadn't just shut her out of the only dream she'd ever had?

No, she couldn't be around them right now.

"You're standing in the childhood bedroom of the home you grew up in after losing a job in the family business," Callie said. "You need to get out of the city and gain some fresh perspective. And it won't cost a thing because you can stay in the main house for free." She held up a hand. "And before you tell me you'd be imposing, think about growing up here. How many times have you offered this house to someone you've met on your travels? Did your family ever care?"

"Not at all." They had six empty bedrooms, and they loved a full house.

"There you go. Same thing. Besides, there're only three people living in that huge house this summer. The oldest brother, Will, his little sister, and Marcella, the house manager."

"Yeah, but it's not like you'll be there. I'll just be this stranger eating their food and sleeping in their bed."

"Okay, you know what? Cook for them. I know Marcella could use the break."

"I could do that. Anything else? I want to pay for my keep."

"Wait," Marco said. "You're seriously considering this?"

Callie turned thoughtful. "Actually, they've just gotten walloped with news of their own. They've got a sister they didn't know about. She's two, and they don't have a nanny yet. So, throw in some babysitting, and they'll be thanking you for staying with them."

Between her six older siblings, she had about a thousand nieces and nephews. Babysitting and cooking she could do. Besides, she had nothing to lose. Literally. "I'm in."

"Babe, stop." Marco turned her to him. "You're not going to *Wyoming*."

White air billowed out of huge, fleshy nostrils, and Delilah jerked to a stop on the driveway. She'd seen a lot of things in her life, but this massive beast with a ginormous rack, beady, hostile eyes, and demon hooves was a first.

Growing up in the city, she came across sketchy types all the time. Basically, she maintained an easy confidence

—as if she wasn't the least bit intimidated—and went on her way.

But this guy…*come on*. He was next-level *huge*. If she took another step, would he charge her? She didn't want to make a ruckus at midnight and wake the whole family, but should she scare him away or at least get the…ranch hands? *Is that who lives on this sprawling piece of land?* She imagined a group of hot cowboys outside their bunkhouse, roasting…wienies? Over a big campfire.

And why the hell was it so cold here? *It's June, for crying out loud*. She wished she hadn't stuffed her sweater into her suitcase. She was freezing.

Well, she had about ten more yards to reach the front door, and she wasn't about to let a moose stop her.

"Hey, handsome. If I weren't so pissed off at my family, about to pass out from exhaustion, and ready to plunge my feet into an ice bath, I'd actually take a moment to admire your majestic badassery. Unfortunately, I am all of those things, so how 'bout you do you, and I'll do me?"

She did *not* want to meet the business end of that rack, but she really did need to get inside, so she'd just treat him like any growly dog she passed in her neighborhood. Like they were besties. "You look like a Carlos. Can I call you Lo? Hey, Lo. How's it hanging?" He did have a massive set of balls between his legs. Looked as uncomfortable as that weighty chandelier on his head.

Move along.

The wheels of her suitcase clacked on the asphalt driveway. She'd asked the driver to let her out at the gate, assuming the house would be right around the bend. *Wrong*.

But…what a house. The moon shone like a spotlight,

casting massive shadows and reflecting off copper flashing and pipes. In spite of its size, the wide expanses of windows and the stone and wood construction made the house look almost part of the landscape. The air, scented with sage, smelled clean and fresh.

Side-eyeing Carlos on the lawn, she hauled her luggage up the porch steps and dropped her tote outside the door. As she slid the key into the lock, she hoped Callie had remembered to alert the household about her arrival. She didn't want alarms going off.

The moment she let herself in, she dragged her luggage into the foyer. Kicking off her wedges, she shut and locked the door, then turned to take in the wide-open space of the first floor.

Unlike her very lived-in family home, this place was spacious and uncluttered, with a lot of leather and wrought iron. Supremely masculine, but with an elegant and thoughtful design.

Knowing she'd get in late, she'd stuffed her sleep clothes and some toiletries into her tote, so she wouldn't have to lug her suitcase up the stairs and wake everyone up. Now all she had to do was find Callie and Fin's bedroom. *Up the stairs, down the long hallway, last door on the left—*

"Hi."

Nearly jumping out of her skin, Delilah whipped around to find the source of that sweet, little voice. Huge shadows loomed across the high-ceilinged room. She scanned the sleek couches, the coffee and side tables, but didn't see anyone.

"Hi."

She sounded so precious. "Hi, sweetheart. Where are you?"

"I here." The kid made it sound like Delilah was the dumbest person she'd ever met.

Heading to the nearest lamp, she fumbled until she found the switch under the shade. The tiny pool of yellow light didn't offer much, but it did allow her to notice a gate at the top of the stairs and tiny little fingers clinging to the top. Little eyes peered at her.

"Well, hey, there. You must be Will's sister."

"I Wooby."

Delilah climbed the stairs to find a cute little girl holding a stuffed animal under one arm. A bounty of dark waves cascaded over her shoulders, and her rosebud mouth matched her name.

"Hi, there, Ruby. I'm Delilah." She reached for the latch, then remembered the little girl didn't know her at all. "May I open the gate?"

Big, wary eyes gazed up at her. "Wheel seeping."

"Right. Well, we don't want to wake him up. Which room is yours?"

The little girl glanced down a long hallway, lit only by a single nightlight. Man, that looked scary. Framed photographs hung on the walls, and most of the doors were closed.

Looking incredibly lost, Ruby rested her chin on the stuffed animal's head.

Her heart squeezed for this little girl who'd lost so much so young. Maybe she should wake someone up? Ruby might be more comfortable with someone she knows. "I'll get Marcella." She was the house manager, after all.

"Cella seeping."

"Yeah, that makes sense. Okay, do you want to show me your room? I'll bet you've got lots of fun toys and awesome books to read. I could read you one." When she babysat her nieces and nephews, sometimes they didn't even get through one whole book before they conked out.

"No, fanks." She stood there in her polka dot pajama short set and watched Delilah with anticipation, like she was waiting for her to break into a song and dance routine.

What're you looking for, sweet girl? "Okay. Let's just sit here and hang out." Maybe she'd tell Ruby a story instead. After she fell asleep, Delilah would carry her to bed. She didn't look like she weighed more than a cannoli.

Unlatching the gate, she stepped inside and sat down on the floor. She patted her lap, but the girl didn't budge. *That's okay.* She'd just sit here until Ruby got comfortable with her. "This morning, before I left for the airport, my brother made our dad's famous Hawaiian French toast." *Because he felt bad for taking away my restaurant.* As he should. *Not this girl's problem.* "He makes it with Portuguese sweet bread and uses a ton of butter so it's super crunchy on the outside and then warm and sweet and gooey on the inside. Do you like French toast? I could make you some in the morning."

Gaze fixed on her, Ruby didn't say anything.

"I like cooking. Like, a lot. Maybe we could cook together. My nephew, Ben, is my favorite sous chef. I even got him a hat and an apron. He's just six, but he's adorable, and he's really into cooking."

There was something in the way Ruby looked at her, anxiety brimming in those beautiful blue eyes. Delilah couldn't help wondering what she was thinking.

The toddler stood close enough that Delilah could smell baby shampoo and feel the heat coming off her little body. She parted her rosebud lips and said, "Where momma?"

The simple question was as jarring as a sudden blast of heavy metal music, and it rendered Delilah speechless.

Clutching what appeared to be a chicken, its big, yellow, floppy legs sticking out under her arms, the little girl looked fragile…forlorn, and Delilah needed to find some words *right the hell now.*

"I—" The weight of sorrow cut off her ability to think, breathe, react.

How did a two-year-old process the fact that her mom wasn't coming back? Delilah had been eighteen when her mom died, and she still reached for the phone every time she had something important to share. It was a fresh hit of grief when she remembered there was no one to call.

Maybe they hadn't told her? Callie had said the mom died a few weeks ago—

Oh, my God. Ruby's been waiting all this time for her mom to come and get her. She wanted to haul that little girl into her arms and hug her until she felt safe again.

But Ruby wouldn't want that from a stranger. She wanted her mom.

"I don't know where your momma is, Ruby." It wasn't her place to answer that question. "But you know what I do know?"

Ruby twisted first one way and then the other, using her whole body to say no.

Delilah didn't know if she should engage in such an important conversation, but she certainly couldn't ignore the question. Totally out of her element, she plowed forward with the only thing she would want to hear. "Your momma loves you with all her heart."

What she would give to hear that voice in her ear just

one more time, feel her mom's arms around her, and know that everything would be all right just because she's there.

The little girl's shoulders relaxed, and she lifted the chicken to cover half her face. Those soulful eyes watched her over the white fur.

"You're her sweet little angel girl." Delilah scraped the hair off the toddler's forehead, tucking it behind her ear. "Your momma loves you so much, Ruby."

Those sad eyes glistened. "See momma?"

Okay, now she needed rain boots to slosh around in the overflow of her weepy heart, but she had to stay strong. The goal was getting Ruby to settle down, so she could fall asleep. "If your momma were here right now, I bet she'd hug you. Can I hug you?" *Please?*

Please let me comfort you.

But Ruby shook her head.

"I bet she'd carry you to your bedroom and get in bed with you with a big pile of books. Can we do that? Read some books together?"

"Want momma."

Yeah, me, too. Well, she couldn't just dump the little girl back in her bed, all alone in a strange room. She had to do something. *She's wide awake.*

As a little girl, Delilah had had a hard time sleeping. Mostly, she'd hated missing out. Her siblings always had friends over, so her home had been alive with music, conversation, and bursts of laughter. It always smelled like popcorn or a mix of cologne and perfume. To get her to sleep, her mom would carry her into the kitchen and bake with her. There was just something soothing about the smell of vanilla and butter, the whir of beaters, the hum of the refrigerator, the heat from the oven, and her mom's quiet conversation.

"I've been traveling all day, and I don't eat airport food, so I'm starving. You want to bake some muffins with me?"

She nodded vigorously. "Wooby hongry."

"Awesome." She lifted her into her arms and headed down the stairs. "Do you like muffins?"

"Shock-let muffins."

Delilah smiled. "Well, I make a mean dark chocolate banana—" Ah—weren't the Bowies extreme athletes? They wouldn't appreciate dessert for breakfast. Then again, this wasn't about power foods. It was about calming a scared and lonely little girl. "You know what? We'll go check out your pantry and see what we can come up with."

At the bottom of the stairs, Delilah made her way across the living room to a gaping, arched doorway that led to the kitchen. "We just have to find the butter and flour and vanilla and sugar…all that stuff. This is going to be so yummy."

"And shock-let. Scock likes shock-let, too. You like shock-let?"

Scock? "Have you seen these hips?" She said it with a big grin, until she realized the impact of her comment. A joke among her friends was one thing, but teaching a little girl not to eat because it might make her fat was a whole other ball game. "Yes, Ruby. I love chocolate. I probably should've been a pastry chef."

Ah. An image of Marco's expression when she'd broken up with him popped her square in the gut.

He'd thought for sure it was a reaction to losing the franchise.

Your career *took a hit. Don't drop a bomb on your whole life.*

But that was exactly what she wanted to do. Blow up her life, so she could start fresh.

Without a clean slate, her thoughts would be tied to salvaging what she had and not building something new. Besides, what if she wound up taking a job in Italy? Los Angeles?

That's the whole point of coming to Wy-freaking-oming. The freedom to figure out the best future for herself.

Running her hand along the wall, she found the switch plate and flipped it on.

Holy mother of God. Kitchens in heaven look like this. White cupboards with glass-faced cabinets, gleaming stainless steel appliances, and huge swaths of granite, marble, and butcher block counter spaces. Two ovens, three sinks, and a massive custom-made refrigerator.

Crossing the spotless hardwood floor to what she hoped was a pantry, she thought about Callie. *You wanted me to have a whole new perspective? Well, I sure as hell got it.* The day before yesterday she was catching a cab for a meeting to get Da Nonna's included in a New York City Food tour, and now she was in Wyoming, talking to a moose and baking with a little girl and her stuffed chicken.

"Oh, Ruby-bean, life can be pretty crazy sometimes, can't it? I'm not comparing my loss to yours—no way—but…man." She opened the door to—*you've got to be kidding me*—a mile of food stored on floor-to-ceiling shelves. "You should've seen my brother's face when I told him I was coming here. To freaking *Calamity*." She made a comical face, and the little girl smiled as she tucked her chin into the chicken's soft, furry head. "For one second there I actually thought he'd change his mind. When I told him I hoped to hit it off with one of the chefs, maybe move to Italy? I thought for sure he'd let me have my franchise."

Instead, he'd smiled sadly and said it sounded like something she would really enjoy.

He'd wished her luck.

"So, there you go." She knew her siblings loved her—didn't question that. And she also believed they thought she had real talent and needed to find the best way for her to express it. *Intellectually, anyway.*

But in her heart? She'd been shut out of the family business, and she didn't know if she'd ever recover.

As she scanned the shelves, she determined to put New York behind her and embrace this new experience. She'd explore the town and its culinary offerings, meet the chefs and learn about local cuisine. "Looks like we're both going to have to find new paths for ourselves, right, Ruby-bean?"

And one day, she was sure, it would all lead back to Da Nonna's. It had to. *It's where I belong.*

Boxes of organic chicken broth, bags of quinoa and farro, and sacks of beans took up the bottom tier. The middle held great big baskets overflowing with beets, kale, carrots, and broccolini. "Would you look at this place? This is every chef's fantasy kitchen."

She found the basics—salt, baking powder, and vanilla—and carried it all to the island. Dumping the ingredients on the black marble, she washed her hands and then, with Ruby still in her arms, got to work.

"Okay, girl, let's do this." It was a little awkward, but she managed to measure the flour and dump it into a big ceramic bowl, all while chatting quietly. When she turned on the hand mixer, the little girl's eyelids drooped, and when Delilah hummed as she stirred in the chunks of dark chocolate, Ruby yawned.

She smiled when the girl's head flopped onto her shoulder, her legs dangling straight down. The chicken landed on the floor. Singing softly, Delilah swayed as she spooned big glops of batter into the silicone muffin cups.

"What the hell's going on?" The deep male voice shattered the quiet.

Chapter Four

Delilah jolted, her hand automatically going to Ruby's back. She turned to see a big, brawny man standing at the entrance to the kitchen.

"Delilah?" With each step forward, he swallowed up air and square footage in the vast kitchen until she felt like she was alone with him in a closet.

She lived in a big city, and she'd traveled around the world. She'd seen men in all shapes, sizes, and colors. But this guy? A wall of muscle, he was hot, commanding, and…intense. He radiated pure testosterone with a tightly leashed energy.

"Yes. Hi. I hope…" She didn't know whether to apologize for making herself right at home in his kitchen or thank him for letting her stay here.

But, since he had his gaze trained on his sister—and not in an *Aw, how cute that my sister's crashed out on you* way—she leaned more toward the apologetic side. "She was awake when I got in."

Those broad shoulders tensed, like Delilah held the little girl hostage, and he was waiting for his opening to knock the wooden spoon out of her hand, grab the girl, and run.

"I didn't wake her up or anything. I…" She didn't normally get tongue-tied, but he was just such a formidable presence, so imposing. He made her feel…guilty.

Well, now, hang on. I haven't done anything wrong.

Shifting the sleeping girl in her arms, she reached out to shake his hand. "Will, right? I'm Delilah." *Duh.* He knows that. "It's so nice to meet you. Thank you for letting me stay with you."

"Here." He reached out, effortlessly lifting Ruby and turning her so that she slumped against him.

The little girl's head lifted, her eyelids barely staying open. "Wheel?" The utter relief in her voice made it sound like she'd been lost at sea for a month, and Will was the Coast Guard. She patted his shoulder, as if making sure *he* was okay.

His gaze rested on that tiny hand, and emotion choked his features. "Yeah, Rubes, it's me."

"Oh." One gush of air shouldn't have contained such contentment…but it did, and it turned Delilah's heart to goo. The little girl wrapped her arms and legs around him the same way Delilah cuddled with her body pillow every night.

"I'll put her to bed." He quickly turned and left the kitchen.

But the image of his broad shoulders straining the width of his white T-shirt and his perfectly round ass in the black athletic shorts lingered.

I have to live with this guy?

Delilah had grown up with four brothers and all their friends. She was totally comfortable around guys. But Will

Bowie? He was that hot guy in school who kept to himself, rarely made eye contact with anyone outside his tight group of athlete friends and, when he gifted a smile to someone, made her feel like the Pope had blessed her right there in the hallway.

Thankfully, she'd only be here two weeks. Those mysterious guys made her uncomfortable. She liked to know where she stood with people.

Shoving the tray into the preheated oven, she dumped the bowls, spoons, and measuring cups into the sink. She was exhausted, but at least the family would have a fun treat in the morning. She wouldn't sponge off them.

"What were you doing with Ruby?"

For the second time, her body jolted at the sound of his commanding voice. With shaky hands, she shut off the faucet and reached for a red and white-striped kitchen towel. "I told you. She was wide awake when I came in tonight."

"If it happens again, I'd appreciate it if you'd put her back to bed. Not…" He gestured vaguely around the kitchen. "Get her all stirred up with lights and activity."

Stirred up? "She was asleep in my arms."

Drawing in a breath that said, *You're getting on my last nerve, but you're a visitor so I'll give you a pass*, he gave a fake and somewhat intimidating smile. "She's only been here since Saturday, and she's not sleeping through the night yet. I'm dealing with it by giving her a routine. So, if you see her up again, just take her back to bed."

"Look, I didn't walk in the door and pull a sleeping child out of bed to keep me company while I baked. She literally started talking to me from the top of the staircase."

When Will didn't like something, every muscle in his

body turned to granite. *Right, so stop arguing with him. You're a guest in his house.* "But, okay, if it happens again, I'll put her to bed." She flipped the faucet on, poured some dishwashing liquid onto a sponge, and scrubbed the mixing bowl.

But she didn't see the sudsy water or the silver bowl. She saw those big, round eyes peering up at her. *Where Momma?* She couldn't even stand the idea that the lost little girl was waiting for her mom to come back. She hit the faucet and reached for a dish towel. "Actually, no, I don't think I can do that."

His expression clouded and, if he'd been intense before, he'd just turned thermonuclear. "You're going to *have* to do that. I'm teaching her to self-soothe at night. She's got to adjust to a new normal, and that's the only way to do it. If she relies on us to put her to sleep, she'll never have the skills to do it herself."

The *only* way? "Hang on. Let me finish. If she'd just been awake and waving to me, I would've put her back to bed. I might've read her a book first, but I certainly wouldn't have baked muffins at midnight with her."

"I don't want you to read her a book. I want you to put her back to bed. You know what? Forget it. Next time it happens, wake me up, and I'll handle it.

Oh, this guy. "Will, she asked me where her mom was."

He flinched, as if she'd just flicked water in his eyes. His mouth opened, but no words came out. Just a slow hiss of breath. And then his shoulders went back. "What'd you say?"

"I didn't know *what* to say, so I told her what I'd want my mom to say to me. That she loves her very much. That she was her mommy's sweet angel."

A look of defeat tipped his head down, drawing her gaze to his gorgeously sculpted thighs and big, bare feet.

"Has she done that before?" she said. "Asked about her mom?"

"Never."

"So she has no understanding about what happened to her parents?"

"She never knew my dad. He…" When he swallowed, his Adam's apple jumped. "He died a little over two years ago. Her mom…no, she doesn't understand anything. I'm supposed to let her come to me with questions, and I'm only supposed to answer the questions she asks—not add my own information."

Ah. So, he'd lost a parent, too. "Well, I think she's waiting for her mom to come pick her up."

Awareness struck, and his jaw slackened. "Her mom went away for a long weekend and never came back." By his expression, if he were watching a movie, he'd hit the scene where the killer's identity had been revealed. "Jesus. She's waiting for her mom." His voice sounded rough, raw with the revelation.

"Yeah, sounds like it. So, it kind of broke my heart. When I was a little girl and couldn't sleep, my mom would take me into the kitchen and bake with me. I thought I'd try it with Ruby."

"No. Don't do that." He must've seen her reaction to his aggressive tone, because he looked…well, frustrated. "Just let me handle it, okay?"

"Sure, yeah. If it happens again, I'll wake you up." She couldn't imagine applying a textbook solution in this situation, but it wasn't her call. This wasn't her family. She turned back to the sink, but his big hand came down on the counter beside her, and she couldn't help looking up at him. All her annoyance washed away when she saw the worry in his eyes.

"It's a tough situation, but we're doing the best we can. We can give her everything…except parents. It sucks for her, but that's just the way it is."

Just give her love. Oodles of kisses and hugs and…love.

She didn't say it, of course. Just turned back to the sink to take care of the mess she'd made. When she glanced back at him, he was gone.

Tightening the backpack's belt, Will glanced at the rooster clock. Six AM. *Right on schedule.* He checked the counter to make sure everything was ready for his protein shake—wait, were they out of almond butter? *Ah, hell.* He grabbed the grocery list and added it.

"Okay, Rubes, ready to go?"

"Go." His sister gave a rallying cry from the backpack.

This kid. Everything was exciting to her. He opened the mud room door and stepped onto the back porch to find Uncle Lachlan stretched out in an Adirondack chair with a steaming mug of coffee. "Hey, old man."

His uncle tipped his chin to the lawn. "Your guest's playing leapfrog with Fred."

In a deep squat, knees practically in her armpits, Delilah shifted her weight forward, lifting her feet off the blue yoga mat. Their rambunctious goat bounded straight for her. "Oh, crap." Will started off the porch.

"Oh, come on. Let him have some fun."

Not that Will could've gotten there in time anyway. Besides, the goat had never hurt anyone in his eight years with the family. Will watched Fred playfully lower his head and ram into her ass, knocking Delilah sideways.

Will trampled down the stairs to get to her, relieved—and a little surprised—when he heard her laughter.

"You nut." She rolled onto her knees and fielded the goat's eager nuzzling with both hands. "What'd I ever do to you?"

He stopped at the bottom of the stairs to watch for a moment.

"Come on, fella." She got up, swiping the grass off her black leggings. "I have to finish, so I'm putting you back where you belong." Fingers tucked into his collar, she walked him to his pen and nudged him through it. Then, she went back to her mat and formed her body into the letter K, face turned up to the sky.

"Gee-yup, Wheel, gee-yup." Ruby's little feet kicked out.

"All right, Rubes." He called up to his uncle, "I'm out of here. See you in an hour and a half."

"Your mom might be up by then," Lachlan said. "So, I'll have found something else to do." Watching the lawn, he sat forward with a big grin.

Will turned just in time to see Fred get up on his hind legs and smack the latch a few times with his nose. The gate swung open, and he raced towards his new friend.

"Delilah," Will called.

"Oh, this is gonna be good." Lachlan chuckled.

Will struck off to save his houseguest. Frolicking towards her, Fred nudged her from behind, knocking her face-down onto the grass. Peals of laughter filled the backyard, and it made Will smile.

She rolled onto her back. "Oh, my God." The goat

kept jumping around her, diving in for attention. "What's the matter with you?" But she was still laughing.

"Come on, Fred." He snatched the goat by the collar and led him back to his pen, twisting the wire around the latch to make sure he couldn't get out. "All right, Ruby, let's hit the road."

"Hit wode, Wheel."

When he turned, he found Delilah heading toward him, a hand shielding her eyes from the bright morning sun. "I guess I missed an important feature of goat entrapment." She reached them and smiled. "I'll remember that."

Will's pulse quickened "Yep." He looked away. "Just twist this wire."

"Got it." She smiled up at Ruby. "Hi, sweetie. You going for a run with Will?"

"Wif Wheel."

"That's sweet of you to take her with you."

"Marcella raised four of us. She's doesn't need to start all over again." Something about this woman's smile, her intelligent brown eyes, and all that bright-blonde hair scrambled his brain.

It didn't happen all that often, a strong attraction like this, but there wasn't a chance he'd go there with Callie's best friend, so he stepped around her. "I'll see you later."

"Wait." Her hand caught his forearm. "I just want to say how sorry I am about last night. It was a difficult situation, but I'm a guest in your home, and I want you to know I'll mind my own business."

"No worries. We're all finding our way." *Go.*

But she had a lost—maybe even sad—look in her eyes that kept him rooted. What had Callie said? Something about Delilah's life going sideways, needing a change in scenery.

Well, he wasn't about to ask her about it. *Not my business.* And yet, still, he found himself saying, "You need anything?" She'd just gotten in last night, knew no one. He could offer her…something.

She looked relieved. "I'll try to stay out of your way, but maybe you could go over a few things with me? One of the reasons I came out here is to meet the chefs in the competition, so if you could point me in the right direction, I'd be grateful."

"There's a train. I can show you when I get back."

"Awesome. Thanks." She beamed a smile so bright it made his blood go fizzy. "Also, it's important to me that I pitch in around here, and since I'm a chef, I'd like to cook for you guys. I just need to know what you guys like to eat."

Normally, Marcella would handle these issues, but he and his brothers had given her the summer off. Between Ruby and a houseguest, he knew Marcella would think she needed to stay.

When he didn't respond right away she said, "Never mind. I'll talk to Marcella. I know you have a schedule to keep."

"I do, but it's summer, so my training schedule's lighter." His body needed to rest after an intense competition season. "I'll be back at seven-thirty. I can show you around then." He'd loan her a car, give her a tour, go over his diet, and then she'd be good to go.

"You don't mind?"

The longer he looked at her, the more he noticed. Like her lush and expressive mouth, her lips, the color of raspberries. The pink in her complexion, and the roundness of her breasts and hips in the Lycra tank top and leggings. Ruby kicked her legs, snapping him out of his daze. "Of course not." With a tight nod and smile, he headed out on his run.

Normally, he dealt with distractions by switching the channel in his brain, aiming his focus on the task at hand. Blocking temptation had never been much of an issue. He didn't need booze or cake or a hookup that badly. No, he kept his eye on the ball. Always.

In this case, switching the channel meant having someone else get Delilah settled in, but Lachlan was unreliable and Marcella needed a break, so Will figured he could handle it.

He thought about the way she laughed, though. The way it lit up her whole face, made her hazel eyes sparkle, and wondered if he might be making a tactical mistake.

Lick.

Under a canopy of trees shading the sidewalk outside Bliss, the town's ice cream parlor, Will forced himself to look away…until she moaned. And then he *had* to see her expression.

"Oh, my God." Delilah's eyelids fluttered closed, and her pink tongue made a slow pass around the edge of her melting ice cream cone.

Delilah Lua turned out to be nothing like he'd expected. Then again, other than her family owning a famous Italian restaurant, Callie hadn't told him much. Maybe he'd expected a dark-haired woman. A harried, fast-talking New Yorker?

Not a blonde beauty with exotically-shaped eyes.

Not sexy as fuck.

Everything about her was sexual. The sway of her hips when she walked, the way her teeth sank into her lush bottom lip when she turned thoughtful, and that luxurious, long hair that shook and shimmied every time she used her hands to tell a story—which was all the damn time.

Expressive, energetic…she turned a basic tour of downtown Calamity into an experience.

Her eyelids popped open, and those warm, hazel eyes trained on him. "What *is* it about this ice cream?"

Just when Will pried his gaze off her mouth to answer, she ran that tongue along her plump bottom lip, kicking the hum of desire in his dick to a full-blown throb. "The owner's the president of the Slow Food Organization. He uses all natural ingredients sourced from local farmers."

"A-ma-zing." She'd spent so much time savoring it—to let the "flavors linger in my mouth"—that the ice cream was dripping. Grinning, she licked it off her fingers. "Best I've ever tasted. Do you mind if I talk to the owner real quick? I promise I won't be long."

Liar. He'd planned on giving her a quick lay-of-the-land. Calamity wasn't that big. Three long streets filled with shops, restaurants, and bars, faced the town green. The historic section sat a few blocks beyond Main Street, complete with wooden boardwalks and the original, now-faded advertisements on the wood and brick buildings built in the early nineteen-hundreds.

But she'd kept ducking into restaurants to check out the décor and meet the chefs. Just before stopping for ice cream, she'd spent twenty minutes with the owner of Coco's Chocolates discussing her "sources" and "process."

He'd never met anyone so interested in food. And people. And…everything. "No problem."

She watched him with those clever eyes that didn't

miss a thing. "I don't want to keep you. If you want to go, I can always catch an Uber back to the ranch."

"I'm good." He turned toward the set of picnic tables under the Ponderosa pine trees. He'd clocked the teenager watching him earlier, so he wasn't surprised when she approached him the moment Delilah went back inside the ice cream parlor.

"Can I get your autograph?" She thrust the napkin and pen out, as if forcing herself to break through her fears. "I want to be just like you."

Will Bowie liked the kid's spirit. "You board?" He reached for the pen. "Or ski?"

"I grew up boarding, but I want to ski half-pipe like you. Especially after what Damien said."

Will didn't care what his closest competitor had to say. For five years the guy had come in second to Will's first and bitched about it every time. *Sore loser.*

He scrawled a note to the kid.

Set goals, stay focused, and take home the gold.
Will Bowie

As he handed the napkin back, the girl said, "I don't believe anything he says."

"Good." But the defiance in her tone got Will's attention. "Thing is, any time you're on top, you're going to have people trying to yank you down. You've got to keep your eye on the prize. You're Teflon, and the negativity's water. Let it roll right off you."

"My dad says Damien's a jackass. Nothing but a showboater. You're…you're perfect. I've never seen anyone ride the rails the way you do."

"Thanks." He shook the teen's hand. "Means a lot."

As she read the note, her eyes widened. She gazed up at Will with a painfully earnest and hopeful expression. "You mean it?"

"You think I'm a superhero?" Will waited for the comment to sink in. "I'm just a guy. I won for two reasons. One, I work hard, and two, I never gave up. Nothing more to it. So, yeah, you can absolutely stand on that podium. You just have to want it more than anything else."

"I do. I totally do. Thank you." With a huge smile, the girl dashed back off to her skateboarding friends.

"Hey." Wiping her mouth with a napkin, Delilah approached him. "Sorry about that."

Most people wanted to see the elk preserve or Bazzo's Mercantile. They got a kick out of taxidermy grizzly bears, antique brothel tokens, or jewelry made of elk ivory, agate, or opal.

Not Delilah. She seemed to find those the least interesting things about the area. With a thoughtful expression, she took in the crowded town green and the sidewalks busy with tourists. After a long hard winter, summer hit with a bang in June, drawing out the residents and attracting visitors. Most used Calamity as a base for their Yellowstone and Grand Teton adventures.

She smiled at the group of teenagers. "You're quite the celebrity in this town."

"I just got back from a pretty big competition. It'll settle down."

"What kind of competition?"

"I ski. Half-pipe."

She glanced to the mountains that jutted out of the earth, snow glistening on their rugged peaks. "You any good?"

"I hold my own."

"I'm totally kidding you right now." She nudged him with her elbow. "I do pop my head out of the kitchen every now and then."

"Yeah? You follow freestyle skiing?"

She laughed. "No, but a good friend of mine—Callie Bell? You might know her?" She gave him a mischievous smile. "She gave me the low-down on the whole family. Besides, I think about a hundred people have congratulated you so far."

"Will, dude." An old friend from high school approached them. "Proud as shit, man." He slapped Will's back.

"Thanks. Delilah, this is my friend Gunther."

She reached to shake his hand. "Nice to meet you."

"Same." He turned his attention to Will. "Dude, your amplitude in the qualifying round?" Gunther tipped his head back and howled with excitement. "Holy shit, I thought you were gonna crash into a satellite or something. Never seen anything like it."

"Thanks."

His friend's gaze darted over Will's shoulder, and the smile faded. "Ah, hell. Looks like you've got company."

Will turned to see a news van and a couple of paparazzi heading up the street toward him.

"And that's my cue to head home." He turned to Delilah. "You ready?"

"Sure."

"Gunther, man, I'll catch up with you later."

His friend nodded. "I'll distract them with my big—"

"Truck?" Will shook his head and smiled before taking off down the street.

Delilah fell into step beside him. "You don't do interviews?"

"I do scheduled interviews before, during, and after events. I don't bring my work home with me." Actually, the paps didn't usually come to Calamity. He thought about Ruby, and a sick feeling churned in his stomach. "They might be after something else."

He'd parked on the other side of town, behind the yoga studio, so he ducked down a quiet side street, hoping to dodge the reporters.

"The fact that a celebrated chef's staying with you?"

"Ha." *If only*. "They might know about Ruby."

"Why would anyone care about your sister?"

She kept right up with him, and he appreciated the hell out of that. Especially in those fancy gold sandals she wore. He gestured to them. "Need me to slow down?"

"Oh, honey, I'm a New Yorker. I can chase down a purse snatcher in heels twice as high and not miss a beat."

He couldn't help smiling.

"So, Ruby?" she asked.

"You remember that World's Worst Boyfriend thing last summer?" His youngest brother had turned into an international meme when a text he sent to a friend went viral. Thousands of spurned lovers from around the world had told their stories on social media, replacing their real-life lover with Fin's name.

"Uh, yeah."

The meme had trended for months. His fiancée, Callie, had even made a museum out of it. "It pretty much put Calamity on the map."

"As adorable as the whole modesty thing is, it's just me here, so let's lay it all out there. It put the four hot Bowie brothers on the map."

Delilah Lua was a trip. "Anyhow, a lot of that attention hasn't died down. They've got fan groups that keep track of what we're doing. They might've found out about Ruby."

"And you don't want the world to know about her?"

Hell no. "We're trying to get her settled and adjusted. She doesn't need reporters in her face." He didn't need to share his real concerns with a houseguest. "But there are plenty of other reasons."

"Like?"

He wanted to be annoyed at her pushiness, but—at least for the next two weeks—she was involved in their lives. She should be aware. "Frankly, we don't want her to become a target."

"The whole billionaire thing?"

He cut her a look. *Bingo.*

"Yikes. You really think that's a possibility?"

Kidnapping the children of billionaires? He and his brothers had grown up with security detail on the ranch, so yes. A very real possibility.

"Will?" a reporter shouted.

Another paparazzi came rushing at him from a side street. "Will, do you have a response to Damien's interview?"

He remembered what the teenager had said just a moment ago. *Especially after what Damien said.*

What's that asshole done now?

"It's not about Ruby." Delilah touched his arm. "Do you want to stop and give them a quick answer? It might get them to leave sooner."

"I'm not dignifying anything Damien Brenner has to say." In the old section of town, they reached the alley between the yoga studio and Callie's museum. Two of the elderly staff came out the door and waved, inviting conversation. Just as Delilah veered toward them—her natural inclination to be open and friendly—he grabbed her hand. "I'll take you there another time."

"What is that place?"

"That's Callie's Museum of Broken Relationships."

"*That's* it? Oh, my God. I have to see it."

"Wait up, Will," a reporter called. "Is there any truth to what Damien said?"

Don't know, don't care. As soon as he got to his truck, he'd get his manager on the phone. See if he could get ahead of whatever trouble Damien had stirred up.

Just as they emerged out of the alley, though, reporters swarmed him. "Will, is it true? Does your family money have anything to do with your wins?" one of them shouted.

Delilah swung around. "What kind of question is that?"

Will caught her upper arm, forcing her to look at him. "Don't engage them."

"Can you verify whether your father invested in any of the Games' sponsors, Will?" someone shouted.

Truck in sight, he dug into his pocket for his keys. He hit the fob and the tail lights flashed. Just before he reached the driver's side door, he heard someone shout, "Running away only makes you look guilty."

Guilty? He wanted to remind them his dad had been gone over two years. *You think he's paying off judges from the grave?* But the whole thing was ridiculous, and he wouldn't validate it with a response.

His manager would put out a statement, shutting down Damien's latest bullshit. Will pulled open the door and stepped on the running board.

"Will!"

Just as he started to close the door, he heard, "How do you feel about being suspended?"

He slammed into the word with the same impact as hitting the ice wall of the half-pipe.

Suspended?

Chapter Five

WHAT THE HELL COULD HE HAVE DONE TO GET suspended? Unless…had Damien uncovered a connection between his dad's investments and a sponsor? If he had, no way would it have come with strings. In the World Freestyle Games, the judges were former athletes, and the idea that they could be bought was laughable. Extreme athletes were in it for the thrill of the sport.

He held the door open for Delilah, and then followed her inside the house. A cartoon blared on the television. "Ruby?" He found the remote and punched it off. "Mom?"

"Hey." Alex, his manager, came out from the kitchen. "We need to talk."

"Hang on a sec. Have you seen Ruby and my mom?"

"Your mom's out back. And Ruby's looking for… something. I don't know."

"She left Ruby alone?"

"I guess so. But she's fine. I saw her a few minutes ago. Look, we've got to talk about this suspension."

"Not until I find her." He breezed past, needing to get eyes on her.

"Will." His manager's harsh tone stopped him. "This is serious. We've got decisions to make."

"My sister's a hell of a lot more important than some bullshit suspension."

But Delilah was already heading into the kitchen. "I got it."

He turned to his manager. "What's going on?"

"A few days ago, Damien ran his mouth off with the press." Alex pulled his phone out of his pocket. "Here. Listen to it yourself." He pressed Play.

On the small screen, a reporter shoved a microphone in Damien's face. "So, here you go again. Always a bridesmaid never a bride. How do you feel about that?"

Damien's amiable demeanor hardened. "It sucks. But I guess if my family was rich as hell, you might see me on the podium seven years in a row."

"Wait, what're you suggesting?" the guy asked.

"The Bowies own half the world," Damien said. "Figure it out."

"Are you suggesting Will Bowie's family *bought* the judges?"

"Look, Will's a great skier, but he didn't outperform me this time," Damien said. "He just didn't. So…come to your own conclusions."

Alex killed the video.

Into the blaring silence came a sugar-sweet voice. "Hi." Ruby, in blue and white polka dot pajamas, came bumping down the carpeted stairs on her butt. Under her arm, she clutched her big, white chicken.

"You okay, Rubes?" When she nodded, he checked the time on the phone. "Why's she still in pajamas?"

"I don't know." His manager lifted both his arms in exasperation. "Come on, Will. This is serious."

"It's almost one o'clock. She should be dressed. She should be playing outside." Will started for her, but his manager caught his arm.

"The League's thinking about *suspending* you. Do you understand the impact of that?"

Heels clacked on the hardwood floor. *Great.* Just what he wanted his mom to hear.

"Suspending him?" In a silk blouse and slim-fitting skirt, his mom looked like she'd just walked off the page of a fashion magazine. "What's going on?"

"We've got an issue with the League," his manager said. "But we're handling it."

"Why?" his mom asked. "What's he done?"

Jesus, not now. "I haven't done anything. Damien's a sore loser who's shooting his mouth off again. No one takes him seriously." He couldn't get suspended based on an unsubstantiated rumor. "This isn't his first tantrum."

"He just accused your family of *buying* the judges, Will," Alex said.

"Is it true?" his mom asked.

He turned away from her, as if to dodge the bullet, but it glanced across his pride nonetheless. "Of course it's not true. It's so ridiculous it doesn't merit discussion."

"It merits a whole lot more than discussion." Alex gave him a hard look. "It merits an investigation."

What? He'd been a League member for nearly two decades. They knew him. They knew his family. "How? It doesn't even make sense. They've got different judges every year. Besides, you think if we pulled a stunt like this for seven years it wouldn't get out? You don't think *one* of them would come forward?"

"You're missing the point. No one thinks you paid off judges." His manager's expression sharpened. "Damien just questioned the integrity of the sport."

"Okay, but they can't suspend me based on some—" Will watched the little girl, still bumping down the staircase. He motioned impatiently for his mom to get her. "Nonsense from a poor sport."

Ruby flashed a grin with her tiny, white Chiclet teeth. "Hi." When she hit the bottom stair, she waved like she was on a float in a parade.

In her enormous chicken slippers, the girl padded over to the coffee table, flung her stuffed chicken on it, and climbed on top. Her little legs stretched out in front of her, and her tumble of auburn hair gleamed in the afternoon light. "Hi." This time her voice wavered, and her elbow lowered a notch.

Delilah reached for her, whispering in her ear, but Ruby firmly shook her head and stayed put.

"They have no choice," his manager said. "People watch sports to see athletes push the boundaries. To do things no one's ever done before. If they think it's fake, they won't watch, and then the money dries up. Look, the half-pipe's new to the Olympics. The League can't afford to lose spectators. So, for the sake of appearances, they have to do an investigation. Keep everything clean and above board."

"Investigate what, exactly?" Will asked. "How are we going to prove that my family doesn't pay off judges? How do you prove a negative?"

"You can't. Which is why I've come up with a solution to make this go away." For some reason, Alex didn't look as confident as he sounded. "People Fuel's been after you for years to be the spokesman for their brand."

Not this again. "I don't do endorsements." Will didn't eat protein bars or drink any of their shit products.

"Yeah, I know that. But you've never had the threat of suspension, either." Alex exhaled harshly. "You want the Olympics, yeah?"

A knee injury had kept him out last time around. Now, at twenty-eight, this next one could be his only shot. He had a lot of trophies and medals, but he didn't have Olympic gold. He wanted it as a finale, to finish out his career.

But, mostly, he wanted it for his dad.

"If this suspension's longer than three months," Alex said. "It could impact your next season."

Which meant he wouldn't make the Olympic team.

"What, exactly, do you need him to do?" his mom asked.

"I just got off the phone with People Fuel. We've worked out a deal that'll make everyone happy. You do a campaign for them, and they'll sign a contract to sponsor the Games for the next five years." Alex shrugged, as if it were that simple.

"What happens to Damien's accusations?" Will asked. "You told me they have to investigate."

"And they will. If you bring them People Fuel, they'll interview a couple of judges, talk to the executor of your dad's estate, and sit down with you. Look, they already know they're not going to find anything, so they're comfortable putting out a statement in a few days that says there's no evidence to support the allegations."

They should stand behind me anyway.

"What's the big deal?" his mom said. "So you do a campaign?"

He thought about that kid in town who'd asked for his

autograph. If he told her to eat a People Fuel bar, she'd eat it. "I can't endorse a product I don't use." The first ingredient listed on the label was sugar. "It's got twenty-nine grams of sugar in one bar."

Alex's gaze swung back up. "Yeah, Will, I know all the reasons you won't do it. Now I'm giving you a damn good one to do it." He lifted both hands as if he couldn't believe he had to convince his client of something so obvious. "It's *advertising*. You do a few commercials and sit for a bunch of photo shoots. You'll get a million bucks in your bank account and everyone will ignore Damien's innuendo."

"Hi." Ruby's bottom lip quivered, her hand falling to the stuffed white chicken nestled in her lap. She looked so damn lost.

But she wasn't. Not anymore. She had Will and his brothers. They'd take care of her.

"Hey, kid." But this issue wasn't just about him, was it? How would the suspension impact his brothers...*her*?

"Why are you hesitating?" his mom said. "He's giving you a chance to clean up your family's reputation."

"The Olympics are eight months away," his manager said. "Do the campaign, and we stay on track."

His dad had been Will's biggest supporter. He'd stood by him at the cost of losing his wife.

Winning that gold medal would prove his dad's support hadn't been for nothing.

"What if you spin the endorsement in a different direction?" Delilah said. "What if you worked it so Will's not actually telling anyone to eat the product? Like maybe you show Will skiing or training, and then an image of the product pops up on the screen."

Well, damn. He had so much tangled up in this suspension—the reputation he'd worked so hard to build, his dad who'd supported him through everything—that he hadn't considered the options. "I like that."

"Won't work." His manager's gaze shifted to Ruby. "They have a specific campaign in mind. They've already sent the contract, which I haven't had a chance to look at but, basically, they're going for family values. They want you as a father figure."

His joints locked. "I'm not a father."

"How do they know about Ruby?" His mom's tone was filled with accusation.

"Maybe from the guardianship papers you filed," Alex said. "Someone from the courthouse might've leaked it."

Ah, that's probably it. "So, the campaign includes Ruby?"

"Yes. They're a good company. Like I said, family-oriented. They donate ten percent of their proceeds to charitable causes. And they think highly of you, Will. You lead a clean life. And now…with the kid."

"Hi?" The little girl's voice cracked, and big, fat tears glistened in her eyes. The fingers resting on her cotton-covered thigh curled into the fabric, making it bunch. She blinked a couple times, her lungs pumping rapidly. Her jaw set, lips pressed together, she looked determined not to cry.

Will couldn't take it. Stepping around his manager, he scooped Ruby off the table and into his arms. Jesus, she didn't weigh more than a boot. With her big blue eyes, she stared at him, her body stiff. Her lower lip trembled, but not a single tear spilled down her cheek.

She studied his features, like she wanted something from him. *No, that's not it.* She wanted to know if she could trust him. *Fuck.* It was like a punch to his chest. This kid. So alone in the world, and yet so damn brave.

She's not alone anymore. She has us. "I've got you. We're here for you." He patted her back.

"Like I said, it's just a few commercials, a few photo shoots. And then your reputation's clean."

Her warm body shifted in his arms, like she was looking for a comfortable position, a place where her body fit with his. "I can't compromise her security to fix my reputation."

"Look, I get it." His manager tipped his head toward Ruby. "It's a tough situation, but you've got to hear me. The integrity of the sport's been called into question. With all the scandals in football and cycling, baseball..." He shook his head. "This sport's too young to risk losing its audience. They have to do something. It's a small price to pay if you wind up on that podium next February."

"It seems to me Will's in a strong negotiating position," Delilah said. "He's just come off a huge win. There's got to be another big-name sponsor who'd love to do a campaign with him. No offense to anyone here, but it's unconscionable to force him to use his sister—a toddler—into doing a national media campaign with him."

Through all the anger and frustration, something else spilled in. Respect. Affection. He had no words for the fact that this stranger was speaking up for him.

Helping him.

"If we had time," Alex said. "I could pitch the idea to other sponsors. But this one's been after Will for years, and they see an opportunity. I've got a few hours to seal this deal before the League has to announce a suspension. So...it's People Fuel or nothing. And they want the family values thing, which includes the kid. It's either that deal or..." He shrugged.

"Well, for goodness' sake," Delilah said. "They can use

an actor. They can't make him use his *sister*. Especially if they know her story."

"People Fuel won't use actors," Alex said. "They want Will and his little sister. They love the story, love that you guys took her in."

Delilah turned towards him, in a way that unconsciously edged out the other two. "What do you think?" She placed a hand on his forearm, and he found the warmth and gentleness of the gesture momentarily distracting.

He shook it off. "I don't like having my arm twisted. It's a shit product—" He looked down at Ruby. Dammit, he'd have to do better with his language. "And I don't want to expose her to a media campaign."

"If they're all about family values, then explain the situation, and maybe give them what they've wanted all along—you. Only, make it so you're not actually telling anyone to use the product. You've got nothing to lose by negotiating."

"He does," his manager said. "I've got maybe an hour or two before the League holds its press conference. I don't have much time to negotiate. And it's going to have to include Ruby." Alex faced him. "What's it going to be, Will?"

A tiny hand landed on his jaw. The slight pressure Ruby exerted had him turning toward a pair of deep blue eyes. "You sad, Wheel?"

His heart swelled painfully at her compassion. "No, kid. I'm good."

"I not *kid*." Her sweet, little-girl voice slayed him. "I Wooby." Her hands cupped Will's cheeks, forcing him to acknowledge her. "Say Wooby."

"Okay, Ruby." He smiled. "You got it."

"And you Wheel. *My* Wheel." She clapped a hand over her mouth to cover a giggle, but nothing could hide those sparkling eyes.

A strange sensation tripped down his spine. It made his heart stutter and his skin prickle.

And it jerked everything into perspective. Not a chance would he put a target on this little girl's back. "Forget it. I'm not endorsing a product I don't believe in, and I'm sure as hell not using Ruby to make my problems go away."

Chapter Six

"HOLY SHIT." DELILAH'S HEART JUMPED INTO HER throat at the sight of the bison blocking the trail. "Are you *trying* to make me wet my pants?"

It ignored her, munching grass.

Until it swung its head up and gave her a threatening look that said, *You wanna start something?*

Fuck my life. But, seriously, where the hell was she? When had the sage meadow ended and the tall grasses and scrubby brush mixed with pine trees begun?

Screw it. Hitching her purse higher on her shoulder, she turned around. "Trail's all yours, buddy."

Hot, tired, and with a monster headache, she wanted to pull out her wand and magically plant herself back in her bedroom. Uh, the Calamity one. Not the one back home.

Ha, definitely not that one.

Whatever. *The only way to it is through it.* She just had to find her way back. The mid-day sun burned her skin—she hadn't even thought to wear a hat or sunscreen. She figured she'd hop on a train and get off in town. Kind of like in New York City.

Crunching leaves caught her attention. *Shit.* Where was it coming from? She didn't see anyone on the trail—ahead or behind. Was it another freaking animal?

"Delilah?"

That familiar voice—deep, confident—filled her with relief. "Oh, thank God." She watched the big, brawny athlete emerge out of the forest. His T-shirt clung to his sweaty body, and his powerful thighs flexed beneath the athletic shorts.

Will Bowie. *Damn.* Well over six feet of hard muscle, smooth, tan skin, short brown hair, and startling blue eyes.

He's gorgeous.

"What're you doing out here?" He sounded like ranch security detail coming upon a trespasser.

But, given the way he was around Ruby, she suspected that was how he handled being concerned about someone. "Excellent question. One I probably should've asked myself about an hour ago."

"You got lost?"

"So completely lost that, if a polar bear came out of the bushes, I wouldn't be even a little surprised." Her natural impulse was to reach out and touch him—she was just a touchy-feely kind of person—but she stopped herself from doing it with him. "You heading back home?"

He nodded with a look that said, *Where else would I be going?*

"Well, I don't know. Maybe you're looking to take down a bison for dinner. Use its pelt for booties and its horns for kitchenware."

He suppressed a smile. "I'm coming back from the gym. Session with my trainer."

She didn't know why he fought his grins so hard. He had these adorable dimples bracketing his mouth, just dying to pop out. "Can I tag along?"

"Sure. Where were you headed?"

"If I tell you, you'll think I'm a bubblehead."

"Try me."

"The train station."

Now, he cracks a smile. "Yeah, you're not anywhere in the vicinity."

"Well, if there hadn't been a Mack truck blocking the trail, I probably would've kept going until I got to Idaho. You know the kind of lost-in-thought where you don't even see your surroundings anymore? You look up and go, Wait, I'm in *Harlem*?"

"Sure. Happens when I run. Work out all my problems that way."

"Yeah, but in Harlem, I can hop on the subway and get right back downtown. In Calamity, I wind up the love slave of Grizzly Adams. Unbelievable."

"You okay?"

She did sound pretty agitated. "Honestly?" She took a deep, calming breath. "I'm so far from okay, if I didn't think a bison would sit on me I'd just want to curl up in the fetal position right here on this trail."

Their shoes crunched on the dirt path, and a hot, dry breeze rustled the leaves. In the quiet, she noted he didn't ask her what was going on. Which meant she should keep her mouth shut. *Leave the poor man alone.*

But she'd been alone with her thoughts for hours, and she couldn't keep them inside a minute longer. "My life changed"—she snapped her fingers—"like that. And I spent the first hour of my walk thinking about taking my brothers and sisters to court. Can you imagine? My *family.*

The same people who wanted to make sure, since I'm the youngest, that I didn't miss out on any of the traditions after my parents died. They all had their own places, but they kept the house, so I'd have a home to come back to during college. We have all our family parties in that house, and they do all the same things my parents did for Thanksgiving and Christmas and birthdays and graduations. The people I love most in the world? I'm thinking about suing them."

She realized she was probably scaring the crap out of him, so she shut her mouth. But he didn't look scared. He looked contemplative.

"Maybe turn back a few pages? Fill in some of the blanks?"

She laughed, though it was more out of relief that she hadn't freaked him out than embarrassment. "Sorry about that. I'll come back later and clean up the word-vomit I left all over the trail. Okay, so you know my family owns Da Nonna's, right?"

He nodded.

"Yeah, so, we all get our own franchise when we turn twenty-six. Except me. My brothers and sisters decided I shouldn't get one because I keep messing with the signature dishes. And, while I hold my hand up and admit I shouldn't have taken liberties in the flagship kitchen, I should be able to do whatever I want in my own restaurant."

"Except it's a franchise. And isn't the nature of a franchise for them all to have the same décor and menu?"

"Yes." She said it snappily because he was right, but she didn't want him to be. "And that's why I quit ranting about suing them and switched to streaming solutions.

Like, what if I start out doing things the way they want, but gradually transition into my *own* signature style?"

"Wouldn't it make more sense to just start your own restaurant?"

She sucked in a sharp breath and took in the tufts of white clouds dotting the deep blue sky. "But then I wouldn't be part of my family's business. I'm not changing it to a French Bistro, for God's sake. I'm adding a different cheese to the minestrone. I'm playing with the tiramisu. It's not like I'm serving sushi." The toe of her Dr. Martin's kicked a stone that clacked into another, the sound surprisingly loud. And, in the quiet space he gave her, the truth crept in. "At the very top level"—she raised a hand over her head—"I'm angry that they told me at my birthday party instead of giving me a heads-up. It made me feel like an outsider. Like they've been scheming against me. And that hurts. But deep down"—she lowered her hand to her hip—"I'm really angry at myself for ignoring my brother."

Suddenly, she was so tired. While she was only carrying a tan leather tote, it felt like she wore a backpack filled with a week's worth of supplies. "He gave me a million chances. He's constantly telling me not to mess with the recipes, but I guess…I thought I knew better. What does he know, right? He got a degree in business. He doesn't know food."

"Is there anything you can do to fix it?"

"There has to be. It's what my parents wanted. I just have to prove to them that my food's good enough to bring in customers. That my restaurant won't fail, and then they'll have the confidence to invest in it."

"So, coming out here…were you trying to punish them?"

Was I? Because she'd been checking her phone constantly, expecting them to beg her to come home, so she guessed, on some level, she'd wanted them to feel bad enough to relent and give her the franchise. "I thought I was coming out here to get away from the only life I've ever known." She thought about that bison, the wooly tufts around its head. "And, boy, did I get it."

"Well, if there's anything I can do to help, let me know."

"I'm not here for vacation. I'd like to meet the chefs—not just the ones in the competition, but the ones in town. I'd like to check out the farms and Farmers Markets, and I'd like to take over the cooking for your family. That is, if you don't mind me experimenting."

"The kitchen's all yours. Cook to your heart's content."

"Okay. Just give me a list of what you can and can't eat."

"Don't worry about me."

"No, I want to feed you. Feeding people's my happy place. I can experiment *and* make the things you like." Wait, had she made it sound like she needed to be chauffered around the entire county? *Better clear that up.* "I actually only need two things from you. A ride into town so I can hit the Chamber of Commerce. They'll have all the information I'll need. And a list of the foods you eat. I'll take it from there."

"Sounds good. Anything else?"

Energy started rolling in and, for the first time in days, she felt stronger, more in control. Damn, it felt good. "Yes. Two more things, actually. Point me in the direction of the train station so I can get to Owl Hoot and meet the chefs. And, just so you know, I've got about five dozen nieces and nephews, so if you need a hand with Ruby, I'd be more than happy to babysit. Okay?"

"After training tomorrow, I'll take you into town. As for food, it's pretty simple. I eat meat, vegetables, nuts, and fruits. Mostly, the first three."

"That's it?"

"Yep. No bread, rice, potatoes, sugar, or alcohol."

"Um, okay. I can work with that. This'll be fun, actually. I'll work on some interesting dishes."

"I don't need fun or interesting. I have an almond butter and banana protein shake when I get back from training in the morning. Either a chicken or salmon salad for lunch—loaded with vegetables. Steak or pork chop for dinner. And lots of sweet potatoes."

"That's…" *Boring*. "Basic. No variety?"

"Nope."

"Okay, then." She didn't think she'd ever met anyone so regimented in her life.

Which was a good thing. He might fascinate her—all that dark, brooding energy, and the way he deftly handled everything being thrown at him—but he was way too uptight for her.

And that meant she wouldn't be crushing on her hot athlete host.

Swiping the perspiration from his forehead, Will yanked open the back door and stomped into the mud room. He'd promised Delilah he'd take her into town this morning, so he'd make his protein shake and then hit the shower.

"Wun, Wheel, wun." Ruby rocked her little body in the backpack.

"Nah, Rubes. We're done." He kicked off his running shoe so hard it slammed into the washing machine. Normally, a ten-mile run would drain all the frustration out of his system.

Not today.

Because one thought kept cycling through his head: the League didn't have to suspend him. They could —*should*—defend him. He suspected they were sticking it to him because he was an outsider. While most competitors trained at the League's facility in Utah, Will had always had a private coach who'd lived on the ranch.

After Brodie's accident, his dad had hired Coach Peterson to teach his sons how to use their bodies—to develop their musculature, flexibility, and strength for their extreme sports adventures in the Tetons.

That's what his dad had said, but Will suspected he'd understood the brothers hadn't wanted to be separated again.

Did he party with his teammates? Not usually, no. So, yeah, he could see how he might be perceived as an outsider. But he supported the team in other, more meaningful, ways.

So, for them to turn against him…it shook his very foundation.

I win because I score higher. Period. It wasn't luck. It wasn't favoritism. And it certainly wasn't money. It was about focus and discipline. Commitment. It was about never giving up.

And, frankly, winning a gold medal was motivation enough. You never wanted to lose again.

Little legs kicked his ribcage. "Gee-yup!"

A smile cracked through his internal rant. "We're done riding. It's time for breakfast."

Time to see Delilah. Just the thought of seeing her bright smile pushed out all the dark thoughts. He unclipped the buckle at his waist and gently loosened the straps from his shoulders, sliding the backpack to the floor. Reaching under her arms, he lifted her out.

"Let's get this hat off you." He untied the ribbon under her chin and peeled the floppy hat off her sweaty head.

A deep, raspy voice came from the kitchen. *Lachlan*. "Want to go see your uncle?"

"No, fanks." She nestled into that spot they'd discovered yesterday, where she molded to him perfectly. "I hongry."

"Then let's fill that little belly."

At the stove, Marcella stirred a big pot, and his uncle poured himself a mug of coffee. The kitchen table sat empty, the pantry door was closed, and he heard no other sound.

Disappointment plucked his nerves. "Where's Delilah?"

"Not up yet." Marcella glanced over her shoulder and gave Ruby a warm, loving smile.

His uncle just stared. With his shock of white hair naturally styled like a pompadour and a full white beard and moustache, he looked at Ruby with an intense and conflicted expression.

Since getting the paternity results, Lachlan hadn't interacted with her much. He and Will's dad had been extremely close. No one had gotten over Mack Bowie's death—and he doubted they ever would—but it seemed hardest on Uncle Lachlan. Mack had been his person.

Seeing his brother's face in Ruby had to be tough. It was for Will, too, but in a sweet way. He had a piece of his dad, alive and warm, in this house again.

"So, how's this gonna work?" Lachlan asked.

"Come here, my darling." Marcella reached for Ruby, but she clung to Will.

I got her, he mouthed, bringing her to the table and settling her on top of the booster seat. Marcella handed him a melamine bowl of oatmeal, and he plopped it down in front her. "Gobble up."

"Gobbo, gobbo." Ruby plunged the spoon into the bowl.

He turned back to Lachlan. "I'll have a nanny hired by the time Fin gets back in August, when he takes over, and then, once everyone's home, we'll look at the calendar and figure out who gets her next."

"You're gonna pass her along like a baton?"

Will shot him a look. *You're bringing this up now?* They could've used his input a week ago. "If you've got a better idea, we're open to it." He strode to the refrigerator and jerked it open. "We've thought about it from all angles, and this is the best plan."

"Scock, scock, scock." Bouncing her stuffed chicken on the table, Ruby shoveled oatmeal into her mouth.

"What'd she just say?"

Will poured himself a glass of unsweetened tea. "Squawk. It's a chicken. Anyhow, once we hire a nanny, we'll have some consistency. I've talked to agencies in Denver, LA, and New York City, and I've set up a few video-conferencing interviews."

"Not gonna be easy finding someone to live out here."

"No, but in the meantime Delilah's in town."

"I'm staying, too," Marcella said.

He stopped before the glass reached his mouth. "You're taking the summer off."

She glanced towards the table. "That was before."

Oh, hell, no. Marcella had come to live with them about a month after his mom had moved out. Hired as a housekeeper, she'd jumped in to fill all the important roles in their lives—not the least of which was caregiver. She needed the break. "You're going. We've got plenty of help between me, my mom, Delilah, and this old man."

"Delilah's only here for two weeks," Marcella said.

He knew that—obviously—so he didn't know why it moved through his body like a cold fluid. It was just…she brought something new and different—*exciting*—to this house. And he liked it. Wanted it.

"Besides, it's too late. I already cancelled my ticket."

Will reached for the cell phone he'd left on the counter.

"What're you doing?" Marcella asked.

He hit their pilot's speed dial. As always, she answered on the first ring. "Hey, Sarah."

"Morning, Will."

"How's it going? Your sister doing better?"

"She's absolutely fine. It was a scare, and she's got some road rash, but luckily nothing more." She drew in a breath, obviously still rattled by the motorcycle accident. "Anyhow, what can I do for you?"

"Glad she's okay. I'm going to hand the phone over so my overworked and underpaid"–Marcella snorted—"house manager can arrange her travel plans with you. She's going to Michigan, and we want her out of our hair as soon as possible."

"Oh, please. You can't live without me and you know it." Marcella grabbed the phone, mouthing, *You sure?*

He held her gaze, wanting to make sure she heard him. "You're right. We can't live without you. But we're covered for the summer, so I want you to go."

She reached up and caressed his cheek. "You're a good boy, Will." Giving him an appreciative smile, she walked into the mud room to take the call.

"So, you're training, you're standing in for Brodie at Owl Hoot while he's out of the country, and you're taking care of the kid?" His uncle's voice was gruff.

"It's my off-season." *And I've been suspended.* "And Brodie hired an event planner. I'm only here if she has questions or problems. Besides, everyone on the board's in town, so she'd turn to them first."

Marcelle swept back into the room, handing off the phone. "Done. But if you need me for any reason, I'm a quick flight away."

"She's a two-year-old. How much trouble can she be?"

The thwack to his head made him whip around. Marcella's arm was cocked back with a dish towel in her hand, ready for a second snap.

"Hey, I'm trying to make sure you enjoy your vacation."

"Delilah seems good with her, yeah?" Lachlan asked.

He thought of that first night, the way Ruby'd been slumped in her arms, the way Delilah had swayed like she was hearing a slow song on a dance floor. "Yeah."

He'd about lost his shit when Delilah told him Ruby'd asked about her mom. He'd immediately understood why his sister hadn't been sleeping.

The first night she'd come to stay with them, he'd caught her in the living room. Up on her knees on the couch, belly pressed against the cushion, she'd stared out the window. That was why they'd put up the gate.

He hadn't known at the time, but she'd been waiting for the flash of headlights in the driveway that signaled her mom coming home.

Fuck. He knew just what that felt like—remembered lying in bed, waiting for the sound of the door, his mom's voice, her heels in the hallway—except he'd been much older. And his mom hadn't *died.*

He had no idea how to explain death to a little girl. Fortunately, he'd found a lot of books on the topic. He'd handle it.

"Seems like a lot of people coming and going, but who's staying?" Lachlan asked.

The truth stabbed him right in the conscience. "Believe me, I worry about the same thing. But what can we do?" He'd find a way to make it work. He had no other choice.

"Tough situation." His uncle looked him in the eye. "She's in good hands."

Coming from his uncle, a man of few words, that meant a lot.

"You ready for some breakfast, old man?" Marcella called.

Will didn't miss the spark of humor in his uncle's eyes. "For your slop?"

"I'm happy to give it to someone who appreciates it." Marcella started to pull away the bowl of oatmeal filled with slices of apricots, almonds, chia seeds, and almond milk, but Lachlan reached out and grabbed it.

With a booted foot, he pulled the chair away and dropped onto it.

"Sorry to say it's not raw bear flesh or whatever it is you usually eat," Marcella said.

"A man gets tired of raw flesh. Gets stuck in my teeth.

Don't mind mixing it up with some gruel every now and then. Makes me feel like I'm atoning for my sins."

Lachlan stuffed a big spoonful into his mouth. For a few moments he and Ruby ate in companionable silence. And then Lachlan lifted a rucksack off the floor and set it on the table.

Untying it, he pulled out a pine cone and examined it in his big, coarse hand. Then, he closed his eyes and sniffed it. "Pine cone." He set it down and carved another spoonful of oatmeal out of the bowl.

Ruby's spoon clattered, as she reached for the pine cone with both hands. She lifted it, sniffed it, then closed her eyes. "Pie co."

Marcella flashed a look to Will, and they shared a smile.

His uncle pulled out a small rock. He held it up to the chandelier over the kitchen table and turned it in different directions. Then, he set it down between them.

Ruby picked it up and held it to the light. "Pwee wock"

"Yeah, it's pretty," Lachlan said. "But it's not just a rock. It's a schist."

"Shist." Ruby pumped her little arm, as if ejecting the rock into outer space.

His uncle leaned over, quietly explaining about the plate-shaped mineral strains.

"Good morning." Delilah's soft voice sounded a little raspy.

Will spun around a little too quickly—*eagerly*—and immediately felt like a fool. Heat rushed up his neck, fanning across his cheeks, and burning the tips of his ears.

"I can't believe I slept so late." Her slightly sunburned face looked fresh and scrubbed clean, her long hair neatly brushed, but her pink plaid tank top was inside-out and didn't match her blue and gray striped pajama shorts. "For the life of me, I couldn't fall asleep."

Will grabbed a glass from the cabinet and filled it with water. He handed it to her. "Headache?"

When she reached for it, their fingers brushed. Their gazes connected, and heat billowed through him.

"The worst." She looked away, drinking greedily. "Thank you. How'd you know?"

"We're sixty-three hundred feet above sea level," Marcella said. "The altitude takes some getting used to. Keep hydrated, and that headache'll go away. Also, sunscreen. Use it all the time."

"Oh, I learned that lesson yesterday." Delilah turned on the faucet and filled her glass again, downing it like a frat boy at a keg stand.

Gusto. That was the word he'd use to describe the way Delilah experienced life.

"I hate to do this to you since you were only supposed to cook the occasional meal," Marcella said. "But I'm leaving tomorrow morning and—"

"Oh, no worries," Delilah said. "I already told Will I'd take over the cooking. Honestly, it'll be my pleasure to cook for them."

"First of all, that one…" Marcella gestured toward Uncle Lachlan who was still canoodling with a fascinated Ruby. "Has his own cabin and spears whatever unfortunate beast happens to cross his property."

Uncle Lachlan lifted his head and gave her a dull look.

"And even if he does wander over here, you're not obligated to feed him."

"She can feed me," his uncle said.

"You want to be fed, show up at a recognized meal

time." She turned to Delilah. "He's like a bison. He does what he wants, when he wants. So, if he just shows up, don't think for a second you have to go out of your way for him. We're not running a diner here."

"I cook for a busy restaurant and a big family, so there'll be plenty of leftovers. He can roll in whenever he wants."

"Guess I know where I'll be spending my time," Lachlan said. "Now that someone's laid out the welcome mat."

"Make him take off his shoes," Marcella said. "Otherwise he'll track scat all over my clean floors."

"Scat?" Delilah's tone held a touch of humor.

Will liked how nothing fazed her. "Poop."

Delilah's eyes went comically wide.

"Anyhow, while I'm gone you'll only have to cook for Will and my little punkin-pie-sweet-pea-muffin-head."

"You never called me cute names like that," Will said.

"You weren't cute."

Uncle Lachlan barked out a laugh.

"Ruby thinks I'm cute. Right, Rubes?"

Her chair scraped back, and her little feet hit the floor. Clutching her chicken, she toddled over to Will, wrapping her arms around his leg. She peered up at Delilah. "You gots my shock-let?"

Delilah dropped to a crouch. "You mean our yummy chocolate banana bran muffins?"

Ruby nodded, thrusting out Scock. "We hongry."

When Delilah cast a questioning look up at him, the direct eye contact hit like a taser to his spine. Thrown, he gave her a tight nod. He didn't want Ruby eating crap, but in that moment, he didn't give a damn. Delilah could do anything she wanted.

"Awesome." She got up and headed toward the pantry, her nicely rounded ass cheeks filling out the pajama shorts in a way that made his entire body wake up and pay attention.

He hung out with a lot of athletes, so he was used to women with toned, tight bodies. Delilah's was softer, rounder, and it unleashed a dangerous desire.

Coming back with a Tupperware container filled with muffins, she popped the lid and held the box out for Ruby. "Here you go." The smell of chocolate wafted out of it.

"Hey, now." Uncle Lachlan practically knocked back his chair to get his big paw on one of them. He shoved half of it in his mouth. "Now that's what I'm talking about."

"Oh, so we finally found something you'll talk about then?" Marcella took one for herself. "Must make for scintillating conversation with the moose."

Delilah held the box out to Will. "I didn't know your diet when I made these, but with you being an athlete and all, I tried to make them as healthy as possible."

"Carbs, sugar, butter…" Marcella shuddered. "That's the work of the devil in this house."

"I didn't use butter, and the only sugar comes from the bananas and apple sauce. That's why I used so many spices."

His uncle grunted with satisfaction, hoisting a second muffin as his vote of approval.

Will watched Ruby pick out the chunks of chocolate and stuff them in her mouth like they were the antidote to the poison in her gruel. His uncle reached for a third muffin.

"Looks like they're a hit." Food didn't tempt Will. Not usually.

But, just then, watching Delilah's teeth sink into the brown cake, her tongue sweep out to lick up the crumbs, her eyelids flutter closed as if reveling in the flavor, that muffin tempted him pretty damn hard.

She swallowed. "You don't have to eat them, but I used buckwheat and wheat flour, some bran, and just a tiny bit of honey. It was unpasteurized, so I thought it'd be okay."

She'd made the effort for him, and he didn't want to let her down. Besides, he was suspended, so what the hell. He bit into the soft cake, and a world of flavor filled his mouth. Cinnamon, cloves, nutmeg, bananas—and that decadent, smooth hit of dark chocolate.

Damn, that's good. He couldn't remember the last time he'd paid attention to the way something tasted.

"That was thoughtful, Delilah," Marcella said. "We'll go over things this morning, and you can make us dinner tonight. Sound good?"

"It sounds great."

"What time?" Lachlan asked.

Marcella's glare made them all laugh. "Apparently, with the right incentive, you *can* keep a schedule?"

"Can I have some of this oatmeal?" Delilah turned to the stove, wooden spoon in hand as she stirred.

Had he ever noticed the slope of a woman's shoulders before? The smooth skin at the back of her thighs? The tumult of long blonde hair looked so fucking sexy hanging down her back. He could imagine what it'd feel like brushing his chest and thighs when she straddled him.

Desire burst in his core, spreading hot and fast. "I'm going to shower." He tried to take a step, but Ruby's hold tightened on his leg. Before he could pry her arms away, Delilah was back in a crouch.

"I'm going shopping today. Would you like to come with me, so you can pick out the stuff you like to eat?"

"No, fanks." She pressed her face into Will's leg.

Marcella gestured to the keys hanging off hooks by the back door. "You're welcome to use any of our cars or trucks."

"Oh." Delilah stood up. "I don't drive."

Uncle Lachlan stopped chewing. "Why not?"

"I grew up in Manhattan. I've never had to."

"Well, I can take you a little later this morning," Marcella said.

"I'm taking her."

All eyes turned to him, Marcella's filled with surprised.

A little uncomfortable, he said, "I told her yesterday I would." They were making it a bigger deal than it was. He could spare an hour or two. Besides, it wasn't like he'd act on this attraction.

He'd never hook up with Callie's best friend. And since when had his self-discipline ever failed him?

"Awesome." She flashed that gorgeous smile, vibrant and fucking sexy.

Except it struck Will that...possibly his resolve had never been tested *quite* to this extent.

Chapter Seven

A SHAFT OF LATE MORNING SUNLIGHT GLANCED across the rooftops, casting a hazy, golden glow over Owl Hoot. Will had only meant to take her into town for groceries, but then he figured he might as well drop her off at the saloon. That was the second item on her list, meeting the chefs.

When they'd arrived, though, she'd been blown away by the costumed reenactors and the buildings renovated to look like a genuine gold-mining town, so he'd given her a tour. He figured he'd take her as far as the restaurant, and then head back home and work through the nanny resumes.

As they strolled along the boardwalk at the far end of town, Delilah kept brushing up against him, touching his arm and tugging his T-shirt to make a point or get his attention.

She'd gotten his attention all right. Her ballsy laugh, her bright energy, and that hair. Jesus, that long, blonde sexy hair. Will curled his hand into a fist.

She did it unconsciously, he was sure. She was just that

type of person. She used her hands to express herself, and she didn't hold anything back. But what she didn't know was that he wanted to touch her skin to find out if it was as soft and smooth as it looked. He wanted to dip his face into her neck, close his eyes, and breathe in her honey-vanilla fragrance.

What *was* it about her? Why did her particular scent —soft, feminine, *sexy*—make him so aware?

Aroused.

And, worse, what was this infuriating rush of happiness he got from being with her?

She stopped walking and rested a hand on the wooden bannister. "I've never seen anything like this." Her tone held awe.

"Yeah, Brodie did a good job."

"It's hard to believe that a year ago this was literally just an old ghost town."

"We've got pictures, if you want to see what it looked like."

"I totally do." She gazed up at him—all warm and interested—and he didn't think he'd ever wanted to know someone's secrets the way he did hers.

It made him a little dizzy.

Turn the channel.

Right. Snapping out of it, he flipped his thoughts to home. "Let's get going." The sooner he hired a nanny, the better off Ruby would be. Besides, he didn't want her spending too much time with his mom, so he struck off toward the saloon.

Less crowded at this end of town, they had the walkway to themselves. "Do you know why it was abandoned?" she asked. "Was it a gold rush thing?"

"It was the original settlement from eighteen ninety-seven, but it was too close to the mountain, so they moved the town a few miles out."

"They just abandoned it?"

"Wasn't much to it. A saloon, a jail, a mercantile…a few other buildings. My dad bought it about fifteen years ago." A couple of actors dressed in period clothes passed by, and Will nodded to them.

She flashed him a crazy smile that said, *Did you see that?* "Was he a history buff?"

"He was but, honestly, I think he bought it because it holds so many memories for us. My brothers and I used to play here. We'd use sticks as guns and have shoot-outs. I always played Butch Cassidy." He smiled at the recollection. "We'd hide out in the old saloon, lock each other up in jail." *Good times.* "I doubt he ever imagined it turned into a living museum." They crossed the dusty street to the next, more crowded, boardwalk.

"Oh." Touching his arm, she gave him a sweet but sad smile. "I bet he'd love it."

"He would." Loss ballooned inside his chest, making it hard to take a full breath, but he wouldn't go there. Not now. "We did a lot of camping growing up, and we'd sit around the fire listening to my dad and Uncle Lachlan tell stories about the rustlers who'd lead their stolen cattle or horses into Jackson Hole."

"Tell me one."

He cast her a quick glance, getting that kick of awareness from the interest sparking in her hazel eyes, the swell of her breasts in the pretty lavender sundress.

He looked away. "I'll tell you why we decided to call the town Owl Hoot. This area was pretty uninhabitable. The Native Americans came into the valley for the bison, the traders came for the beavers, but the land and weather weren't hospitable enough for anyone to make a home here. It's also shaped like a bowl with only a few passages in, which made it a perfect place for people who didn't want to be found. Rustlers would steal Montana horses, hide out in the valley—Jackson Hole—long enough to change their brands, and then sell them to cowboys in Utah or Idaho."

"So this whole area was founded by outlaws?"

He smiled. "Badasses, yeah."

She squeezed his bicep. "I guess that explains the streak of independence in your family."

A pulse of electricity shot through his limbs. It wasn't just the touch, he realized. It was the way she seemed to like him. Admire him. "Yeah, so, like I said there weren't many ways to get in, and since they were rustling and trying to avoid the law, they had to take the most treacherous routes. They called the passage Owl Hoot because they ran the horses and cattle in at night."

"Oh, I love that. What a great story." They'd neared the center of town, and she smiled at the costumed actors tying up their horses to iron hitching posts. "It's funny because I've traveled a lot, but I've never seen anything like Wyoming. From the plane, the land looked brown and… desolate. I thought it'd be sad here, but it's gorgeous and so different from anywhere I've ever been."

"Wait'll you hit the trails." He stopped himself from offering to take her out on the ATVs. *You've shown her around. That's enough.* When they reached a crowd surrounding a street scene, they stopped to watch.

She smiled like she'd never seen anything so delightful as a jailor hauling a drunk by the back of his neck. Her complexion was so smooth and creamy, and she had the cutest dimple.

He wanted to punch himself in the face. *Why am I giving my houseguest a tour of this town instead of taking care of business at home?* "Let's go." He continued on, ushering his thoughts towards his sister.

Funny thing, he actually missed the little girl. After his shower that morning, he'd come downstairs ready to get her, only to find his mom had taken her into town. His disappointment had surprised him.

When they reached the saloon, he said, "Okay, we're here."

"What's going on?" She pointed to the people waiting to get in.

"We're doing family meals this week."

"I thought the town doesn't open until Friday?"

"It doesn't. But, to iron out the kinks before we officially open, we're doing a trial run, so it's open to friends, family, and town employees. Everything's free."

"That's such a great idea. Your brother thought of everything."

"Yeah, so…enjoy. Lachlan will pick you up whenever you want."

"Or I can just take the train. Now that I know where it is." Her eyebrows lifted, and she gave him a smile.

She was so pretty. He'd seen plenty of beautiful women in his life, but they didn't make him feel like *this.* Like hitting the rails at slightly the wrong angle and not knowing whether you'd correct in time or crash. *Turn the channel.* "See you."

"Will?"

They were right in the middle of pedestrian traffic, so he took a step back towards the saloon wall.

"I know you don't need a houseguest on top of everything else you've got going on, so thank you. For taking me out today and just…being so nice. All I wanted was to take my mind off the stuff going on at home, and I sure got it."

"Is my suspension and finding out my dad got someone pregnant right before he died doing the trick?"

"Oh, man. No offense, but I think I'll keep my own problems."

"No offense taken."

"I have to say, you're handling the suspension incredibly well." She gave him a knowing look. "But I suspect you're a still waters kind of guy."

"I can't get worked up over things I can't control." *Really? Is that why you didn't sleep last night?* Every time he'd start to drift off he'd remember the suspension, and it would send a shockwave through him.

"The injustice of it, though." Delilah shook her head.

You got that right. "Yeah. I won't lie, it's grinding through me. People have always made fun of us for our discipline. We don't party much or get trashed, don't crash cars or sleep with local girls."

Clearly, that last detail got her attention, but she didn't press him on it. "So it sucks that we've worked so hard and sacrificed so much, only to have some jerk tear it all down."

She gave him a compassionate smile. "What're you going to do about it?"

It killed him to say it, but… "Nothing."

"*Nothing?*"

"It'll fix itself. Anyone who knows the sport, my friends and family, the people that matter, gets what's going on. And, since the investigation can't turn anything up, I'll be exonerated." But a truth flickered somewhere in his brain. Being exonerated wasn't the same thing as restoring his reputation.

"There must be something you can do, right?"

"Jumping up and down and waving my arms will only make it worse. Like I said, my friends and family know the truth."

"Well, I didn't mean anything *aerobic*, but I get your point."

She was cute, and he wanted more. More touching, more of her humor. He wanted to feed her fresh-picked strawberries from Marcella's garden, watch her eyes go wide from the juicy sweetness. He wanted her alone in his truck. In his bedroom. Under the covers. More…

Go. "You ready to meet some chefs?"

"Totally. Hey, maybe I'll even hit it off with one of them and get a job out of it. But, even if I don't, I'm bound to learn something, right? Chefs of this caliber wouldn't come out here unless there was something special about the place."

"A hundred thousand special things."

She eyed him curiously.

"One of them's taking home a hundred grand."

"That's the prize?"

He nodded.

Her eyes went wide. "A hundred thousand dollars?"

"How else would we get them out here?"

She gestured to the Tetons, the town, and then her hand swept from his head to his boots, making him laugh.

"They might come out for a visit, but the whole summer?" he said. "We had to make it worth their while."

"I thought they got a shot at running the spa restaurant?"

"Some of them don't want that. I know Chef

Mathilda doesn't." She wouldn't walk away from her Michelin-starred restaurant. "Two of them are looking for a change, so they might be interested. Chef Alonso came to work on his cookbook. But the search for an executive chef is separate from the competition. That's something the board will decide, and it'll be based on more than the food they prepare. The chefs came for the event itself, the exposure, the change from their routine…and the hundred grand."

"That's a lot of money." She looked lost in thought, and he liked watching her mind work. "If I applied for a small business loan, I'd have *two* hundred grand." A switch flipped, and thoughtfulness turned to excitement. "I could open the franchise myself." She touched his arm like it was the most natural thing in the world.

Something deep inside him stirred. He'd felt attraction and interest plenty of times before, but never this craving, this thrumming…*imperative* to be with a woman, and it shocked the hell out of him.

"I know the first event starts at the end of the week," she said. "And I know you've already got your five chefs, but is there room for one more?"

Before he could answer, she said, "You're outlaws. What do you care how many chefs are in the competition, right?"

He got that she was excited, but he wasn't sure she had all the information. "There are six events total, one a week." Except they had two weeks to complete the final event. "You'd have to stay the whole summer."

"I can do that." But then excitement flattened to worry. "I'd have to get a job, though, and find a place to live. That can't be too hard, right?"

"You're not going to find either in the middle of the

summer tourist season. But if you're in the competition, you'd get lodging and a stipend like the others."

Her hands covered her mouth, her eyes glittering with happiness. "Will you let me in?"

"I'm not involved with the competition in any way. I can't imagine Brodie having a problem adding a sixth chef, but you'd have to meet the same criteria as the others."

"Which means?"

"The board wanted chefs with visibility, accomplishments, something that makes them stand out."

"I won the American Culinary Federation Student Chef of the year, and I run one of the most famous restaurants in New York City. Plus, I've apprenticed with—"

He raised a hand to stop her. "I have nothing to do with it. I'll put you in touch with Chris. He's running the show."

She reached into her giant leather tote and pulled out a tablet. "What's his email address?"

Will cracked a smile. He liked her style.

"What? The first event is Friday night, right?"

He nodded.

"Then, I've got to get cracking. I can at least introduce myself and send my resume."

The moment he gave her Chris's email address, her fingers went flying over the keypad.

He had no idea whether they'd let her enter this late in the game, but he couldn't help wondering what it'd mean for him. Lodging meant she'd likely live with him, since all the other houses on the property were taken. If she'd proved such a distraction in a few days, imagine an entire summer with her. More of her smooth legs curled under her as she read to Ruby on the couch, of her rocking out to some song on the radio in his truck, of watching her animated expressions as she chatted with the butcher in the grocery store.

Christ.

"Okay. Done." She slipped her tablet back into her tote. "One of my brother's reasons for not giving me a franchise is because the start-up costs come out of the estate which, obviously, impacts everybody. But if I come up with the money myself, he won't be able to stop me." Hope shone in her eyes. "I'd have to learn high altitude cooking, but do you know how fun this would be for me? I'd get to check out all the local farms and ranches and Farmers Market. You must have sustainable farms out here, right?"

"We do. But, before you get carried away, it might be too late. Like you said, the first event is at the end of this week."

What about Ruby? He didn't want her getting too close to their houseguest, and it would be impossible not to get attached to her. Delilah had a way about her—warm, lively—she sucked everyone into her orbit with her warmth and curiosity, her genuine interest.

"I do have the credentials, though." She covered her mouth with a hand, eyes glittering. "Oh, my God, this would be the most amazing thing. On so many levels. I mean, even if I didn't win, I'd still have so much fun learning about the local cuisine. And I'd get to be with Ruby. I don't know what it is about that little girl, but she just grabbed my heart, you know? She's so strong. I love her spirit. Ack, I'm getting carried away. I'll shut up. I'm just so excited." She took a step forward and then stopped. "Wait, just one more thing. What kind of lodging are we talking about? I've heard stories about your infamous bunkhouse."

The bunkhouse. They'd had some wild times there. "You could talk to Chris, see what arrangements the board can make for you. Or…you could stay in the main house. With me and Ruby."

"You wouldn't mind?" Her tone straddled the line between wary and thrilled.

"Not at all."

She hurled herself into his arms, pressing that warm, soft body against his, and he knew in an instant he'd made a fatal mistake.

He stayed disciplined by shutting out distraction, and there wasn't a chance in hell he'd be able to resist this woman.

There'd be no channel to turn. It'd be the Delilah Show, twenty-four-seven.

And he couldn't remember ever wanting anything more.

The roar of conversation hit him the minute he entered the saloon. Five tables, covered in white linen and loaded with serving dishes, lined up against the wall of windows that overlooked the mountains. The chefs chatted with guests and handed out white plates filled with steaming samples of their food.

Whether or not she got into the competition, she still wanted to meet the chefs, so he might as well introduce her to them. *Then*, he'd head home.

Cut it out. Will believed in honesty, so he should probably stop lying to himself. He *wanted* to hang out with her and, since he didn't have to be home until his meeting with the trainer at four, he should just relax. He had all night to go over the resumes.

"Probably not the best time to meet them," Delilah said. "But I'd love to see what they've made." She broke out in a huge grin. "See who I'm competing against."

"You do realize I have no pull in this whatsoever?"

"Oh, I know." She turned serious. "I'm not trying to manipulate you, Will. If you want me to stop talking about it with you, I totally understand."

"No." He never wanted to shut down her enthusiasm. "As long as you know my world is completely separate from this, then you can talk about it all you want."

"I do. I swear."

"Hey, man." An old friend from high school came up and clapped him on the shoulder, leaning in for a hug.

The look of concern made Will think he should've waited a few more days until the novelty of being a *fucking cheater* had faded before coming into town.

To hell with that. I've done nothing wrong. "Jimmy. How's it going?"

"Good, good. I—"

Nope. Don't want to hear it. "This is Delilah, Callie's friend. She's a chef from New York City."

Jimmy and Delilah shook hands, but his friend swung right back to Will. "I'm gutted, man. I can't believe what that little shit's done to you."

"Where I come from," Delilah said in her sexy voice. "It's called Small Dick Syndrome."

Jimmy's mouth gaped open, and then he burst out laughing. "That's exactly right." He draped an arm around Will's shoulder. "We all know it's bullshit. Just want you to know that. No one here buys it. Not for a second. Your dad was a good man. The best."

"Yeah, he was. Thanks, man."

"Everyone here knows how hard you and your brothers train. We know—"

"Oh, my gosh," Delilah said. "I *love* this restaurant." She gestured to the shiny brass bar, the burgundy leather booths and dark-stained wood paneling.

Affection for her blasted away his frustration. She'd read him well, and he appreciated the shift in conversation.

"Your brother really held true to the architecture and décor of the period. It's like I've gone back in time." She gazed up at him. "Only with way better food. Do you smell that? I'm starving."

"Jimmy, we're going to grab some lunch. I'll catch up with you later?"

"Sure thing." His friend returned to his booth.

"Hey, Will," the hostess called from podium. "It's all buffet, so grab a plate and get busy."

He gave her a nod in thanks.

"You're staying?" Delilah asked.

That was the thing about her, he realized. She didn't hide her happiness. Didn't play games. *I like that.* "Yeah. I'll sit with you."

"Cool." She watched the chefs in pure awe. "Look at them. I mean, they're all so out of my league and, yet, I think I could hold my own with them. I really do." She reached for his hand, clasped it, and gave it a squeeze. "I want this. I really do. I mean, I looked at their bios on the plane, and there's no question they've got way more experience." She went rigid, her eyes wide, before breaking out in a smile. "Oh, my God." She dug into her tote for the tablet and powered it up.

"What's going on?"

"I got a review, from the top food critic in Manhattan.

He thinks my food's 'magnificent.'" Pride and confidence made her rosy complexion glow.

Will wouldn't get involved, but he sure as hell hoped the board let her into the competition. He wanted her beauty—her smile, her positive energy—in his house. In his life. "When you're done with that, go grab some food. I'll get us a table."

She looked up from her screen. "What do you want?"

"Nothing." He'd already had his protein shake. He wouldn't eat again until noon. But she looked disappointed, so he said, "Bring me whatever meat looks good." She'd learn pretty quickly that food was fuel to him.

"Spoken like a non-foodie. Protein and veggies. I got you." She gave him a thoughtful expression. "You know, if you let me, I can give you exactly the kind of food you're used to but with actual flavor. If I promise not to use butter or oil or anything like that, would you at least try something I make?"

There was no censure in her tone. Just interest. He liked that. "Of course."

"You train three hundred and sixty-five days a year? No breaks?"

"Training's my job, so I do it five days a week. I take weekends off, and I travel a lot, so no, not three hundred and sixty-five days a year."

"I'm going to take a wild guess and say that your idea of fun on the weekend involves hiking or mountain biking, so…closer to three hundred and sixty? Give or take a day or two?"

He couldn't help the smile from spreading. "How do you know I don't fish? Or play solitaire? I could have all kinds of sedate hobbies."

She took a slow and bold pass from his neck, down the

slope of his shoulder to his bicep, across his chest—sliding from one pec to the other—and then back up to his eyes. "Just a hunch."

He burst out laughing. "Okay, you're right. But I learned early on that it's just not worth taking a break. It's too hard to get back into shape after slacking off. Especially at my age."

"Yeah, you old fart. Do you miss anything? Beer, pot, cake?"

"I don't know." He'd never really thought about it.

"You don't know?" She had a mischievous smile. "Come on, you must've gotten drunk in college, pulled all-nighters and lived off coffee and day-old pizza?"

He gave a one-shouldered shrug.

"Oh, my God, you didn't, did you?"

"I've been competing since I was eleven. Not a lot of opportunity to party."

"Hey, Will." The hostess—Lindy, if he recalled—approached, arms balancing several plates. "Thought I'd get you started before all the food ran out."

"Thank you."

They followed her to a booth and slid in on either side, facing each other. Delilah watched as the hostess set down each plate. "This looks fantastic." She glanced up. "Thank you."

But the hostess barely spared her a glance, and Will didn't care for that. "Lindy, this is Delilah. She's a chef."

"Nice to meet you."

Given her wide eyes as she took in the various platters, Delilah didn't seem the least bit bothered by Lindy's flat tone.

"Let me know if I can get you anything else." Lindy

lingered, suggestion in her eyes, and Will decided to kill it right there.

"We've got it. Thank you."

The moment the hostess left, Delilah unfolded her napkin and set it on her lap. "I kind of wanted to get the food myself so I could see which chef made what." She eyed the food like she didn't know where to start. "But this looks amazing."

He did a quick sweep of the plates. One held cheeses, slices of crusty baguette, grapes, fresh figs, and almonds. Another had small bowls of what looked like couscous, polenta, and creamy mashed potatoes. Not much for him to eat. He started to slide out of the booth to find some of that grilled meat he could smell, but Delilah plunged a fork into the potatoes, and he wasn't going to miss this show for anything.

"Mm." She closed her eyes and moaned. "Oh, my God, these are unbelievable."

He could imagine her making that sound in a whole other context.

She shuddered. "This is so good. I think they put ancho chiles in the potatoes. Can you imagine?" She stabbed a fork into a stalk of asparagus and bit off the tip. She chewed, eyes closing again. "What the heck did they put on this? It's got a serious bite." She reached for her water glass. "One of those chefs knows her southwestern spices. That's really good."

"I'm questioning my life choices right now."

"You should be. Man, oh, man. This is good." She dipped her fork into the polenta and turned it his way. "One bite."

"I'll pass, thanks." *So, you can resist cheesy polenta that smells out of this world but not the woman sitting across from you?* "I'm going to see what kind of meat they've got. Want anything?"

"Oh, you know, maybe just one of everything?" Her eyes sparkled with humor.

But as he slid to the edge of the bench seat, he heard his name coming from the table behind him.

"I know he wouldn't *cheat*."

He recognized the voice. *Tim*. A friend from high school. He shot a look to Delilah. *Like I told you*. His friends and family knew Damien was full of shit.

"But," Tim continued. "Could he have benefitted in some way from his family money? I know they wouldn't pay anyone off—that doesn't make sense—but the judges might favor him because he's rich."

Will froze. *Are you fucking kidding me?*

He'd grown up with Tim. They'd skied together.

My dad took you in when your parents kicked you out for three months senior year.

"Benefit how?"

That sounded like Kylie. He'd been on the ski team with her in college.

"It's numerical," she said. "They get a *score*. There's one for execution of tricks, variety of tricks, difficulty, pipe use, and amplitude."

"Or maybe the League wants him to win," someone said. "Maybe it brings in more sponsors when Will's going for his seventh, eighth or ninth win. It's the hype."

"That's a good point," Tim said. "He gives something like ten scholarships to the League every year. And it doesn't have to be conscious. They might just like him, so they give him higher scores."

"The judges are former skiers," Kylie said. "That doesn't make any sense. You guys are being ridiculous, and it sucks that you're giving Damien's bullshit any credibility."

"I don't know," Tim said. "I'm just saying it might be possible."

It's possible? His friends thought he benefitted from his dad's money?

"Can we get out of here?" Delilah said. "I've lost my appetite." She shifted out of the booth, gliding by Tim's table. "Must be the stink of disloyalty in the air."

Will pushed open the door, letting Delilah pass through, and walked out into the bright sunlight, sick to his stomach that the guys who knew him, had grown up skiing with him, questioned his integrity.

Delilah slid her big, black sunglasses on, making her look like a movie star. "Why didn't you say anything?"

"There's nothing to say." He started off towards his truck, his boots thundering on the boardwalk.

"Yes, there is. And if *you're* not going to, then I sure as hell will."

"Don't bother."

"Will, come on. You have to defend yourself."

"I do. Every time I hit the half-pipe." *Words don't mean shit.*

At the end of the walkway, he hopped off. Noticing he was heading into one of the staged shoot-outs, he cut through the alley between two buildings.

He didn't hear her footsteps on the dirt, so he turned around. She wasn't there. He jogged back to find her heading into the saloon. "Delilah, stop. Where're you going?"

"I'm going to tell them what I think about their stupid, disloyal faces."

"No, you're not. I have to get home to Ruby." His sister had spent more than enough time with his mother.

Shooting an evil eye to the saloon doors, she relented and hustled beside him to his truck.

He pulled his keys out of his jeans' pocket. "Look, it's not just impacting me. A bunch of judges have already held press conferences. Their integrity's been called into question just as much as mine. They're refusing to judge again."

"Does Damien realize what he's done here? And why would he even want to win now that he's stirred up all this trouble? He'll never know if he won because you're out of the running or if he really deserved it."

"Trust me, Damien believes he deserves it. He thinks because he does more spins that he's the better skier. But that's not how the competition works. It's based on technical skills. You have to execute them better than everyone else. If you don't stomp your landing, or if you don't get enough amplitude, you lose points. It's that simple. Damien thinks he should win because his tricks have more flash."

"Well, you can't just let him get away with it. You have to do something."

"Nothing for me to do." He hit the keypad and got into the truck.

She got in on the other side and slammed the door, shutting out the world. "What about the Olympics?"

"What about it?"

"You're going to stand at the top of the half-pipe, ready to do your thing, and even though the investigation's cleared your name, won't it still be at the back of people's minds? Won't your fans discuss it in their living rooms and in sports bars just like they did back there?" She pointed a thumb behind her.

"Yes." The word came out hard, dirty, like he'd just spit it out of his mouth.

"So, is there anything you can do that will kill the whole thing for good? Anything that will prove, beyond a shadow of a doubt, that you've earned your medals?"

And just like that the anger cleared. He shoved the key in the ignition, every cell in his body shifting, heating up, slamming into each other.

There sure as hell is.

Chapter Eight

When his mom left the family, he'd felt powerless. Discipline, *structure*, had restored his sense of control.

Damien pulling this stunt? Wiping out all the years of hard work? It snatched the rug out from under him all over again.

Until now. Delilah had reminded him there *was* something he could do, the ultimate competition that would obliterate all the bullshit rumors.

Freefest.

As soon as he got home, he'd add his name to the roster. Because he'd go to the Olympics with a clear record, he'd bring home the ultimate gold medal for his dad's trophy case, and he'd shut down Damien Brenner, once and for all.

As they passed the fairgrounds, the sea of white tents caught Delilah's attention. "What's that?"

"Farmers Market." He already knew how much she wanted to go, and since his fingers itched to sign up for the competition, he flipped the turn signal.

"Are we going?"

"You go."

"Are you sure?"

"Just keep it brief, okay?" He pulled into the dirt parking lot and eased into a spot. "We can come back tomorrow after my work-out."

"Awesome. I'll just take a quick look around to get an idea what they sell."

The minute he put the gearshift into Park, Delilah flicked the latch on her seatbelt, and hopped out of the truck. "Give me ten minutes."

He pulled his phone out of the console and got out of the truck, leaning against the fender as he tapped out a text message to his manager.

Entering Freefest.

Ready to compose the same thing to his brothers, he smiled when his phone vibrated with a call. *Alex.* He smiled as he answered. "That got your attention."

"You're not doing Freefest. Are you crazy?" Rarely did his manager, normally cool as a cucumber, shout. "You've got the *Olympics*."

"Think I know that."

"I couldn't believe you entered last year, but I was damn glad you didn't go through with it."

The world of skiing was divided by freestyle competitors and freeriders. The first group practiced tricks until they could perform them on muscle memory alone. The second didn't care about technical performances. They rode the mountains for the sheer joy of it. For the rush.

So, after the season ended, the best skiers in the world met in a secret location to compete against each other. Just skiers and the terrain. No media, no sponsors, no agenda. Just athletes judging each other. Whoever went home with that trophy knew he'd outperformed every other skier in the world.

Last year, bad weather had hit the mountain, and just about all the freestyle athletes had pulled out. With the competition season approaching, they couldn't take the risk.

He'd take it now.

"You've got nothing to prove, Will. You hear me? Let me handle it on my end."

"There's no other way *to* handle Damien's accusation." *Thank you, Delilah, for reminding me of that.* "The League's investigation is bullshit. They'll, what? Talk to the sponsors, the judges? Everyone will deny it, and the case will be closed. But it won't change anything for me. It won't remove the question at the back of everyone's mind." *Could he have done it?*

"Don't screw up what could be your last shot at Olympic gold by doing something as reckless as Freefest."

"I have to." He gazed up at the dark gray mountains. "That medal won't mean shit if people are wondering if my dad bought my previous wins, so I'm clearing my name now in the only way that matters."

"Dammit, Will. You're making a mistake here."

He turned his back on the Farmers Market and lowered his voice. "For ten years I didn't win. And, every single time I lost, I felt like shit. I wanted to quit, but I didn't. I went back harder. Trained smarter, adjusted my diet, did everything I could to get better. And then, one day, I finally won. The whole world talked about me like I was some overnight success, but that's only because I wasn't on their radar before that point, so they didn't see the work I put in—the failures I racked up. I will be damned if I let Damien take away what it took seventeen years to achieve. I'm not asking for your opinion on this, Alex. I'm doing it."

As they roared down the highway, Delilah scanned the grass-covered preserve for signs of an elk. She didn't see any but, then, she'd heard they only came down in winter.

Using an earpiece, Will, in total warrior mode, discussed his plans with Fin.

He'd already talked to the other two brothers. Their resistance only splashed butane onto his resolve. And there was nothing hotter than his you-can't-stop-me, I-can-move-mountains-with-my-bare-hands-if-I-set-my-mind-to-it attitude.

No wonder he's a champion.

Just hearing his voice—powerful, determined—brought about a strange fluttering in her belly.

Her work was so all-consuming that she didn't tend to date guys with Will's intensity. She liked the fun ones, the wild ones. The ones who didn't think too hard or require too much of her. Ones who let her loosen the release valve every now and then.

But those guys…frankly, there was no chance of her falling in love with them. Will, though…there was something so appealing about him. She suspected his intensity, if he ever fell in love, would translate to ardor, and he'd be all-in. He'd want everything from his woman—and he'd give everything he had.

An image struck. Her, on her back in bed, Will looming over her with that passion, that fire in his eyes directed towards her. His hunger for her, his possessive touch…desire jolted through her.

She'd bet her life he wasn't the kind of man to just get himself off. He was the kind who paid attention to every sound and movement his partner made. The kind who'd read her responses. Because he cared. Because he sank that deeply into the few people who mattered to him.

The image in her mind shifted to Will leaning closer. Close enough to set her heart thundering. To see the crystalline blue of his eyes. And then he kissed her. Not a soft press of lips, a gentle, Hey-is-this-okay? No, it was, a freaking open-up-that-mouth-and-let-me-in-before-I-die-without-the-potent-taste-of-you make-out session.

A current of desire ripped through her so powerfully she had to squeeze her thighs together and turn away so he wouldn't catch it on her face. She'd never thought about sex—love—this way before. As something so…consuming.

And why on earth she was thinking about *Will* this way, she had no idea. She wasn't going to have *sex* with him. He'd been kind enough to let her stay in his home during a really turbulent time in his life. He didn't need the complication of a fling.

Besides, there's only one thing I should be thinking about. Because, somehow, turning tail and escaping to the wild west might have just turned into a once-in-a-lifetime opportunity.

Glancing down at her phone, she scrolled back to the email Chris had sent while she'd been squeezing tomatoes.

Hey, Delilah. No objections to adding a sixth chef. I've already forwarded your resume and that review to the other board members. With the opening this weekend, we're meeting pretty much every day. I'll bring it up with them this afternoon. Get back to you soonest.

Chris.

The thrill of it seized her. What if they let her in? She'd go up against some of the greatest chefs in the world.

"Later." Will cut the connection, his knuckles white on the steering wheel.

"Everything good? Your brothers didn't scare you off?"

He watched the road ahead with a look of an invading conqueror. "You want to know when you wipe out?" He cut a look her way. That hint of a smile made her pulse quicken. "When you let doubt in. The moment you question yourself, you screw up."

"Total mind control." She'd take that advice with her into the competition. "That's got to take some serious discipline."

"It does. And, yes, your mental game is everything."

"I guess you'll need to start training right away." Would she see him less? It had only been a few days, but she liked spending time with him. Really liked it. But, of course, if things went her way, she'd be just as busy. It was probably for the best if they focused on their own goals.

"Oh, yeah. Post season training's nothing more than maintenance. Event training's a whole other ballgame. After my run, I'll hit the gym, so that'll be four hours in the morning and a couple hours in the afternoon to go over film." His fingers flexed on the steering wheel. "I need to find a nanny."

Wow, he was totally in the zone. She shook off the hit of disappointment, reminded herself she'd only known him a minute. It wasn't like she was losing anything. "I heard from Chris. He said they don't mind adding a sixth chef. They'll get back to me this afternoon." Only one thought tempered her optimism. "Do you think your brother will mind me joining?" Will had only talked to Brodie about Freefest.

"Not at all." One side of his mouth curved up. "He'll like upping the stakes."

"I'm sure I don't stand a chance in hell of winning, but I'm going to give it all I've got." Because it wasn't just about the money. No, it was about proving to her siblings she was good enough to open her own restaurant.

Every bite was magnificent, every flavor lingered so lovingly on my tongue that I didn't want to move onto the next course

If Harry Morgenstern believed in her, why didn't her siblings?

When she shifted in her seat, she noticed Will's foul expression. "What's that for?"

"What?"

She waved a hand at his face. "That." She matched her expression to his.

He took a hand off the wheel and turned it palm-up. It was a *what the fuck* gesture. "Can you imagine if I had that attitude at the starting block? If I looked out at the course and thought, I don't stand a chance of winning, but I'll give it all I've got."

Awareness locked into place. "You'd break your neck."

"That's right."

"It's all about the mental game."

He nodded firmly.

He was right. She had to get her siblings out of her head. She was a trained chef who'd packed in a whole hell of a lot of learning and apprenticing over the course of her life.

I can totally do this. "What's the first challenge?"

"Opening night, they've got five bartenders competing

to make a signature cocktail for the resort, and the chefs are presenting hors d'oeuvres." Just as he turned into the driveway and paused for the gate to open, his phone vibrated. He checked the screen and then answered with a smile. "What's up, old man?"

Whoever he was talking to spoke a mile a minute. Will's features went rigid. "Have you searched every room in the house? Closets, cabinets—shit, okay."

Alarm hit her skin like a bucket of ice. "Ruby?"

But he didn't answer her. "Call the police. Call everyone we know. We'll do a sweep of the area. I'm almost there." He tossed the phone into the cup holder and floored it.

"Ruby?" she said again.

"She's gone."

"What does that mean?" Lost in the house? Because the idea that she'd wandered off on this three hundred thousand acre ranch…was unthinkable.

"It means my fucking mother wasn't paying attention."

The moment the house came into sight, Delilah threw off her seatbelt. Trucks lined the driveway, pulled over haphazardly. A man in a black Polo shirt and jeans ran across the meadow.

Will hit the brakes, and they both jumped out of the truck.

Her fragile gold sandals slowed her down, so she kicked them off and ran up the asphalt in her bare feet. As she reached the house, she found Mrs. Bowie on the porch, looking pale and frightened.

"How long has she been missing?" Delilah said.

"I don't know. Maybe half an hour."

How could she not know? "Where'd you last see her?"

"I put her down for a nap. For God's sake, I made sure the gate was locked."

"Did you have the baby monitor on?"

"Of course. I didn't hear a thing."

Well, that couldn't be true. Ruby always made noise.

Worry crimped the skin around the older woman's eyes. "But there's a pile of books on the floor. She must've used them to climb over it."

If she had, she'd have tumbled down the stairs. The wedge of space between the gate and floor was too narrow for a little girl to safely land. Delilah brushed past her and hurried up the stairs. She strode down the hallway, blood pumping with determination. There was only one place Ruby wanted to be: with Will.

The woman's heels clacked on the wood floor. "I already checked the bedrooms. That's the first place I looked."

"Did you check Will's closet?"

"I checked everywhere. Under beds, in cabinets. Everywhere. She only wants Will. She doesn't want anyone else. And she doesn't listen."

Delilah tuned her out, slapping Will's door open with the palm of her hand. She made a quick scan, taking in the hastily made bed—the covers tossed back to expose navy sheets, the jeans draped over the back of a chair, and the open door to the balcony.

"Ruby?" She raced across the room and stepped out into the bright sunshine, but she didn't see the little girl. Hands gripping the bannister, she peered below to a grassy area that surrounded a sand volleyball court. "Ruby." Her voice carried on a warm breeze.

Whipping back around, she nearly ran into Mrs.

Bowie. *Move.* "Excuse me." She hurried into the closet. "Ruby? Sweetie?" She was so sure she'd hear that sweet little voice that when it didn't come, her heart thundered. Where was she?

She hurried down the stairs to grab her phone and found a text from Will.

Anything?

She checked the time stamp. Four minutes ago. *Dammit.* She shot him back a text. ***No. You?***

He responded right away. ***Check the backyard gate. Let me know if it's closed. If it is, she couldn't have gotten out that way.***

Beyond the back fence lay bears, coyotes, elk, wolves…danger. Delilah spun around and dashed through the house.

Mrs. Bowie followed her across the living room. "I don't know how she got by me. I was sitting right here." She gestured to the couch.

Delilah flew out the back door. A wide slate terrace gave way to the enormous pool with lush plantings and waterfalls. Hedges and willows kept the stone wall surrounding the backyard hidden, but she easily found her way to the tall iron gate. She finally released a breath when she found it securely latched.

She shot Will a text. ***Closed.***

Her phone rang as soon as she hit send. "Will?"

"We got her."

"Where was she?" But he'd already disconnected. She hurried back into the cool house and found Mrs. Bowie in the kitchen. "They found her."

"Oh, thank God. Where?"

Without answering, she brushed right past her to get to Ruby. The moment she hit the living room, the front door burst open and Will entered, followed by Lachlan. Ruby clung to her brother, her features flushed and sweaty.

Relief hit her in such a rush, her body flooded with adrenaline, making her shaky and weak. Blood roared in her ears with the imperative to get to that little girl. "*Ruby*." She threw her arms around their backs, both of them hot and damp. "I'm so glad you're okay."

The three of them stood in a tight circle, the only sound their harsh breathing.

Ruby had been outside. *Alone*.

Delilah thought of that moose her first night in town, yesterday's bison. Three hundred thousand acres of meadow and forest. She could've gotten lost. She could've gotten hurt.

But Ruby didn't look scared. She didn't even look relieved. In fact, a vein throbbed in her temple, and she gave Will a fierce look. "You go way. No, no, no. Dat bad, Wheel." And then her tone turned stern. "Wooby go wif you."

Will looked tortured. "You went shopping with Grandma."

Chest rising and falling too quickly, Ruby looked on the verge of tears. But not a single one spilled over. Instead, she shrieked, "*Go wif you*."

Brother and sister faced off, both of them equally stubborn. Until Will's stern façade faltered. He was torn, and Delilah wondered which way he'd fall.

Love her.

Reassure her.

"Do you see what I had to deal with?" his mom said. "First, I had to force her into a car seat. And then she threw a tantrum in the dress shop. I finally had to bring her back home. We didn't get a thing."

But Will ignored her, focused exclusively on his sister. "I work, Ruby. I can't be with you all the time, but you've got Uncle Lachlan and Marcella and lots of other people here with you."

Delilah noted the omission of his mom.

"No, no, no. Wooby wif *Wheel.*" She gave a toss of her head to emphasize his name.

"Not all the time." He started to set her down, but she clung to him.

Oh, come on, Will. Now is not the time to establish her "routine."

Just hold her until she settles down.

But he pried her fingers off his arms and lowered her. When her legs refused to straighten, he looked to Lachlan, who quickly moved in.

"Come on, kid. They're delivering the swing set today. Let's go outside and you can tell me where you want it."

Ruby kicked and twisted in his arms, but Lachlan wrapped his big, burly arms around her and whisked her away. An electric energy filled the space she left behind.

Will's chin tipped down, hands on his hips. Delilah should go. Leave mother and son to talk it out, but the silence, the crackling tension, locked her in place.

After a moment, he looked to the staircase with a thoughtful expression. "How'd she get over that gate without falling head over ass?"

"I have no idea. I was right there." Mrs. Bowie pointed to the couch. "She couldn't have gotten past me."

The look he gave his mom would have sent a sane person to her knees. "But she did."

"I don't know how." His mom looked defiant. "I only

left the room to make myself a cup of tea. Otherwise, I was here the whole time, and she didn't make a peep."

Will tensed. "You shut off the monitor, didn't you?"

Delilah had only been here a few days, but she'd never known Ruby to be quiet during nap time. She always chatted with Squawk or hummed.

Mrs. Bowie looked away.

"You were pissed at her for not cooperating in the store." Though his tone held no emotion, the flatness sounded menacing. "You probably tossed her in bed the minute you got home. When she kept making a fuss, you shut off the monitor. Went about your business."

"There's a gate at the top of the stairs, all the doors down that hallway are closed, the doorknobs have safety covers..." Her tone turned belligerent. "How could she possibly get out?"

So she'd turned off the monitor *and* gone about her business. *There's no way a two-year-old could've made it out of the house if this woman had been paying attention.*

"She's just like you were," Mrs. Bowie said. "Stubborn and difficult. And *you're* just like your father. You're not doing her any favors by catering to her every whim."

Will's expression hardened. "You used to tell everybody how you only had four boys because you kept hoping for a girl. Well, here she is. A girl. And she's still not what you had in mind."

"With a firm hand, she'll be—"

"You'll never get to find out what she'll be." With a tense jaw and rigid shoulders, he looked her hard in the eye. "It's time for you to go."

Without a word, his mom swept out of the room. Her heels clicked on the hardwood floor. She got halfway up the stairs when she stopped and looked down at him.

"It's a shame your brothers aren't in town to handle this mess."

The moment she disappeared down the hallway, Delilah said, "Not your number one fan, huh?"

He didn't smile. "She can't stand me." He headed into the kitchen, and she followed.

She could see where he'd get that impression. "You're her son. She loves you. She just doesn't like being challenged."

"No, she actually can't stand me." He watched out the window as Lachlan and Ruby, on their hands and knees, set leaves onto the surface of the pool, like colorful little boats.

His uncle put something on Ruby's arm, and she sat back on her heels, utterly enthralled.

"Brodie's supposed to be the seven-time world champion," Will said. "Not me. He's the one who's supposed to be the Olympian."

What? She didn't say a word, leaving the space open for him to say more if he wanted.

He kept his gaze trained on Ruby. "My mom's right. Ruby's a lot like I was. A little hellion. I caused her a lot of trouble." He sucked in a breath. "But the last straw was when my brothers and I went skiing during a supermoon."

Oh, no. She cringed. "How old were you?"

"I was eleven. Had it all planned out. Earlier in the day we'd left our skis on the other side of the fence, so we didn't make a sound when we snuck out. We hiked to the Bowie Pass, which is the widest. I deliberately chose the easiest, safest run, but I guess the shadows threw off his judgement." His features pinched as though watching the reel of it in his mind. "Brodie went right off the cliff. Busted his knee pretty bad."

"That must've been terrifying." But he was all right now, wasn't he? Callie had never mentioned an issue with Brodie.

"She already had a hard time with me, but that was it. She was done."

"Well, not literally. It was just a scary situation. People say things they don't mean all the time. Especially when they're upset."

He scrubbed his clean-shaven jaw. "After his surgery, she took my brothers with her to New York City."

"For how long?"

"She meant it to be permanent, but if she thought raising boys in the mountains was tough, she found it ten times worse in Manhattan. When the three of them went through the ice at the Central Park Pond, that was it for her. She sent them all back here." He glanced at her. "Mothering wasn't really her thing."

Pressed so close together in the mud room, aware of the clean scent of his clothes, the warmth from his skin, she understood him in a whole new light. "I'm pretty sure you just skimmed over the worst part of the story."

For the first time, she saw the little boy that still kicked around inside him. That hint of vulnerability transformed him from a formidable champion to a guy just as wounded by life as everyone else. She wanted to get up on her toes and kiss him.

God, that mouth. That beautiful, sexy mouth.

She seriously hated what his mother had done to him. "Your mom left you behind?"

"Yeah. My parents didn't know, but I heard the whole conversation. I waited for them to get home from the ER so I could see how Brodie was, but when I heard them arguing I didn't come downstairs. It was a pretty brutal fight. She threatened my dad. Said if he didn't send me to boarding school or do something about me once and for all she was leaving. And my dad said…" The barest hint of a smile softened his features. "My dad said there was nothing wrong with me. I was a kid." A bittersweet affection sparked in his smile. "And there wasn't a chance he was giving me to someone else to raise. That, if she had a problem with me, it was up to her to figure out a better way to reach me. He said we don't discard our children. We work with them until we get them on the right path."

"What a good man." She said it in a whisper, and she couldn't miss the way his skin bubbled with gooseflesh. She wanted to run her fingers over the bumps. "I wish I'd met him."

"You'd have loved him. You both have big personalities."

Will didn't give many compliments, so when he did… it just…it meant a lot. "So, how are you to blame for Brodie not being in the Olympics? He was, what, nine years old when he got injured?"

"Brodie was a phenom. After the injury, my dad hired a full-time coach to teach us how to use our bodies, how to move and react. If we were going to run amuck, he wanted us as safe as possible. So, as soon as Brodie finished his physical therapy, he was back on the slopes, and he was amazing. Best out of all of us." He gave a wry grin. "And then, two months away from the Olympics, he hurt his knee again. Wasn't even skiing. The doctor told him if anything else happened, he could do permanent damage. So he quit, and my mom never forgave me."

Now that she understood him a little better, the lines around his eyes that crinkled with concern took on a whole new meaning. She'd mistook cockiness for worry that he was being judged. His mom had done a number on him. "That's really terrible. I hope your dad and uncle made you understand that it's your mom who's messed up. Not you."

His brows lifted in surprise. "I was a handful."

"Good. That's how kids are supposed to be. And if she watched you the same way she watched Ruby today, then I'm not surprised you guys didn't have more bad accidents."

One half of his mouth lifted. "I like that about you."

"What?"

"You've got my back." His smile widened, a tenderness softening his eyes. "You're good people, Delilah Lua."

Something flowed between them, something hot and magical, and her pulse raced.

But, like flipping a switch, he looked back out the window. "I don't know what I'm doing with her."

"Ruby?" she asked.

He nodded.

"You're doing a great job."

"I'm so far out of my element here. It's tough enough raising a kid, but one who just lost her mom? Jesus. I…I don't want to mess this up."

"It's not always going to be like this."

He turned to her, eyes begging for answers.

"In time, when she feels safe, she won't want to spend every minute with you. She'll get bored and want to play. She'll make friends. But, until then, maybe you could just let her have you."

"But that's the whole thing. She can't have me."

"What're you talking about? You're her brother. She has you forever." *He's overthinking this.*

"But I'm only in charge of her for three months. Then,

my brother takes over. Three months after that, she'll have someone else. She can't attach to me."

"Who should she attach to?" She hoped that didn't sound sarcastic. She meant it seriously.

"All of us."

"But *you're* here now." How did she get through to him? "Will, your sister needs you right now, today. You might not know what you're doing, but I promise you'll never go wrong by giving her the love and security she's so desperate for."

"Look, I'm not winging it here. I'm reading books. I'm learning how to handle the situation."

"She's not a situation. She's your sister. And if she can't get attached to you, then I don't know what kind of woman she's going to become. She can't just be chauffeured from one activity to another. Taken shopping, given meals. She's not a plant that you water daily. Do you know how lonely she's going to be? I know it's none of my business. I haven't even been here a week, but I know she's already attached to you. And it hurts to watch you push her away."

"I work. We all have jobs, just like any other guardian. Just like her mom did." He perked up. "Her mom was a flight attendant, so Ruby's used to babysitters. That's what it'll be like here. She'll get used to it."

"Is that what the books say?"

"Yeah, Delilah." He registered her sarcasm and shook his head. "That's exactly what the books say." He reached for the doorknob and headed outside

Chapter Nine

MOVEMENT STARTLED HIM AWAKE. EARLY MORNING light streamed in from around the edges of his curtains. Will tuned into the monitor but only heard silence. Ruby was all right.

He needed a full eight hours of sleep in order to put in the kind of training he'd do for Freefest, so he rolled over, determined to shut down his mind and get in a few more hours. Closing his eyes, he visualized the rails, his skis scraping along the narrow pipes. Turning his shoulder hard, he took flight off the bars and—

"Gee-yup, gee-yup." The whispered voice accompanied a rocking sensation.

Will jackknifed up. *What the hell?* He fumbled for the switch on his lamp. Warm yellow light spilled across his navy comforter, illuminating the frail pajama-clad back of the little girl sitting on his bed. Book on her lap, her long dark hair bounced with her quiet movements.

"Ruby?"

Face lit up, she crawled over to him, dragging the open

book. Will hadn't even adjusted the pillows before she'd nestled up against him. "Yook. Hawsey."

The assault of her warm, cotton-clad body and hair that smelled like sunshine on a field of wildflowers ignited every protective cell in his body. "Yeah, Ruby. That's a horse." *What time is it?* He reached for his phone. Five-fifty four. His alarm would go off in six minutes.

Didn't make sense to take her back to bed.

"Weed." She thrust the book at him.

What was he going to do with this girl? None of the advice from the books worked with her. She did what she wanted to do…joyfully. "Ruby, you know the deal. You have to wait until I come get you in the morning."

"I wake, Wheel." She nudged the book. "Weed." She curled up like a kitten against his ribcage, those little knees tilting towards him, her butt against his arm.

Of course he wanted to read to her. How could he not? But if he gave into her now, she'd make a habit of crawling into his bed and asking him to read. They'd do this every morning.

Would that be so bad?

Delilah would tell him to do it. To give her what she needs right now.

But he wasn't sure he should be taking advice from a woman whose rebellious streak cost her a family franchise. He'd been rebellious, too. *Look where it got me.*

Still, it was hard to say no to such a sweet, simple request. He pushed up higher and looked at the page. A horse, dog, skunk, and squirrel had to work together to get a stuffed animal back to its owner, a red-haired, freckled little girl who lived on the farm and took care of them all.

Ruby glanced up with that sparkly smile, an adoring

look in her eyes, and his heart about exploded. She trusted him. Needed him.

A prickly heat skidded down his arms. He didn't want to hurt her. She'd come to trust him, and then he'd leave. Fin would take over, and then Gray. Then Brodie. How many times could she open her heart only to have the person she trusted bail?

It'd make her feel all alone in the world, and that would change her. Make her hard, closed off. "We're not reading, Ruby." Structure would make her feel safe, keep her on the right path. "I told you to wait in your room until I get you."

Her features crunched in confusion and…hurt. "You weed, Wheel. Weed to me."

"We read at night before bed. Not at…" He picked up his phone. "Five fifty-six in the morning. Now, if you want, we can read when I get back from my work-out." *Good concession.* "And we can read before dinner. But you stay in your room until I come get you."

He swung his legs out of bed and reached for the athletic shorts he'd tossed on the chair. When he turned back, he found her standing on the mattress in her polka dot pajamas and puffy chicken slippers with her arms held high.

He reached for her, anticipating that moment when she clung to him, relieved when she did because he knew it wouldn't be long before she stopped loving him so unabashedly. When she'd come to understand he wasn't hers.

Or did he mean she wasn't his?

And it sucked because he wished she could have the stability she deserved. He just had to get her used to the way her life would be in this house.

Delilah had grown up in a brownstone—which meant vertical living. From street level, a set of stairs led down to the kitchen and family room on the bottom level. The first floor held the living room and formal dining area. All the bedrooms were on the second and third floors.

Her parents had worked all the time, and her dad had a problem throwing things out, so every floor was cluttered. The comfortable kind, though, with stacks of books against the walls, piles of papers waiting to be filed on the baby grand piano. Side tables held coasters and mugs with the dregs of coffee or tea.

Maybe because she was the youngest, but she'd always loved that evidence of her family around her. That sense that her people had pressed pause on whatever they were doing and would be right back.

The Bowie house couldn't be more different. With its massive rooms, high ceilings, and plate-glass windows that let the outdoors in, every room looked ready for a photo shoot with *Architectural Digest*. No piles of books—other than the ones artfully arranged—no unwashed plate with the crumbs of a quiche on the tines of a fork, and no shoes kicked off.

It made her miss home. The way it used to be, before her parents had died. She missed following the trail of her dad's aftershave to find him fixing whatever plumbing or electrical issue had befallen the big, old house. She wanted to walk into the kitchen and find her mom pouring boiling water from the kettle into mugs. She wanted to snatch a biscotti off a saucer and bite it before her mom could yank it out of her hands. *That's for your dad. Get your own.*

But, mostly, she was confused. Her brothers and sisters always praised her food. They thought she had a true gift. *So why not give me my franchise and trust me to rock the hell out of it?*

Phone in hand, she knew it was time to talk to her brother. They hadn't spoken since the day after her birthday party, and she needed to make peace with him. She loved him. She loved all her siblings, and she hated being on the outs with them. Plus, she needed to let them know her change in plans.

She'd heard back from Chris. She was in. They'd let her into the competition.

Every time she thought about it, fear immediately squelched the blossoming roar of joy.

Those other five competitors? They were a big deal. Chef Mathilda had a Michelin star, for crying out loud.

She had to keep reminding herself that she had an award, a great review from Harry Morgenstern, and more experience packed into her twenty-six years than most chefs had in a lifetime.

She could do this. Most importantly, if—no, *when*—she won, she'd get her franchise and the respect of her siblings. *Eyes on the prize.*

She stepped onto the balcony and hit her brother's speed dial. As the phone rang, she imagined hanging the Da Nonna's sign over the funky little space she'd always loved on Bleecker Street. Almost cave-like, it had stone walls and a bay window that overlooked the lively neighborhood.

Of course, she'd stay true to Da Nonna's standard décor, but she'd add some things that reminded her of her mom and dad. *Oh.* Maybe she could commission some mixed media pieces from Callie. Like her Dad's felt Fedora he liked to wear while shoveling snow. Her mom's strands of pearls and the Pez dispenser collection.

Pick up, Joe. I really want to talk to you.

The leaves shivered as an early morning breeze sailed across the pale green sage meadow. *Holy shit.* This view. Billowing white clouds shifted across a vast expanse of bright blue sky, skimming the tops of jarring mountain peaks. Jackson Hole, in all its splendor, was laid out before her. She breathed in the clean air, scented with sage and wildflowers and slightly chilled with snow run-off.

Her brother answered, breathless, right before voicemail would've picked up. "Delilah?"

"Hey." Hurt had built up a thick wall of resentment and frustration, but the sound of his voice knocked it all tumbling down.

"I've missed you, keiki."

She could hear kitchen noises in the background. Someone shouting, something clattering. "I miss you, too." A terrible wave of homesickness crested over her.

"What do you think of Wyoming?"

"It's great here, actually. Nothing like I expected."

"Good. Listen, I'm in the middle of the conversation with Tortolli I should've had a month ago, but I've got your flight information right here. We're looking forward to seeing you next week."

"Well, hang on. That's why I'm calling." It struck her that this call had the potential to change everything. Telling her oldest brother—a man twelve years her senior, who'd made sure she got to experience her family in the same way he had--that she was staying here for the summer could make him back down and give her the franchise. He'd want her to come home.

In a few days she could be back with her big, crazy

family. Back to the life she'd lived before this teeny, tiny glitch of Calamity, Wyoming.

The drag and pull in her soul surprised her. Not to go home, but to stay here. The competition excited her, the idea that she could beat those world-class chefs, the acknowledgement of her talents.

And, of course, Will. She could fall so hard for that man. "Joe, I'm staying here for the summer."

"What're you talking about? You're not staying in *Wyoming*. Why would you do that?" He must've set the phone down because she could hear him talking to someone, but it was muffled and faraway-sounding.

"Joe? *Joe*."

He came back on the line. "Come on, Delilah. Don't punish me. I know you think I'm being too hard on you, but you have to know it was a very difficult decision for us to make. In the end, we made the right one—not only for our business but for *you*."

She hardened. "The right decision for me is getting my franchise. It's what Dad and Mom wanted, and it's what I've earned. Look, I take full responsibility for Harry Morgenstern's review. You've told me a thousand times not to mess with the recipes, and I let my ego get in the way. I shouldn't have done that in the flagship restaurant, and I'm genuinely sorry."

"I...thank you. That's nice to hear."

"But I should be able to do whatever I want with my own restaurant. And that's why I'm staying in Calamity. The Bowies are running a competition. Five—well, now, *six* of the best chefs in the world are competing for a grand prize of a hundred thousand dollars. I'm going to use that money to start my franchise, and that way I won't touch any of the estate money. You guys won't be investing."

Her brother was quiet.

With each moment that ticked by, her anxiety grew. "Joe? Are you still there?"

"Yeah, I'm here." He sounded defeated.

Well, she was sorry to upset him, but she wasn't backing down. "I'm not going to fail you. I'll keep the décor the same. I'll even keep the menu mostly the same, but I'm going to have some other items. Seasonal dishes, a specials board. It'll be all right, I promise." *Trust me. Trust my cooking.*

"Delilah…no."

No? If she came up with the money herself, he didn't have a say in this. "It's in the will that I get a franchise."

"That's right. A *franchise*. I can't have you opening a restaurant with our name and décor and then have it be a different style of food."

"I thought you liked my food."

"I do. But it's not Nonna Abelli's, and that's what we sell. You can't open a McDonald's and sell pad thai and falafel. I'm sorry, Delilah. I love you. I think you're amazingly talented, but you can't open a franchise."

In her apartment in the city, lights flashed across her ceiling all night long. Sometimes red from cruisers, but mostly white headlights. Here, in Callie and Fin's bedroom at the back of the house, she had…pure darkness.

It was unnerving. Mostly, because her mind compensated for the silence with endless streams of thoughts.

Like the call with her brother. He'd definitively cut her out of the family business. Like, no hope. And it was like he'd pulled out her heart with his bare hands. Because that restaurant was her dad, her mom, her childhood. *My life.*

Joe kept the house so she could have Christmas morning in the family room off the kitchen and Thanksgiving in the formal dining room upstairs, but her memories, her heart, was in Da Nonna's kitchen. The utility closet still had the same step stool her mom had bought from Grace's Hardware so Delilah could stand in front of her dad while he stuffed shells and beat whipping cream.

She'd done her homework at the table by the window, while the wait staff set up for dinner, her mom's voice on the phone taking reservations, her dad bustling about as he fielded one distribution problem after another.

She'd absorbed the smells and sounds of that restaurant into every fiber of her being.

But Delilah was not the sort to wallow in self-pity. *That's not my style*. She had a competition to win. The first event was tomorrow—well, tonight. It had to be past midnight by now. Ideas for hors d'oeuvres swirled and spun, spitting out images now and then, a toast point, a clam shell, a dollop of sour cream. Her go-to ingredients in New York City didn't interest her. She wanted to use what grew here.

Thanks to the Chamber of Commerce, she'd put together a list of the Farmers Markets and sustainable farms and ranches in the region. She couldn't wait to visit them and talk to the owners to see what grew locally and who provided the products that didn't come from the area.

Okay, guess what? I'm not going to fall asleep.

Throwing back the covers, she dropped out of the enormous bed and snatched her brother's Cornell T-shirt off the floor. She pulled it on and jammed her feet into flip flops. Opening the door, she nearly had a heart attack when she found Ruby waiting in the hallway.

"Oh, sweet pea." The moment she reached for the little

girl, acting on her impulse to bring her into the kitchen with her—she stopped herself. She couldn't live here and ignore Will's rules. "Can't sleep?"

"I hongry."

What harm could there be in getting her a yogurt?

Will doesn't want you to. That's reason enough. "How 'bout we make pancakes for breakfast? I'll put some chocolate chips in them, okay?"

She lifted the arm that didn't hold Squawk, ready to go. "Make cakes."

"We can't do it now, Ruby, because it's the middle of the night." *She says, as she's heading downstairs to get to work like it's afternoon. Confusing much?* "But I promise we'll make them in the morning."

"It morneen." Ruby tossed Squawk over the gate and then kicked off her puffy chicken slippers. Clutching the white rods, she hoisted herself up. Like a monkey, she got a grip of the bar between her toes, gaining the traction she needed to climb higher. It took her all of two seconds to get to the top of the gate.

"Ruby." Sorry, but she couldn't help laughing. Nothing would stop this girl from getting what she wanted. Hooking an arm around her waist, Delilah pulled the little girl off the gate and turned her in her arms.

"Make cakes now?"

How the hell did Will say no to this fierce little girl? Everything in her screamed to take Ruby downstairs and make the damn pancakes. *It's the right thing to do*. Forcing her to stay in that strange bedroom, scared and alone, was plain wrong.

But…dammit, she had to honor Will's wishes. "Sweetheart, we can—"

"Ruby." That deep, rumbly voice startled the hell out of her.

Will stalked towards them. If she'd had a black light, she'd see the angry fluorescence radiating off him. Before he even reached them, Ruby hurled herself toward him, forcing him to lunge forward.

The three of them stood so close she could smell him, the scent of laundry detergent, the hint of pine forest, and the unique essence of *Will.*

He adjusted his sister in his arms, cupping her chin so she'd pay attention. "You need to stay in bed until I come get you. Do you understand?"

"Wheel." It was a chastising tone, as if he was just being ridiculous.

And it was exactly that kind of confidence that made Delilah love this child so damn much.

"Wally make cake. Shock-let cake. Come wif us."

Wally? Funny, because her nephew couldn't say Delilah either and called her La-lee. She'd always gotten a kick out of that, but she loved Wally even more. *The whole world should call me that.*

Chef Wally.

"No, Ruby." He rocked that stern, commanding tone, but the hilarious part was that Ruby couldn't have cared less. "If you want pancakes for breakfast, you have to go back to bed right now, and you have to stay there until I come get you in the morning." He headed toward her bedroom.

"Wake now. Wally make cake."

They slipped inside her room and, even though she knew she should go downstairs, Delilah waited, listening. She should get into the kitchen—*that's where her ideas popped*—and start thinking about a list of possible ingredients, but she couldn't move. Which was stupid because she shouldn't be so invested in this family that wasn't hers.

But she just really needed Will to make his sister feel safe right now. *Love her, Will.*

Sheets rustled, the mattress squeaked, and she imagined his big body sitting on the edge of her bed as he tucked her in.

"You can make pancakes for breakfast, Ruby. Not in the middle of the night." The bed squeaked again. "Goodnight." His bare feet padded toward the door and then stopped. "Ruby." This time his tone tried really hard to be stern. "What did I tell you? Get back in bed until I come get you in the morning."

"No. Wif you, Wheel."

Something was different in her voice, something wobbly, and it broke Delilah's heart. If he put that little girl back to bed right now, she'd didn't think she could stand it.

It might not be her place to rock Ruby to sleep with the whir of the beaters and the hum of the refrigerator like her mom had done for her, but she knew it would soothe her—and that was all that mattered.

She's scared.

She misses her mom.

He had to know Ruby wasn't going to sleep, that he was sentencing her to more terrifying loneliness. She'd sit in that stupid half-crib baby bed thing all alone in the dark, fear turning shadows into monsters and creaks into howls, wondering what the hell was taking her mom so long to come get her.

"Do you want to run with me in the morning?"

"Yes." Oh, that tiny, little voice. Scared, yet holding strong in the face of the man she'd chosen to love.

"Then you need to get back in bed and go to sleep. If you do, I'll take you on a run with me."

Ruby sighed, the bed squeaked.

"Good night, Ruby. I'll see you in a few hours."

She should go, skedaddle before she got caught listening in the hallway. But the room went excruciatingly silent.

And it took everything Delilah had not to peek inside and see what was happening.

Chapter Ten

She's killing me.

Will stood in the room that smelled of baby powder and raspberry jam and watched Ruby's lower lip wobble. *It's one in the morning. She has to learn to sleep through the night.*

What the hell am I supposed to do?

On one side, he had the books telling him to put her back to bed. On the other, he had Delilah warning him Ruby was scared in this room. That she needed Will to stay with her until she felt safe enough to fall asleep.

Delilah was an intuitive, impulsive woman, and—oddly—he trusted her. But she wasn't an expert, and this situation was too important to screw up.

So, what should he do? Let Delilah take her to the kitchen and make pancakes?

It had worked that first night. No doubt, Ruby had been crashed out in Delilah's arms. *Point for Delilah.*

But the books promised if he stuck with the program, she'd adjust more quickly to her new world. And what was more important? Satisfying her immediate needs or helping her become a well-adjusted young woman? *Point for the books.*

He didn't know.

He just didn't fucking know.

And he wished like hell his dad were here to help him. But he wasn't, and his brothers weren't in town, so it was all on him.

He'd talked to an old friend of his dad's yesterday, a retired therapist. She'd confirmed everything the books said: enforce the routine so she adjusted to her new normal. The first few weeks would be tough, but she'd be better off for it in the long run.

Trust me, Will. Consistency will make her feel safe, loved.

Point for the therapist.

Every step he took out of her room tugged on the thread that tied him to that little girl.

But…he had to go with the therapist's advice.

Walking away required him to draw on every ounce of his discipline, but he had to trust that Ruby wanted to run with him badly enough that she'd stay in bed. He knew she would.

That's what the therapist says, anyway.

He walked down the hallway, visualizing her in bed, breaths evening out. That sweet baby face relaxed as she dozed off.

When he reached the gate, though, he couldn't help himself. He had to check.

Please don't be there, Ruby.

He glanced back.

His spirit crashed when he found her standing in the hallway, watching him with sad eyes.

Consistency will make her feel safe, loved.

He didn't want to do this. He wanted to light a match

and burn the words that were about to come out of his mouth. But he had a job to do. A tough one. And, in the end, it would help her settle in.

He drew in a breath. "I told you, that if you wanted to go on a run with me in the morning, you needed to stay in bed until I come get you."

She sucked in a shuddery breath. The orange glow from the night light he'd plugged into the hallway socket made the welling tears glitter.

"So, that means you can't come with me tomorrow, Ruby."

"Come wif you."

"No, Ruby. Not tomorrow. Because you didn't stay in your room." His pulse raced. "Now get back to bed so you can come with me on Tuesday."

She stood there watching him.

"Do you want to come with me on Tuesday?" How the hell did she know what Tuesday meant? *Shut up.* He had to trust the professionals.

She nodded.

"Then get back to bed and wait for me to come get you in the morning."

Her bottom lip trembled, and she looked like she wanted to break down and bawl like the baby she was, but finally—*thank Christ*—she turned and went back into her room.

He turned around to go down the stairs and walked right into Delilah.

"We need to talk." She whipped around.

He nodded and followed her down the stairs and across the living room.

She flipped the switch, and he squinted against the bright lights of the white kitchen. Throwing open a cabinet, she pulled out a silver bowl and slammed it on the counter. Silverware jostled as a utensil drawer jerked open.

"You wanted to talk?" He needed to get to sleep. He needed eight hours a night, no exceptions.

"I did. I do. I'm just too damn angry right now. Give me a minute."

"Yeah, well, I'm frustrated, too. I get that you want to give Ruby what she needs *in this moment*, but there's more at stake for me. I'm setting her up for *life*. It's my job to help her become a well-adjusted person." He squeezed his eyes closed, fingers pressing hard on his forehead. "She's my sister. I can't mess up with her." He had to be thoughtful, do research, in this very complicated and delicate situation.

All that was positive and bright about Delilah boiled off, leaving a hard ball of anger. "I understand."

She didn't, but that was okay. Delilah came from a good place. She led by the heart, and he wasn't angry with her.

She pried the lid off the flour tub. "Thank you for letting me stay here. I really appreciate it." Scooping out a cup, she dropped it into the bowl, white dust flying up. "But, since I'll be in town longer than we discussed, I should probably find someplace else to live. Callie mentioned the bunk house?"

"I told you that you can stay here." His reaction surprised him. It was for the best that she move out, wasn't it? He didn't need the distraction, and Ruby didn't need to get attached to someone who wasn't staying.

"Honestly?" She set the measuring spoons down. "I can't stand watching what you're doing to Ruby. I can't stand her alone in that bedroom, when she's wide awake. And I know it's not my business. I know you're doing what you think is best, but *I* know it's wrong. I just do. She's *terrified*, Will. And you just mindfucked her to get her stay in a room that scares the crap out of her."

"You think I want to turn her away?"

"I think you need your eight hours a night." She tipped her chin toward the metal sign hanging in the mud room.

Eat well, train hard, sleep = champion.

Coach had designed that when Will was thirteen and struggling with his tricks. It had remained there ever since. "I do, but you're wrong if you think this is about me. I've done a lot of research on this, and I'm using a program that works."

"A *program*? That *works?* She's not a project. She's not an assignment. She's a little girl who lost her mom, and all she wants is for someone to hug her. Kiss her all over her face. Snuggle with her. She needs—"

"Yeah, Delilah, I know exactly what she needs. Her mom. A dad. But I can't give her that." *Jesus fuck.* "You think this isn't tearing me apart? And hearing your perspective only makes it worse. Of course, I don't want her up there terrified, but I also know the sooner I get her used to her new normal, the sooner she'll feel safe and loved. Look, I don't want you to move out. I want you to stay, but if you can't respect what I'm doing..." He did not need this shit. He took in a deep breath, settled himself. *This is just business. She's a houseguest.* "The bunkhouse is taken, and so are the cottages. But I'll see what else I can come up with." Dammit, he shouldn't care. He should be relieved.

And he would be. He turned to go, when she called out to him.

"Will…I know I'm making it harder. I feel terrible about sticking my nose where it doesn't belong. I'm really, genuinely sorry." She came closer. "You're a good man. A really good one, and I know I should stay out of it—I promised myself I would…but I don't care what the books say. She needs your love."

"It's not just books. I'm talking to a therapist."

"You are?"

"An old friend of my dad's. She's helping me out."

"Okay." She looked back to the bowl and wooden spoon.

"Okay, you understand that I'm doing what's best for her?" *And you'll respect it so you can stay here and keep my house full of your smiles?*

"No. Okay, I understand that you're doing what a therapist who doesn't live here and has never met Ruby or seen her wide awake in the middle of the night is telling you to do. Because I can guarantee, if she was the one who found Ruby climbing the gate at midnight, ready to party with the pancakes, she would give you totally different advice. She would understand that Ruby's wondering when her mom's coming back to get her. And that, while she's waiting, she's chosen her big, stubborn brother to love her and make her feel safe. And she'd tell you to go into that bedroom right now and crawl into bed with her and read her a story until she falls asleep."

He stepped closer to her. "And what happens after I move on? Is she going to crawl into bed with Fin and Callie? Will she even give two shits when it's Gray's shift? Or will she give up altogether? It sucks right now, but I have to get her to sleep through the night, so she can learn to do it on her own. The best gift I can give her is teaching her to self-sooth. *Independence*."

"Later, Will. Do all of that later. Right now, tonight, make her feel safe."

"That's exactly what I'm doing. Trying to make her feel safe."

"With rules and routine?"

"Yes, Delilah."

"Come on, Will. She needs your reassurance not your stupid rules."

"I *know* it works." Jesus, he was shouting now. "Because it worked for me."

Her features sharpened with curiosity.

Shit. Well, he'd opened up that can of worms. Maybe she should hear it so she'd understand. "When my mom left, when she took my brothers and moved to New York, I went from having a big, loud family to just…me."

She looked sick about it.

"Before, my dad worked all the time, and my mom didn't do much with us, but my brothers and I were inseparable. We were wild and crazy and loud and…fucking *happy*. So, without them, I was alone."

"That had to have been so scary."

Deeply, terrifyingly lonely. "It was." He'd never told anyone about this before. Not his brothers, not his father. No one.

"Just like Ruby is right now," Delilah said. "Only you were older, so you understood what was going on."

"I suppose, at eleven, I should have understood, but I really didn't. My life changed overnight. One day I had a big, loud family, and the next morning it was just me and my dad. It took a few months for him to get things in order, but he wound up retiring. He hired Marcella and

Coach, and from that point on they gave me a schedule and expectations and rules. And it worked. I can tell you from experience, the feelings of helplessness and loss and fear…it all went away with that routine. So, when I hear the therapist telling me to give Ruby consistency, it fits with what worked for me. That structure my dad imposed? It worked. It made me feel safe."

She pushed off the counter and wrapped her arms around him. "Will," she whispered.

He didn't know what to do with all her softness and warmth and…and…sweetness. She was just too much for him. He wanted to push her away, tell her he was fine, to go make her pancakes or whatever she was making. He just couldn't get his arms to cooperate.

But, instead of reading his body language, his impulsive houseguest hugged him tighter, her hands caressing his back.

It unnerved him. And, oh, fuck, that telltale tingling at the base of his spine meant the blood was rushing to his dick, making him hard.

He breathed in the scent of her shampoo—like an expensive perfume—and felt the swish of her silky hair on his bare arms.

Her hips shifted, her pelvis grazing his hardening erection, and instead of pushing back, she gazed up at him with a goddamn look in her eyes that burned through whatever was left of his discipline, because he knew that just one lick of her lips would make him lose it completely.

His arms hooked around her back, his hand pressing the top swell of her ass. That mouth, wet from her tongue, parted with an invitation he didn't know if he could resist.

"You're a good man, Will. Misguided, but good."

"Misguided?"

That sexy mouth turned into a mischievous grin. "Yeah. You really are." And then the connection snapped when she withdrew her arms and turned back to the counter. "I'll see about finding somewhere else to stay in the morning."

"Delilah?"

When she turned to him, he knew. He didn't want to let her go.

"All the chefs are staying on the ranch so they can take the train into Owl Hoot. The choice is yours, obviously, where you want to live, but the invitation is still open for you to stay here."

Will wasn't a stupid man. He knew something good when he saw it. And Delilah Lua was a gift. She brought a lightness and joy to this house it'd never had.

And, even if it was only for six weeks, he and Ruby would damn well take all she had to offer.

On three and a half hours of sleep, Will bounded down the stairs, ready to train. He might've slacked off for a couple of weeks, but it wouldn't take much to get back into shape.

Amped with the kind of determination he hadn't felt in years, he laid out his day in his mind. Run, protein shake, shower, gym. He'd spend two hours working on the trampoline, backflip burpees, plyometrics, weights...*fuck, yeah.*

Yesterday, he'd hired one of the coaches on Fin's staff to train him exclusively. This guy traveled with his brother on his wild-ass freeriding adventures, so he was in good hands.

Used to particular noises in the mornings—Marcella listening to NPR or the whir of the blender, Will got a hit of surprise at the music blasting from the kitchen.

In the middle of the living room, he faltered. Delilah and Ruby shook their asses to Pharrell William's *Happy*. Ruby mimicked Delilah's every move, her little bottom bopping side to side.

Delilah's long, white-blonde hair whirled like ribbons, and her radiant smile hit the striking surface of his heart, igniting his blood. She was the most beautiful woman he'd ever seen. Like some kind of fairy, she sprinkled her inner joy on every moment, making the mundane vibrant and extraordinary.

He needed to get going, so he made his way across the living room, but then he heard that squeal of delight. "Wheel." Little feet slapped on the hardwood floor as she ran straight to him.

"Dance wif me, Wheel. Dance." She gazed up at him with those glittering, adoring eyes.

An unwanted memory slapped him hard. He'd been no older than five, giddy with happiness to see his mom walk in the door. He'd run straight into her legs, hugging them for all he was worth.

He'd felt pure elation to have her home…until she'd looked at him like he was a dog that'd just rolled in moose shit.

He would never forget that feeling. Like she'd punched him in the chest, knocking the wind out of him. At the same time, though, he distinctly remembered pushing through the uncomfortable sensation that he'd done something wrong just so he could get into her arms. Anything to get that hug.

She'd tried to walk away, her foot giving a little kick, as

if to flick him off, and then she strode into the kitchen, dropping her shopping bags on the table.

The thing was, Brodie, Gray, Fin? They'd just kept playing with their Nerf guns. It was only Will who'd wanted too much.

And it had creeped her out.

He'd creeped her out.

He had to make sure Ruby never felt like that, but she also needed to understand that he worked for a living. How did he draw those lines in a way that a two-year-old understood them?

He dropped to a crouch. "Ruby, I have to go to work now."

"Wun, Wheel. C'mon." She reached for his hand, turning toward the kitchen.

"No, Ruby. You didn't stay in bed last night, remember? That means you can't run with me today. If you stay in bed tonight, you can come running with me tomorrow."

That little face scrunched up in confusion.

He knew what Delilah was thinking. *She doesn't remember last night.*

She's lost and alone. She needs you.

Or maybe that wasn't Delilah at all. Maybe that was his heart. "But I'll be back in four hours and we can do something fun then."

He started to get up, but she shouted, "Go wif you."

He thought about the therapist's advice. *Stay firm. Give her a hug, and then walk out the door. Just be sure to follow through with your promises.*

"I'll be back at ten." Fueled by the expert's advice, Will stood and headed toward the door. He got about two feet when the volume went back up and a hand latched onto his wrist. With Ruby in her arms, Delilah spun him around. "Dance with us, Will."

When he opened his mouth to object, she said, "Two minutes out of your schedule."

With her hair loose and the red Cornell T-shirt draped over her hips to cover her ass, Delilah looked fierce and wild and free.

And he wanted her more than he could ever remember wanting anything.

"I don't dance." But even as the said he words, he started moving.

Ruby's eyes lit up, and she hurled herself at him. He picked her up, and she bounced in his arms, jabbing her fists into the air. This girl was pure, raw, unadulterated happiness.

And he loved it. Loved her joy, loved...

Loved that she'd chosen him. *Damn.* He couldn't explain it, but he did.

Something popped in his chest, heat gushing out, and it struck him that he'd been on autopilot for a long time—maybe as long as seventeen years. That structure his dad and Coach imposed had been his lifeline, and he'd latched onto it with both hands.

He'd clung to it all these years because it had paid off. He'd won the World Games *seven* times.

But...what else had he done?

He'd never once asked himself that question.

Until Ruby and Delilah had entered his life, his highest high had been his love for his family, and his lowest low had been the loss of his dad. Other than that, he didn't think he'd had much of an emotional life.

These two crazy girls, both laughing with total abandon, kicked him into overdrive. And as much as he knew he should walk away and get on with his training program, his heart couldn't find a single reason not to dance with them.

Two minutes out of your schedule.

Yeah, he could do that. He reached for Delilah, the three of them connected, touching, dancing in place. Locked together on this wavelength of music, happiness, and deep, unbridled affection.

And then Ruby wrapped her arms around his neck and buried her face right in the crook. Her breath hot, her fingers pressing hard into his skin, she held onto him like...well, like a scared little girl who needed a hug pretty desperately.

The hug he'd denied her while trying to teach her some kind of life lesson.

Emotion swept through him, so hard and high he thought it might knock out his knees. He let go of Delilah and wrapped both arms around Ruby's frail, little back.

Swaying in place, his body heated up. His heart thundered. Damn, this little girl. He wanted to give her the world. Every single thing she could ever need, but that wasn't the way it was going to work for her.

He should let her go. He visualized handing her off to Delilah and walking out the door. Imagined his feet hitting the trail, his arms pumping...and yet he let his hand sweep across her back. Let his eyes close. Let himself just hold her.

Her whole body relaxed against him, and she let out a sigh so deep her little body shuddered with it.

He had to find a balance, right? Between giving her love and letting her get too attached. Because what would happen if he kept hugging her and holding her and reading to her and snuggling in bed with her...and then he just left? Walked out the door and didn't see her for months. What would happen when he handed her off to Fin?

What the fuck would happen then?

She'd feel rejected. *Ha. Rejected.* As if that word came close to describing what it felt like to have the person you count on leave you. *Destroyed.* That's how he'd felt when he'd finally figured out that every time the phone rang, every time tires rumbled on the driveway—it just wasn't going to be his mom wanting to be with him.

He had to find balance, yes. And that meant making sure she didn't get too attached. "I have to go." He pulled back, but she only clung more tightly. He'd danced with her, given her a hug. He'd shown her he cared. And now he had to show her he had to go to work.

He gave Delilah a look. *Help me.*

She stepped in, put her hands on Ruby's waist, but his sister clung to his T-shirt. And as Delilah got a better hold on her, Ruby started kicking her legs out like she was frantically trying to swim back to the lifeboat that was slowly drifting away.

"Go wif you."

Pain scraped him raw at the sight of her wild-eyed and hurt, and he turned away from them and hightailed it out the door.

He had no fucking idea what he was doing, but making his sister cry was a total fail.

What the hell did balance mean?

Was he ever going to get this right?

Chapter Eleven

After the incident with Ruby that morning, Delilah had thought for sure Will's heart had finally cracked open. She'd expected him to be softer, more open.

Nope. Four hours later, he'd come home from training with an intense focus and a clear agenda: read one book to Ruby, take a ten-minute shower, dress, eat, and sort through the stack of nanny applications.

Maybe she should've left him alone, but Ruby'd been as giddy as a puppy dog when he'd come in through the mud room door, her little bottom swinging as she'd toddled over to her big, sweaty brother.

Delilah had seen his expression, and she'd known in an instant it wasn't going to go Ruby's way, so she'd caught up with the little girl, both of them running toward him with their sticky, chocolate chip cookie dough-covered hands. His stern demeanor had fractured the slightest bit.

To his credit, after he'd gotten some work done, he'd hung out with them and, when she'd asked where he thought she might get figs for the hors d'oeuvre she'd decided to make, he'd offered to take her to this hydroponic farm.

But now, while she followed the owner through the three-story vertical greenhouse, she glanced at Will, hanging back, arms crossed over his powerful chest, and she realized she needed to figure out her own transportation from now on. *He not only doesn't want to be here, but he doesn't have the time.*

He's training, for God's sake.

"In our facility, we produce as much as a five-acre farm." The owner gestured to the three-story conveyor belts filled with bright green plants, the tomatoes just starting to turn red.

She took it all in. "This is amazing." The motor purred quietly, and the humid warehouse-size room smelled like herbs. "I learned about hydroponic farms in culinary school, but I've never seen one."

"You haven't lived at sixty-three hundred feet above sea level before," the owner said. "As Will can tell you, our winters are brutal and can last all the way into May. Once a big storm hits, there goes our truck deliveries. With this facility alone, we can produce one hundred thousand pounds of fresh produce annually, using ninety-percent less water with no need for soil, *and* we take up way less land space."

As he led them further down the way, she smiled at Will. "Doesn't it smell good in here?" The basil grew alongside the tomato, making her mouth water for *caprese*.

"Plus," the owner continued. "The growth rate's thirty to fifty percent faster than a soil plant, and the yields are much greater."

"I can't believe you're growing figs." *Of all things!*

"Well, that's a funny story. I certainly hadn't planned

on growing them, but they're my wife's favorite. She grew up with a fig tree in her backyard, so she's been on me to give it a try here. It's working, and we're getting a surprisingly good response to them, so we're growing even more." They'd reached the end of the warehouse. "How about we head into the tasting kitchen so you can sample some? I've got some other produce for you, too."

"I'd love it."

"Great. Let me get a head start. You look around, and I'll see you there in a few minutes."

"Perfect. Thank you." As soon as he left, she turned to Will. "I can't believe this. Thank you so much for taking me here."

His expression remained shuttered.

"I didn't think I stood a chance of pulling off this dish."

He nodded. "Glad it worked out."

Okay, he was obviously pissed that she'd wasted half his day. "We can skip the tasting room. I know you have a meeting with your coach and want to get back to Ruby. I don't need to taste the figs before I buy them."

"Ruby's at the park with my uncle, and I'm not meeting my coach until four. Besides, I'm pretty sure you *do* want to try them before you buy them."

Busted. She wouldn't serve them without sampling them, so buying dozens only to find out they were tasteless would be a waste of time and money. "Well, I'll make it quick. I know you don't want to be here."

He shrugged. "I'm fine."

"You're not pissed?"

"Not at all." It was the confusion in his tone that convinced her.

"Okay..." She exhaled. "I'm just...I'm used to very

expressive people. I know what everyone in my family's thinking all the time. With you…I don't know."

The owner stood in a doorway, smiling at them. "Looks like my wife got it all set up, so we're ready when you are."

"Awesome. We'll be right there."

He ducked back out, leaving them alone again. "I feel like I'm always pissing you off." They made their way to the end of the row of conveyor belts. "I made you dance this morning, and now this farm…"

"I offered to bring you here."

"Because I don't drive. I just hate not knowing what you're thinking."

He reached around her to hold the door open, and then they started down a long hallway. "I'm thinking that I don't have time to drive you around town."

"You just said—"

He stopped, bracing his hands against the wall, caging her in. "I'm thinking about Freefest, and how fucking important it is that I get my head on right, that I focus and visualize and do all the things I need to do so I don't *die* on that mountain."

God, that look. So intense. *Electrifying*. "I don't want to be a burden. I can get around by myself."

But he didn't look at her like he was pissed or annoyed. No, with his nostrils flaring like that, he looked like he wanted to use both hands to rip her dress wide open and drop his face in her cleavage. And she wasn't entirely sure she'd stop him.

Her pulse fluttered out of control, and desire streamed through her.

He lowered his mouth to her ear, his voice deep and husky. "But it doesn't seem to matter what I'm *thinking*, because it doesn't stop my heart from feeling funny when I watch you talking about produce with a dude wearing toe shoes. It doesn't keep me from realizing that I've known a lot of women in my life but none of them—until you—has ever surprised me. It doesn't seem to matter that I'm really good—and I mean expert level—at blocking out distractions and staying focused because, somehow, you've tangled up my wiring. I'm supposed to be thinking about my thrust or my amplitude or page thirty-six in *How to Raise Your Orphan Sister*, but I can't concentrate because you keep getting under my skin, and there's not a damn thing I can do about it."

His chest was right there—close, but not touching. His mouth, a whisper away, and her body yearned for him to close the last inch of distance between them.

"I can't stop from breaking into a run every damn afternoon, so I can get home to you. I hold my breath because I want to open the door and find you in the kitchen and when you're not there I hate it. I could easily hire some high school or college kid to drive you around this summer. Maybe get you a scooter—anything so that *I* don't have to do it, but I will be goddamned if I let someone else be the one to take you places. That's for me. That's *my* gift."

Every cell in her body opened up and started singing and clapping to a gospel tune. But she was in a hallway, and the farm owner was waiting for her. "Well, that must be very inconvenient for a man like you."

He smiled, and it was like a bright yellow dandelion pushing up through a crack in the cement. It floored her. "You have no idea."

"If it helps, you're not my type."

He stepped close enough that his body brushed hers,

and she could smell the sun in his cotton T-shirt and the fresh mountain air scent of him that drove her wild. "No?"

"Not at all. You're too disciplined. Too…tidy."

"Would it help if I…" He brought both hands to his head and messed up his hair.

She laughed because it was short enough that it couldn't really get messed up. "A little."

"How about if I got some ink. Like maybe a sunburst right here." He brought her hand to his chest, just slightly off-center.

"And ruin that perfect skin?" She shook her head. "Besides, it wouldn't matter what you did. I like a man who can surprise me. Not someone so regimented that I can predict—"

His strong arm wrapped around her back, and he hauled her to him, pressing his warm, soft mouth on top of hers. And then he kissed her.

It was so good, so unexpected, that she practically soared right out of her body. Her pulse quickened, and she had to squeeze her hands into fists to keep from scraping them through his hair.

I could fall so hard for this man.

He parted his lips, and the way he licked across her bottom one had her drawing in a sharp breath as pleasure bloomed across her skin. He took advantage of her surprise by sweeping his tongue into her mouth, tilting his head, and kissing her like the clock was ticking, and he'd never get this chance again.

Sensation flooded her, making her nerves hum and her knees go weak.

"Excuse me."

The voice tore them apart, and they pulled back to find a young woman with a colorful scarf wrapped around her head slip past them in the narrow hallway, arms laden with two platters.

Delilah brought her fingertips to her mouth. "We should…" She cleared her throat and pushed past him, the cool air washing over her, drawing her back to reality.

And the reality was, if she thought she'd had a type, she'd been kissing the wrong guys all along.

The train pulled into the station, and Ruby pumped her arm. "Choo choo." Giggling, she tucked her elbows to her sides and lowered her face into Squawk's furry head.

"You liked that train ride?" Will descended the stairs onto the platform, holding her tight against him.

Actors in period costumes—well-to-do couples, gun slingers, an ironsmith, a banker—roamed the dirt streets and boardwalks, and the town was filled with friends, family, and town employees, ready to launch Owl Hoot.

She pointed over his shoulder to the train. "Go 'gain."

"We'll take the train home, but right now let's go check on Wally. It's her big night." The other chefs had been in town long enough to hire help and get their dishes together. Being so far behind the curve had made Delilah nervous, so he wanted to give her support.

"See Wally?"

She seemed as excited as he was. "Yeah." As he climbed the boardwalk steps and made his way to the saloon, his phone vibrated. When he saw Gray's name, he stepped aside to take the call. "Hey."

"Heard you kicked Mom out."

Great. He could just imagine how she'd spin it. "I don't know what she told you, but—"

"Hey, man," Gray said. "No grief from me. You did the right thing. She's got no business in our house."

Even though he didn't regret his decision, it still relieved him to get his brother's support.

"Besides," Gray said in his deep, rumbly voice. "That's Dad's kid. Mom's got no relationship to her."

Ruby bounced Squawk on his shoulder, murmuring to herself.

"Little girl." He watched her, lost in her own little world, and it made him smile.

"What's that?"

"She's not a kid. She's a little girl."

Gray went quiet. And then, "She's cool?"

"She's amazing." He was starting to sound sappy. "How'd your heat go?"

"Did okay."

Gray. His brother downplayed everything. Swore he didn't care about winning—it was the thrill of the ride. "You make the finals?"

"Yeah."

A rustling sound let him know someone had snatched the phone out of his brother's hand. "Dude, he's like the wave whisperer." Sounded like Amelia, one of the surfer's in Gray's posse. "He caught a fuckin' *ten*, and he was legit shredding those barrels."

"Cool." Will never understood why his brother didn't take surfing and boarding seriously. He could be a champion. "Listen, I've got to go. Can you put Gray back on?"

After a brief hand-off, his brother came back on the line. "Yeah, man. I'm here."

"When you coming home?"

"You need me now? I can fly out tomorrow."

He knew without a doubt Gray would give up his

tournament if Will was in a bind. "Nah, it's all good. Thanks, though. Good luck tomorrow." Disconnecting, he transferred Ruby to his other arm and pushed open the doors of the restaurant.

A crowd gathered around the bar to watch the bartenders in action. Each contestant had a different style of mixing drinks and interacting. The judges—travel writers and food critics—wore lanyards and carried clipboards, as they took notes.

The winner of the best signature cocktail for the Owl Hoot Spa restaurant would get twenty-five grand, but it'd be the board members who'd decide which bartender they'd hire.

Already waiters had started circulating with the chefs' hors d'oeuvres, though the dishes would remain anonymous until the winner was announced.

"Hey, cutie." A waitress carrying a platter rubbed a finger on Ruby's plump cheek. "You want something to eat?"

His sister scrunched her nose and shook her head, making Will laugh. He grabbed a toast point and an extra napkin. "Thanks."

"Sure thing." The waitress gave him a wink and moved on.

Will dumped the smoked salmon and dill into the napkin and handed off the plain bread to his sister.

"Fank you."

As he headed into the kitchen, she ripped a big bite off and chewed like it was a turkey leg. "Dis good, Wheel. 'Nudder?"

"Sure, Rubes. I'll get you some more."

At various stations around the kitchen, the chefs worked like there was one minute left on the clock, and they'd barely begun. Sweat gleamed on their foreheads, and one of them barked orders at her sous chef.

He didn't know if the board had told the contestants that, when it came to hiring for the spa restaurant, the decision would be based on more than the menu, taste, and presentation. Personality mattered, too, since they'd have to work with the chef on a daily basis.

Bad behavior wouldn't be tolerated. The Bowies and their friends didn't like prima donnas or people in power who treated their staff like they were anything less than an equal.

"Wally!" Ruby pointed with such enthusiasm she practically fell out of his arms.

Delilah, in a white chef's apron that covered her gorgeous body, stood by the walk-in pantry, arms loaded with a basket of some feathery green herb.

She chatted with the dishwasher like she'd just bumped into an old friend in the supermarket. Her free arm moved like a conductor's, orchestrating the emotions that played across her face. She used her hands, her body, her voice to illustrate her words, and he found her utterly and completely captivating.

She lit him up. Flicked every damn switch inside him to *On*.

Gesticulating as she told her story, Delilah nearly dropped the basket, but the dishwasher stepped forward to help her. They both laughed, and it was at that moment she spied Will. Surprise turned to something softer when she saw Ruby. She gave the guy a smile before making her way over to them.

"Did you guys come to visit me?" She blew a raspberry on Ruby's cheek. "Or my food?"

Ruby pressed a hand to the damp patch of skin and giggled. "She kissed me, Wheel."

"I saw that. You're a lucky girl."

"Kiss Wheel." Ruby cupped each of their cheeks and pushed their faces together.

Laughing, Delilah brushed her lips across the corner of his mouth, but he caught a whiff of her honey-vanilla scent, and desire roared to life inside him. Catching the back of her neck, he held her in place as he kissed her on the mouth—gently, softly—way too aware of the sexy plump of her bottom lip.

Oh, Jesus. Sensation flooded him, and when her lips parted and he got that hit of wet heat, he wanted to slide his tongue inside and claim her mouth.

"You kissy kiss." Ruby's voice rang like a chime.

Remembering he was in a kitchen and Delilah needed to get her hors d'oeuvres out, he pulled back, letting his gaze linger on her lush, raspberry mouth, still wet from his kissy kiss.

She gazed into his eyes, not backing down, not embarrassed, just smiling with a hot promise of more to come. "You sure know how to distract a girl." But then she turned her attention to his sister. "You hungry, little one?"

Ruby nodded.

"Let's see what I've got for you."

"Shock-let!" Ruby shouted with glee.

"I *wish* I had some of that." She led them to her station—just a small counter in a corner of the kitchen. Handing Ruby a curved bread crisp that looked like a lace basket, she pointed to the pewter tray. "What do you think?"

"What happened to the figs?" They'd bought dozens of them. Instead she'd piled onto the curved bread crisp some kind of beef with a crusty edge, a dollop of jam, and a sprig of a feathery herb—dill? The simple but artistic presentation didn't look anything like what the other chefs had prepared. The ones he'd seen in passing looked far more elaborate and hearty.

"You sound disappointed." She watched him with concern.

"I was expecting figs." He didn't want to let her down, but he respected her enough to tell her the truth. "But yours looks a little simple compared to the others."

"Oh, I never compare myself to other chefs. I just have to go with my instincts." She picked one up. "Try it."

He popped a crisp into his mouth and bit down. The crunch of toast contrasted with the juicy, flavor-filled bite of the meat. The jam gave it a tart and sweet punch. "This is outstanding."

"Yeah?" She eyed her dish with a furrowed brow. "I toasted the bread in this shape to reflect Jackson Hole, since you said the valley was shaped like a bowl. I wanted to do something with indigenous animals, and I really like how the bison roam free on the land—"

"This is bison?"

"Yes. They're all over your property, so Lachlan took me to Wild Buffalo Ranch, and I bought some of their meat. It was a little out of my comfort zone, but I left there totally impressed with their sustainable ecosystem concept. Anyhow, I tried different crusts, but I went with espresso to make it look like their thick, wooly hides. Do you see?"

He liked to think of her as impulsive, changing her mind on a whim—from a fig dish to bison—but he'd mischaracterized her. She was incredibly thoughtful.

She was *intuitive*. Not impulsive.

And she impressed the hell out of him. "I do."

"It's a little early for the huckleberries, but I really wanted that chunky, moist hit of both sweet and tart. What do you think?"

"I think…it's unlike anything I've ever tasted but, even more, I'm impressed with how much thought you put into it. It represents Wyoming. And our ranch."

It struck Will that he'd never met anybody who paid such close attention. Who cared as much as she did. Delilah got completely invested in the things that mattered to her.

And for the first time in his life he wanted a woman—this woman—to care that much about *him*.

Which is ridiculous since she's leaving in six weeks.

Not that he could have her anyhow. *You don't piss in your own pool.* A mountain man down to his bones, his dad didn't have many rules for his boys but, in a small town like Calamity, he'd wanted them to be on good terms with everyone. That meant he didn't want his four sons messing around with the women. *That applies to house-guests. Especially, when she's Callie's closest friend.*

"There's something missing, though, right? The presentation, it's missing color." She checked her watch. "Okay, come on. Think. The chutney's dark like the meat and the crisp. I need…"

"Fowers." Ruby pointed to a waiter carrying a tray of small glass vases filled with wildflowers.

A smile burst across Delilah's face, and she cupped Ruby's plump cheeks. "You, little girl, are a genius." She swept across the room and yanked a handful of stems out of a giant stainless steel sink. Plucking off the bright yellow heads, she sprinkled a few on each piece. "Bingo." She stepped back and took it all in. "Perfect."

Her creamy complexion, her powerful confidence, all that hair tied up at the back of her neck…she was just so vibrant and sexy.

Perspiration broke out on his forehead, and the kitchen grew uncomfortably warm. "We'll let you finish up. See you out there."

"Toast, peeze." Ruby held her hand out for another crisp, and Delilah kissed the little girl's palm before placing the bread in it.

Will didn't like the hammering of his heart, but he was a man who faced his fears. He turned back around. "Delilah?"

With a handful of brilliant yellow petals, she looked up from her platter.

"If your brother came to town tonight and offered you your own Da Nonna's, would you take it?"

Her gaze shifted to Ruby, and her expression turned thoughtful.

He liked that about her. He could trust her to tell the truth.

"Yes." Her determination wobbled for a moment. "It's…my family. I'd have to."

As the warm water rushed over her soapy hands, Delilah thought about her immediate reaction to Will's question, the way her heart had seized. It would mean the world to have her brother show up and tell her he believed in her enough to support her franchise.

At the same time, though, she'd had a stab of fear. She didn't want to leave Will and his sister, the competition, and this sprawling ranch filled with ice-cold creeks and wild animals, cabins, trails, and teal-colored lakes.

These feelings for Will…she couldn't explain it. He *wasn't* her type, and yet she wanted to spend every damn minute with him. And that kiss in the hydroponic farm?

She'd never had a kiss like that. Something so electric, so *erotic*. It had uncorked this desperate need for more. It wasn't just exciting to kiss in the hallway outside the tasting kitchen…it had called on something deep, primal. *Him.*

Mine.

She'd had this crazy feeling like, if she didn't get closer to him, *meld* with him, she would combust.

Shutting off the faucet, she reached for a clean dish towel.

No question, Will was an intimidating man. His energy bristled with purpose, and he didn't waste a single moment, word, or calorie. Everywhere he went, people stopped and watched him. It was almost comical when someone froze in the middle of licking an ice cream cone to take him in. Women eyed him with want and possession; men eyed him with awe and envy.

But nobody saw those moments when he held his sister and agonized over whether he was doing right by her. No one saw him curled up in her bed reading books, as she bounced Squawk in her lap.

And the way he looks at me? That carnal hunger—the promise of what he'd do to her body if they were alone—*Glory be*—it sent a direct hit to her heart, making her giddy.

She liked him, for sure. But that kiss made her realize she more than liked him.

God, she had to have him. Just had to.

"You coming?"

She turned to find Chef Alonso, the only one remaining in the kitchen, at the double doors. "Absolutely."

Time to mingle, she set the towel down and followed him out. She couldn't wait to take in everyone's expressions as they tasted her food.

A crush of people filled the dining room with laughter and conversation. Some dressed casually in jeans and T-shirts, others more formally. Little kids darted through the crowd, and waiters carried silver trays.

Each chef had her own white-clothed table, and guests could read the placard to see the ingredients. Delilah had written a little story on her card, explaining why she'd chosen the elements.

An older man stood at her table with a glass of wine in one hand and her hors d'oeuvre in the other. She could only see him in profile, but he was eyeballing it carefully, as if deconstructing it. She hoped he liked what he saw, because it was really pretty. And it tasted great.

She still had the flavor on her tongue. The juicy, tender meat against the crunch of the espresso and salt crust, and the blast of the chutney profile just made a huge flavor party in her mouth.

She couldn't wait to see his expression when he bit into it. A couple joined him, and he turned to acknowledge them.

Awareness snapped, jarring her and immersing her in a cold fog.

Harry Morgenstern.

No. It couldn't be.

He wouldn't come to *Calamity*.

What, were the judges getting a hundred grand, too?

Why on earth would the *New York Times Daily's* food critic judge *this* competition?

Fighting the crowd, she made her way across the room. Next to the hostess's podium, she read the poster board resting on an easel. It welcomed family and friends to the pre-launch party, invited them to participate in the judging by filling out score cards, and then listed the guest travel writers and food critics.

And there it was. *Harry Morgenstern, The New York Times Daily food critic.*

Her initial shock—having that slice of New York infiltrate her little bubble—gave way to a slow tide of happiness. *This man loves my food.*

Maybe—just maybe—she had a shot here.

Delilah slammed the medicine cabinet closed and squeezed toothpaste onto her brush.

She could not get the image of tonight's scoresheet out of her head.

Not complex enough?

Seriously, how was my hors d'oeuvre not complex enough?

The dishes were anonymous, so Harry hadn't known it was hers, but come on. That bite was plenty complex. He was a New Yorker, born and raised, so maybe he wasn't used to these uniquely western flavors.

Well, he'd have to get used to them, because she was using all locally sourced ingredients. She had a flash of the spa restaurant under her helm. She'd go all-out with the spirit of Calamity—she'd make it almost kitschy. In fact, she'd name her dishes after the outlaws who settled the west.

Oh, I like that.

Actually, that gave her a direction for the final event, a menu for the restaurant and samples of some of the dishes. *Yes.*

As she rinsed off her toothbrush, she thought about Chef Mathilda's expression when she found out she'd won, all cool and confident. What must it feel like to have a starred Michelin restaurant? To be so good at what you do that you became used to the accolades?

If Delilah had won, she'd have been jumping up and down and smiling so hard her face would shatter like a dropped plate. *Total newbie.* She headed to bed but wondered how Ruby was doing. Was she sleeping? She'd just check real quick.

As quietly as possible, she opened her door and peered into the hallway. *Please be asleep Ruby.*

Not a sound—or a little girl—in the hallway.

However, she did see a shaft of yellow light spilling onto the hardwood floor from the bedroom across the hall.

Shouldn't he be sleeping? She padded quietly to Will's door and tapped lightly.

"Yeah?"

Oh, she loved his deep, raspy voice. Pushing the door wider, she peered into his room. "Everything okay?" She knew what eight hours of sleep meant to him.

He sat up in bed, pillows bunched behind his back, laptop propped on a mess of blue blanket, and wearing the sexiest tortoise shell glasses she'd ever seen.

His chin tilted down, as his gaze went from her red-tipped toes, up her bare legs, to her breasts stretching the tank top, to her mouth. "I didn't hear you out there. How do you move so quietly?"

"Well, first, I'm not a wild boy who crashes through

the house like what you're probably used to but, secondly, you're the oldest kid, so I'm guessing you did whatever you wanted and if anyone complained you knocked heads. I'm the youngest. Everyone was always shoving me out of the room or yelling at me to go back to bed." She gestured to the laptop and stack of papers beside him. "What's keeping you up so late?"

"I had video-conferences with three candidates today."

Ah, the nanny search. She stepped further in the room. "How'd that go?"

"The first one was humorless. Ruby needs someone like you, someone who makes life fun, so that won't work."

A flush of joy spread through her. *I'm fun? Well, yeah, I* am *fun, but I love that he thinks so.*

"The second one didn't think she could handle the isolation of the ranch, and the last one wanted to know if her boyfriend could move out here with her."

On his long dresser, snow globes glittered in the light from his bedside lamp. She picked one up and tipped it over. Tiny snowflakes cascaded over the Taj Mahal. "What'd you tell her?" When he didn't answer right away, she glanced over and found him staring at her all lazy-eyed. No lie, she *loved* the way he looked at her.

"I told her she'd be a live-in nanny and that her time would be spent with Ruby. Then, she asked if he could live in the house with us. He's 'really into boarding' and would love to 'talk shop' with us."

"Ah, okay." Setting the Taj Mahal globe down, she picked up one with the Palazzo Vecchio in it. She shook it and watched the glitter slowly rain down. "You've got more interviews tomorrow, though, right?"

"Yeah." His voice turned rougher, and he cleared his throat. "What's up?"

"Nothing." Bringing the snow globe with her, she sat on his mattress, tucking one leg under her. "Just restless after my crushing loss." She smiled, as she turned the globe upside down again and gently shook it. "Thought for sure I had Harry in my pocket."

I appreciated the way the chef incorporated local flavors, but it just wasn't complex enough.

"He doesn't know which chef made your dish."

"No, I know. I don't take it personally."

His eyebrows shot up.

"Okay, fine." She laughed. "I take it personally. But it's the *not complex enough* part that gets me. I wanted to take a Sharpie and write, It is *totally* complex enough." She watched the flakes drift and glitter. "My dish might've looked simple, but each element had so many layers."

"He might just be one of those guys you can't please."

"Chef Mathilda pleased him just fine."

"She's the one who did that three-cheese thing?"

She nodded. "Gougères."

"It was just bread stuffed with cheese."

"Well, I tasted some nutmeg, some pepper, but yeah, it wasn't hugely complex."

"I've never tasted anything like your chutney before, and, believe me, when you grow up around here you've had every possible way to use a huckleberry. And that crust on your meat?"

When people liked her food, it lit a warm glow right in her very center. But when Will liked it…it gave her a shiver of delight.

"It was more than just espresso and salt, right?"

"Oh, yeah, it had chili powder, coriander, oregano and

pepper. But, I mean, the thing is, when you say a chef's food isn't complex…it's the highest insult. Because that's literally what we do. That's what sets us apart from someone who tosses a patty on the grill, flips it, and slaps it on a bun. We layer in flavor."

"You definitely did that."

"I did. I seared the meat, I toasted and ground my own coriander, I added fresh dill. I put in a splash of soy sauce to give it that umami punch, you know?" By his expression, she realized he had no idea what she was talking about. "I'm saying our whole objective is to give our dishes the kind of complexity that makes them stand out. I *know* my dish was complex, so I can only assume he meant it wasn't *as* complex as the others."

"I'm no food expert, but yours had more going on than any of the others. Hands down. It was like the flavors kept elbowing each other out of the way to get to my taste buds."

"Did you try any of the others?"

He nodded, but his gaze had lowered to her mouth. He went lazy-lidded again, as if he'd lost his train of thought.

She held up the globe. "Tell me the story?"

"No story." The color flooding his cheeks said otherwise.

"A big bruiser like you collecting snow globes? Come on. This has got to be a good one." She crossed her legs, settling in.

One corner of his mouth tugged up, but he didn't say anything.

"Is this how you pull the ladies in? 'You wanna see my snow globe collection?'" She used a cheesy masculine voice.

He laughed. "The ladies don't see my…collection."

"You drape a cloth over them?"

He laughed. "No. I don't have sleepovers."

"Ever? Why not?"

"Because I don't want to make Marcella or anyone else uncomfortable. Can you imagine if we all brought home our…ladies?"

"So that's what all those houses all over the ranch are for. Do you each have your own?"

"Our own house?"

"Your own hookup lair."

"Nah. I'm not into hookups anymore."

"*What*? I know you don't have a girlfriend, and there's no way a guy like you is celibate. Explain."

He shrugged, like it was no big deal. "It was fun in high school and college, but it got…uncomfortable."

"I don't even know what that means. You did it so much you threw your back out and now the old sciatica's acting up? You've slept with every woman in town and now avoid CVS and grocery stores?"

"No. I just don't like the imbalance of it."

"What imbalance? The nature of a hookup is a one-time thing. You both have fun."

"Do you really want to have this conversation?"

"Oh, honey, I'm wide awake now." She made a *gimme* motion with her fingers.

"I don't normally have this kind of conversation with houseguests."

"Pretty sure we moved past that when you kissed me at the hydroponic farm."

More color tinged his cheeks.

She leaned in. "You know what's got me on the edge of my seat here?"

He waited.

"You're all serious and reserved…" She paused to see if she could elicit a response, but other than the slackening of his jaw he gave nothing away. "But, underneath, there's this raging testosterone that I suspect you keep on a tight leash. And it makes me incredibly curious. What does it take…what kind of woman makes you…*snap*."

His features tightened, his gaze narrowed. "Sweetheart, you don't want to unclip my leash."

"Unfortunately..." She sighed. "I kind of do."

His energy went feral, like if she turned on the lights she'd see his hairs standing on end, but he clenched those muscles down hard.

She leaned back, away from the gale force winds billowing out of all that restrained lust. "No, I get it. I do. You're all about Ruby and training and don't want things to get messy. So, go back to explaining why you don't do hookups."

"Delilah." His voice sounded harsh, like he'd just dragged it across asphalt.

"What? We're just hanging out."

His gaze dropped to her breasts and then to her bare legs.

"In my jammies." She grinned.

"You overestimate my ability to keep it leashed."

"Okay, come *on*. I'm not even trying here. I'm not flipping my hair or licking my lips or brushing my boobies against your arm."

"You don't need to do any of that." With a grimace, he shifted his laptop.

And she understood that, unless she wanted to climb onto his lap and relieve the boner he was undoubtedly sporting under that computer, she'd better stop playing with him. "So, the imbalance?"

"Jesus." He squeezed his eyes closed, and it looked like he might be counting to a hundred…million billion. But then he drew in a deep breath, and the tension eased—slightly—in his shoulders. "It's not that big a deal. I'm just not into kissing women I don't know. That I don't feel something for. And I don't go down on a stranger, either. Which means the hookup isn't reciprocal, and that doesn't feel right."

"Okay, but if you've never had a girlfriend, and you don't hook up…? I mean, no way a guy like you isn't getting any."

"Really? You can't come up with any other scenarios? I said I don't go down on women I don't *know*."

"Oh, my God, Will. You've got a little black book?" She thought of how many months out of the year he traveled for his competitions. "A 'friend' in every port?"

He shrugged. "I have friends that I travel with. Friends who ski competitively. So, when we're together, we…"

"Fuck. Go on. Say it." She shouldn't be rattling his cage. Not unless she wanted to let the beast out.

Only, she really, really wanted him out and prowling. She wanted those big hands on her ass, his thighs straddling her hips. She wanted to see him, all of him. She wanted to taste him.

But he had too much self-control. "We spend time together."

"I don't do hookups, either. Never have. Just not my thing."

"Yeah? What's your thing?"

A startling image popped into her mind. Will on his knees behind her, hands on her hips, that first rush of bliss as he slid inside her. She imagined his hands cupping her breasts, and her whole body went hot and hungry. *You're my thing.* "Every boyfriend I've ever had, I've worked with. You know, school, kitchen, whatever. I always work super long hours, so I just can't give anyone the kind of commitment he deserves." It was kind of sad, wasn't it? That she was twenty-six, and she'd never been in love? "I know you've never had a girlfriend, but have you ever been crazy about someone? Like a high school crush? Or a woman you ski with?"

"No. I don't think I'm built that way. I don't...give much weight to that sort of thing."

That sort of thing?

His phone vibrated, and he reached for it on the nightstand. His brow furrowed when he read the screen. "It's my manager. He never calls this late." He gave her a look that asked, *You mind if I take it?*

She gestured to the phone. *Of course not.*

"This can't be good." He hit Accept.

Chapter Twelve

"ARE YOU ON YOUR COMPUTER RIGHT NOW?" ALEX asked.

"Yeah, why?" Tearing his attention away from Delilah physically hurt. All of his senses were attuned to her. To her scent, the bounce of her breasts, and the teasing smile that had him talking about things he didn't share with anyone.

But his manger wouldn't have called if it hadn't been important, so Will lifted the lid of his laptop and rubbed a finger on the mouse to wake it up.

"Damien's taken it to the next level. It's all over Sports-News.com."

"What is?" When the screen came to life, he started to put the address into the search bar.

"Just go to his YouTube page. You'll see it there."

He typed in YouTube instead. "Do I really want to see this right now?" *When I have Delilah all to myself in my bedroom?* One glance at her had him wanting to hang up. All that bright, blonde hair—*Jesus*—he wanted it wrapped around his fist. Wanted it spread all over his thighs. He pressed the laptop down, though it did nothing to relieve the pressure of his hard-on.

But, yeah, he probably should deal with whatever problem Damien had stirred up now.

"Up to you," Alex said.

"Does it have to do with the investigation?"

"You know, I don't think Damien gives a damn about that, and I don't think it was his intention to get you suspended. He seems out to prove he's the better athlete."

"He's not." The way Delilah stroked the rounded top of his snow globe made his cock go hard and need surge through his body. Imagining her fingers wrapped around him sent a volt of electricity through him. *Fuck me, I want her.*

What had he told her? *I don't give much weight to that sort of thing.*

Until now. He'd neglected to tell her that part.

"You on that page yet?" Alex sounded impatient.

"Listen, I've got…company. I'll look at it in the morning." He had Delilah all to himself, and he wasn't giving that up.

"Okay, call me if you want to talk about it."

"Sure. Thanks." He tossed the phone aside.

She tipped a chin toward his laptop. "What's going on?"

"More of Damien's bullshit."

"What is it this time?"

"Don't know."

"Well, let's find out. Maybe we can get ahead of it."

We. "You get this involved in all your friends' lives?" She had a little birthmark—tiny thing—right at her temple, and he wanted to kiss it.

What the hell was the matter with him?

"No. Just the ones I care about." She tapped the laptop. "Come on. Let's see."

"It doesn't matter what he comes up with. I'll prove it on the terrain."

"Yeah, but you know what? As long as Damien's the only storyteller, a lot of people are going to buy into it." She rolled forward, twisting around so she could sit between him and the nightstand. Once settled, she shifted the computer so it straddled both their laps. "Let's not let him control the narrative."

Smart woman. Her hair brushed over him, and the insanely soft skin of her arm pressed against his. If he didn't distract himself with the video, he was going to tumble her back on his mattress and kiss the ever-loving hell out of her. He clicked Play.

Damien had posted a split screen of the final run of the World Games event. On one side Will performed a cork 1080, while Damien, on the other side, pulled a switch double-cork 1260.

Will couldn't imagine why the hell he'd do that, since it would only show that Damien hadn't gotten enough amplitude.

Good. Let them see the damn hand drag, too.

His body tightened in anticipation of his next move when the film cut off, and the screen went black. "Fuckin' hell." The footage ended before Will's back-to-back double-cork 1440s.

And, of course, before Damien's hand drag.

What a pissant, only showing my 1080 and cutting out his technical faults.

A moment later, Damien appeared, talking to the camera. "Look, I never meant to cause this kind of trouble. I'm only pointing out that, yeah, Will's good, but he's not better than every other competitor for the past seven years. And I'm showing you the footage so you can see that, while he might be good technically, he doesn't have guts."

"Is that one of the judging criteria, asshole?" Delilah kept her gaze on the screen, shaking her head. "Guts?"

Will paused the video. "Look, anyone who launches himself off a twenty-two-foot ice wall—and then pops another twenty feet above the lip of the pipe—has guts. The difference between me and Damien is that he thinks the more spins he pulls off the better his score should be. But it's not about flash. It's about style and flow. It's about control. It might look cool to pull off extra rotations, but if your arms are flailing and you're not grabbing your skis, if you botch your landing…then you didn't pull off your ride. It's that simple." He pushed Play.

"I'm tired of talking about it," Damien said. "And that's why I put up the footage. See for yourself. I take more chances, I do riskier tricks, and…let's just put it out there, I put it all out on the line because I fucking love this sport."

"You're saying Will doesn't?" an off-camera voice said.

Damien shrugged. "I don't know much about him. He keeps to himself. But I do know he doesn't have heart."

"*Ha.*" Delilah shook her head. "What a douchebag."

"Forget it." Will closed the laptop, reaching across her to put it and his glasses on the nightstand. His arm brushed across her breasts, covered in only the thin cotton of her tank top. He breathed in her vanilla and honey scent, the expensive shampoo, and his soul woke up and just fucking *yearned.*

He jerked his arm back. *See, that's the thing.* Will had always been a needy fucker. He'd learned at an early age to switch it off, and he had to do that now. Forget that she was Callie's friend, she was leaving in five weeks. There was no point to any of this attraction.

Besides, nothing mattered more than Ruby, and he wasn't going to create an unstable home environment by getting involved with a houseguest.

But, before he could tell her it was time to get some sleep, she picked up the snow globe. "Tell me." She pretty much whispered the words, like lovers would do on a Sunday morning under the covers.

He needed her to go. There was no way to hide his hard-on, not with her soft skin brushing his arm and her bare breasts underneath that tank top. *Make it quick.* "It's not a big deal. My parents traveled a lot when I was a kid, and I was that whiny little bitch who pitched a fit every time they left."

"So, they started a tradition of bringing you a snow globe from each place they went?"

Well, this is embarrassing. "Pretty much."

"You're not a very good storyteller." She smiled, soft, teasing…fucking sexy.

"We probably shouldn't tell stories in my bed."

Her gaze dipped to his lap, and her eyes flared. She took in a soft inhalation. "All right, just tell me this one thing, and then I'll go."

"There's really nothing to say. They brought a few back, but then my mom left and that was it."

"Dude." She tipped her chin toward his dresser. "That's more than a few."

Yeah. "The rest I bought myself."

Her hand went to this thigh—dangerously closed to his painful erection—and she gave a gentle squeeze.

Meant, he was sure, to offer compassion, but it had an entirely different effect.

"Go, Delilah. Get some sleep." It sounded meaner than he'd intended.

She hesitated, but then she got up and headed for the door, her ass ripe as a peach in those pajama shorts. At the threshold, she turned back to him. "Damien's wrong, you know. You've got plenty of heart. You don't show it much, but when you love, you love hard. And that's really hot."

Fuck, she didn't know what those words meant to him. About his heart. He flicked off the lamp, knocking all the pillows off the bed but one, and settling in. He wanted to close his eyes, but he waited until the pale orange shaft of light spilling in from the hallway disappeared.

It didn't.

And then he heard, "What you don't have is courage."

Her voice hit him like a slap, sending a stinging shot of adrenaline through him.

"And I'm not talking about the kind that lets you ride down the spine of a mountain on sticks. I'm talking the kind where you risk your heart. Your mom's a bitch. No offense, but she's awful. Pushing you away? Making you feel needy? That's messed up, but that's her issue. Not yours."

"Delilah. I have a four-hour workout starting at six in the morning. We're done with this conversation."

"Yeah, yeah." But she didn't go. She stood there, one foot on top of the other, one hand on the door frame. "The thing is, I'm not sure anyone's ever told you this stuff before. Your brothers are younger, and your uncle's kind of…"

"Eccentric."

"Well, okay, sure. But I was going to say detached. So, he might not have pointed out that your mom made you feel like your love, your *affection,* was ugly. You were a little boy with a pure and big heart, and you loved unabashedly. It literally makes me sick to my stomach to imagine you throwing yourself at your mom, only to have her scrape you off. To picture you climbing onto her lap and having her push you away. Don't you know how thrilled most moms would be to have their little boy so happy to see them? You have to know that the normal response would be to grab you and hug you and love you all up." Her tone sounded imploring, like she couldn't believe he didn't get it. "Her response…it wasn't normal, Will."

He could still hear that brittle voice in his head. *Leave me alone. Jesus. Can't you find something to do?*

He didn't want to remember any of that. It still hurt.

No, it embarrassed him.

But Delilah didn't know, so she stuck her finger on the wound and pressed down hard. "And it kills me because you're doing it to Ruby, and you don't even realize it."

Oh, hell, no. She'd gone too far. He threw off the covers and got to his feet. "That's bullshit." He stalked closer to her. "I don't shove her off my lap, and I sure as hell never tell her to leave me alone."

"No, you don't." She stepped right up to him. "It's not about the words. Think about it for a second. Ruby lights up the minute she sees you, and do you know what your expression says? *Don't.* Don't love me like this. Don't need me like this. Is it as harsh as your mom was to you? Not even close. But does it matter? When you tell Ruby to go back to bed or she can't run with you or when you tell her you don't have time to dance with her, Ruby's not hearing that you want her to get into the swing of things here."

Every word hit his skin like a pellet.

Forcing him to listen.

"She's hearing that you don't want her. And if you don't believe me, step back into your old shoes and remember what it felt like to love your mom so, so much, only to have her push you away." She put her hands on his chest, her tone turning urgent. "I know it's none of my business and, believe me, I try to stay out of it, but I can't just sit back and watch this happen. I see how much you want to do right by her, and I'm telling you that you're doing it wrong. I know you don't want to crush Ruby's spirit the same way your mom crushed yours, but you're doing it."

"I'm doing the best I can."

"Yeah, I know that. I know your intentions are good. But I'm telling you what's actually happening here." She blew out a frustrated breath. "I'm not sure anyone's told you this before, so at the cost of really pissing you off, I'm just going to say it. You didn't need your mom *too much*. You were a sweet, open-hearted little boy, and your mother shut you down. You let that shallow, cold woman snatch the spirit right out of you." She got up on her toes and placed her warm palms on his chest. "And, just so you know? It's still there. I see glimpses of it with Ruby, and in the way you talk to your brothers. You're a man who loves hard and feels things deeply. That's beautiful and human, and I hate your mom for stealing that from you."

He stood there, a massive ball of confusion swarming in his head. As badly as he wanted to get her out of his room, he needed to haul her up against him. He wanted to kiss that mouth that said all the right things and shut those eyes that saw him better than anyone ever had.

"You don't think Ruby's love is ugly, do you? You're not repulsed by the way she wants you to carry her and hold her, right? Think about that, Will. Your mom's reaction to you was twisted. There was something wrong with *her*—not with her beautiful little boy."

The force of that idea made his heart thunder. He told his feet to step back, to disconnect from the warm touch of her hands, but he couldn't move. Because he wanted more. So much fucking more it terrified him.

Her scent filled his senses, her touch enflamed him, and her words…Jesus, she wrecked him.

"I'll let you get some sleep." Only instead of leaving, her fingers curled in his T-shirt. "Promise me you'll think about what I said? The next time Ruby comes running at you with all that joy and love, let her see how much you care about her. You're all about getting her settled in. You want to make her feel safe. Well, there's only one way to do that. *Love* her." She let go of his shirt and took a step back, the nightlight in the hallway casting a bronze glow to her body, accentuating the flare of her hips, the curve of her breasts, and making her hair gleam. "Spoil her with love."

The band of tension reining him in was a hair away from snapping. "Goodnight, Delilah."

But she didn't go anywhere. Instead, she drew in a breath. "Since I've already gone too far, I might as well tell you one more thing. I think there's a reason you've never had a girlfriend. I think you might be afraid that if you love somebody you'll be too needy. It makes sense, right? That's what happened with your mom, and I think if you see it—really get that—then you can get past it. And, once you do, you're going to be an amazing boyfriend. Because, I've only been here a short time, but I can already tell. When you do fall in love? You're going to love her so hard. And be loyal and generous and—"

He closed the distance between them—a rush of air that kicked her scent up around them—bent his knees and cupped her lush ass.

"Oh." The breath whooshed out of her when her back hit the wall.

His blood went hot, his cock turned into a steel bar, and he kissed her. Kissed her with all the desire he'd fought and stuffed down. *You're the only one I want like that.*

Her arms settled on his shoulders, her fingernails scraping into his hair, and her legs wrapped around his hips. All that silky hair slid over his arms, and his need for her split wide open. Desire gushed out, so raw, so primal, he knew he had to get to the bed where he could press himself fully against her.

Kicking the door shut, he lifted her and, with his last thread of rational thought, remembered to lock it. He couldn't stop kissing her, her mouth so soft, so warm, so thrilling.

The moment he set her on the bed, she got up on her knees. "Wait."

No.

Shit.

Fuck.

But her greedy smile reassured him that she wasn't anywhere near done with him. In fact, her teeth sank into her bottom lip and she looked like she was beholding a great feast. Her gaze flicked up, as she reached for the bottom of his shirt. "I get to unwrap you."

Oh, yeah, she was hot. She was everything he'd imagined her to be. Free, wild. Totally uninhibited.

It took every ounce of restraint he had to keep from reaching behind his neck and tearing his shirt off, because the magnetic forcefield was so strong he needed their bodies pressed together right the fuck now. His soul contracted into a marble that rolled around in its empty chamber, and he knew the moment she wrapped herself around him, she'd set him free.

But he would wait; she could do anything she wanted to him. Breathing erratic, limbs shaking, he stood there while she slowly lifted the shirt. Her warm hand caressed the flat plane of his abdomen, the sensation so erotic his muscles clenched, turning it concave. She swept up his ribcage, a finger circling his nipple. "You're so hot, Will. I can't believe I get to touch you." Her palm fanned out, gliding up to his shoulder, and then she dropped the shirt and wrapped her arms around his neck. "I lied. When I said you don't surprise me? You surprise me every day. With your honesty and your humility. Your kindness and loyalty. You're the most caring and amazing man, and I just want it all. I want everything you've got."

"Done." Grabbing her wrists, he pried her off and took a step back, so he could toss his shirt and yank down his shorts. Kicking them aside, he lunged for her. She fell onto her back, hiking herself on her elbows up to the pillows. All that pretty blonde hair spilling across his navy sheets sent a hard kick of lust to his cock, and he licked the smile right off her mouth. Oh, holy hell, the slick heat, the slide of her tongue, and the little moans of urgency worked him into a frenzy.

Cool it. He didn't need to overwhelm her. "You smell

good." As he kissed his way down her throat, she arched her back, her hips rising to grind against his.

She grabbed his ass. "Oh, my God. I've never touched a body like yours. You're so hot and hard and beautiful."

"Take off your shirt, Delilah."

She didn't want to take her hands off him, but when he growled at her all commanding like that? She dragged up the hem, and he helped whisk it over her head. It went sailing. Her bra followed.

"Look at you. *Jesus.*" Cupping a breast, he held her gaze as he licked a circle around her nipple. Her eyes rolled back in her head, and she thrust upwards. *Fuck, yeah.* He sucked the hard bead into his mouth, letting his tongue swirl and flick the tip. He loved the way she squirmed beneath him. Lavishing the same attention on her other breast, his hand swept down her smooth belly until he found the wet heat between her legs.

"Will." She shifted restlessly, thighs parting, hips rocking. "Touch me." She said it breathlessly, desperately, and it made him wild.

Slipping a finger inside, he found her slick and ready for him, but he needed to give her more. *She deserves everything.* He pressed open-mouth kisses down her stomach until he reached the patch of curls between her legs. Holding her thighs, he licked until his tongue met with her soft, slick flesh. With one hand he reached for her breast, cupping it and gently pinching her nipple. He slid another finger inside her, and then a third, rubbing the sensitive patch that had her crying out.

When his tongue found her pleasure point, her hands gripped his hair, tugging and pulling, her legs shifting restlessly on either side of his head.

"Oh. Oh, *God.* I've never...it's so good. *Will.*" She

gasped, drawing her knees up. Her bottom arched off the mattress, as her body twisted and shook with an orgasm.

His cock ached for release, but he stayed with her as she rode through fresh waves of contractions. The moment her ass hit the bed, she let out a deeply satisfied sigh, and he was on top of her, kissing her, licking into that mouth that turned him on in a way no other ever had.

Reaching into the nightstand drawer, he grabbed a condom and tore off the wrapper with his teeth. Just as he lowered his hand, she sat up and grabbed it from him.

"Hang on." Pushing on his shoulders, she forced him to sit back on his heels, his cock jutting straight up. She reached for him. "I want to do it." She said it with such hunger, a new wave of desire surged through him.

He had to get inside her, had to be with her. "Do whatever you want." *I'm all yours.*

"Oh, lucky, lucky me." When she gripped him at the base and squeezed, he thrust into her hand and let out a strangled cry.

Her expression turned carnal. Keeping a tight grip, she slid her hand up to the crown, rubbing a thumb around it. He gasped at the almost painful sensation. "Too much?"

"Nothing you do is too much." *I want everything. Every single thing you have to give.*

"How 'bout this?" She lowered her mouth and licked a circle around the head.

The extreme pleasure had his hips bucking. Her mouth closed over him, and she sucked him in so hard and deep he had to brace his hands behind him and rock into her mouth. "Fuck, Delilah. I can't…*fuck.*" He was going to come. His limbs trembled, and a riot of sensation exploded at the base of his spine. "Let me inside you. Please."

Dammit. He hated how desperate he sounded. Fucking hated it. *Get a hold of yourself.*

But her eyes went molten hot, and she released him. It took two hands to get the mouth of the condom around his head, and she licked her bottom lip while she tugged it down.

Falling back on the pillows, she reached for him. "Do me."

He couldn't help it. He laughed out loud. She was funny and fun and sexy and caring.

She's fucking everything.

And Will wanted her with the kind of crazy abandon that scared the shit out of him.

Because he could never have her. She lived in New York. That would never change. Her entire family lived there. She'd—

"Hey." She lifted up, scraping her fingers through his hair. "You with me?"

Feeling a little foolish, he smiled. He had right now, and he'd take whatever she had to give. "Yeah."

"I mean, I already got mine, so if you need to flip through some nudie magazines or watch some porn to get yourself going again…feel free."

That teasing grin. He had to fist his cock, squeezing to alleviate some pressure. "I don't think I've ever wanted anyone as much as I want you."

"Show me." She lay back down, reaching for him.

Lowering himself, he felt electric energy spark between their bodies, the pull and draw, the force of gravity, his moon to her brilliant sun. He immersed himself in her scent, her smooth skin, and the grip of her fingers on his ass.

"Now, Will. I want you so much I can't stand it."

Squeezing his eyes closed, he eased into her hot, tight channel. He had to bite back against the powerful impulse to fuck her raw. *Do not lose your shit on this woman.* Once he'd buried himself inside her slick heat, he braced his hands on either side of her and started pumping, slow and with a flick of his hips so that he'd brush over her clit.

He watched her expression, watched her eyes turn glassy, her jaw slacken, so he moved faster, and it felt so fucking good he almost couldn't stand it.

Her hands clasped his wrists. "I'm not some delicate flower."

"What?"

"You're holding back on me. I can feel it. *Show* me."

The beast growled, but he held her gaze, asking. *You sure?*

Her legs squeezed his waist, and her eyes turned all sultry. "I want to feel it, Will. Show me how much you want me."

He transferred his weight to one arm, cupping her ass with the other, and nudging her to roll over. The moment she did, she got on her knees and hiked her bottom up in the air. He clapped a hand on one fleshy cheek and squeezed. Fierce need rolled through him. "You don't know what you're asking."

"Yeah, I do."

He lunged forward, his cock wedging in the crack of her ass, and cupped her breasts. She rocked hard against him, and he nuzzled her ear. "Then I'll show you exactly how much I want you." Sitting back, he grabbed her hips and pulled her toward him, thrusting inside.

"*Will.*"

The louder her cries, the more frantic her rocking, the higher the tide of lust rose. Watching her ass cheeks shake, her hair shimmy and bounce, gleaming in the lamplight, unleashed all the pent-up desire, and he hammered into her. Her fingers gripped the sheets, pulling and twisting, and he reached between her legs to find her clit.

Her head jerked back, and she moaned. "Oh, God."

Their skin slapped, the smell of their desire filled his senses, overwhelming him. Desperate for release, he let go of her hip and pinched her nipple while circling her clit faster.

Her body stiffened, convulsed, and her head jerked back with a cry. *Fuck, yeah.* Delilah Lua was spectacular. Need turned desperate, frantic, winding him up so tightly he couldn't breathe. He grabbed her hips and slammed into her with wild abandon.

A freight train roared in his head, and he shot so hard spots danced behind his eyelids. Body rigid, he held her to him, as he shouted his released. Wave after wave of pleasure crashed over him, until he nearly blacked out. "Jesus." He collapsed beside her, throwing an arm across her back.

She pushed the hair out of her eyes. "I know." Grinning, she rolled onto her back and stared up at the ceiling. "I don't even know what just happened."

He felt good. Happy. It was like nothing he'd ever experienced. "Give me a minute to catch my breath and we can start over from the top. I'll replay everything in slow motion."

"That's my champion." Her voice sleepy, she curled up against him, hitching one leg across his hip, an arm over his chest. Her head nestled in against his rib cage. "I tell you what, Will Bowie, you came right out of nowhere and stole my heart."

. . .

His phone vibrated on the nightstand, jarring him out of a deep sleep. So used to waking up alone, the body draped across him gave him a start. Slowly, images seeped in. Delilah's hot mouth on his cock, the taste of her on his tongue, the supple weight of her breasts in his hands.

Fuck, yes. Best night of my life.

"Get it." She nudged him. "Could be important."

He reached across her and grabbed it, but his vision was too blurry to read the screen. "Yeah?"

"Will?"

The confusion in his manager's voice snapped him awake. *What time is it? Where am I supposed to be?* "Yeah, what's up?"

"I thought you'd be out running. I was going to leave a message. Listen, I've got good news. The League's got nothing, so they're winding up the investigation."

"That's great. I assume they'll make a statement, fully exonerating me?"

Delilah lifted up on an elbow, blinking sleepily, and gave him a thumbs-up.

"My next call is your attorney. You bet your ass they'll make an announcement."

"What time is it?" Delilah reached for the alarm clock, turning it in her direction. "Oh, my God. It's *seven*."

"Shit, Ruby." He threw off his covers and raced to the windows, jerking open the curtains.

"Who's that?" his manager asked. "Will, where the hell are you?"

"I'll get her." Delilah turned her tank top right-side out. "Don't worry."

"Listen, Alex, I have to go." *Where are my shorts?* The bedroom floor looked like a Mardi Gras parade had passed through it. Since when did he let things go like this?

"Why aren't you on your run?" Alex asked.

"I overslept." He nabbed his shorts off the ottoman and stepped into them, tucking the phone between his cheek and neck.

"You *overslept*? Will, who's in the room with you? Tell me you're not fucking your houseguest?"

"Alex." His tone held such threat, Delilah stopped hitching up her panties. "Don't ever talk about her like that."

"Jesus Christ. Now is not the time to start something up with that chef."

He grabbed a T-shirt off the floor. "This is none of your business."

Delilah looked apologetic, and he shook his head. *Not your fault.*

"It's seven in the morning, and you're not running. If you're not running, I'm going to bet you're slacking off in other ways. Did you get eight hours of sleep last night?"

No.

"Freefest is in five weeks. You're supposed to be in peak training right now, and *that's* my business. The details aren't important—I don't care if it's the chef or a farm animal. What I care about is your schedule. There's no winning without discipline, and you're not showing discipline right now. Pull your head out of your ass before it's too late."

His manager disconnected, and Will rubbed his forehead. When he turned, he saw Delilah had heard every word. But he couldn't worry about her right then. "I have to get Ruby." He had his shirt on inside out, but he didn't stop to fix it. He hurried out of his room.

He couldn't make his sister stay in bed until morning if he wasn't going to show up on time. Dammit, he'd let her down. But the moment he got into the hallway, the smell of bacon hit him and he heard noises in the kitchen. Uncle Lachlan said something that made Ruby shout, "Dat not wight."

Will was thankful his uncle had stepped in this time, but next time—no. There wouldn't be a next time.

Delilah came up behind him. "You okay?"

At the top of the stairs, he turned to face her. He thought about telling her they'd talk about it later. That they'd try to find a way to make it work out. Because he did want to be with her.

Best night of my fucking life.

But everything Alex said was right. He had too much on his plate already, and he had to focus on Freefest and Ruby.

"I have to get back on track."

Hurt pinched the skin around her eyes. "And you can't do that with me in your bed."

"No, I can't. I'm sorry."

"So, what was last night? I thought you don't do hookups?"

"Honestly, Delilah, I've never wanted anyone the way I want you. But—"

She lifted a hand to shut him up. "Yeah. I know. We got carried away." She gestured toward the kitchen. "Sounds like Lachlan's got everything under control. I'm going to shower."

Watching her walk away felt wrong. He should reach for her, kiss her good morning, and tell her how amazing last night had been. And, yet, there was no getting around it. Now wasn't the time to start something up with her.

It was all about time management. He needed eight hours of sleep and four hours of training. Another hour with his coach to review the day's work. The rest of his time belonged to Ruby, and that included getting her set up with a nanny.

There weren't enough hours in the day to give a relationship with Delilah the attention it deserved. Maybe if they'd met at a different time—*no*. She still lived in New York.

The discussion was a non-starter. He had no more room in his life for Delilah than she had for him in hers.

He'd been too abrupt, though, so he'd talk to her about it when he got back from his run. And then he'd let her go about her business with the competition, while he took care of his.

Turning back around, the walk to his shower felt like a death march.

But he knew that, as soon as he changed the channel, he'd be fine. *That's how it's always worked.*

Sucked, though, to get a taste of something he couldn't keep.

Chapter Thirteen

You're an idiot.

Delilah lifted a golden pear out of one of the boxes of goodies Lachlan had just dropped off from the Farmers Market.

She could not *believe* she'd slept with Will last night.

Why did she do this? Get involved with the guys she worked with?

With Marco, it had been fun from the start. Stolen make-out sessions in the pantry, sneaky hands in the busy kitchen. Day-long rides on the back of his Harley along the Hudson River. Fun.

But with Will—sensation tore across her skin. That had been the hottest sex of her life. He'd been so intense, so powerful, so…*God.* He'd devoured her. She couldn't stop thinking about his big, strong hands, the way they'd worshipped her.

Stop it. She lifted a pear to breathe it in. *Mm, just perfect.* It would be juicy and sweet. The grainy fruit with a creamy custard and a buttery crust…yes, a tart would be perfect. For the second event, celebrating the opening of

Owl Hoot's outdoor amphitheater, they needed to create picnic baskets. She'd come in third the first competition; she'd be damned if she scored lower in the second.

She looked down at her notes.

Duck and wild mushroom terrine with a crusty baguette.
Mediterranean potato salad with feta and olives.
Berry and custard tart.

Picking up a pen, she scratched out berry. Once she'd seen the glorious, ripe pears, she'd known she had to incorporate them somehow. *Oh, what about a baked chocolate cream with ginger-poached pears?*

Too messy for a picnic

She'd stick with the tart.

The back door rattled, and voices filled the mud room. Ruby chattered, and Will answered in his deep, sexy voice.

She'd had that voice in her ear last night. It had made her toes curl.

Desire streaked through her, a meteor lighting up all her secret places. He didn't need to see her reaction to him, so she went to the sink and flipped on the faucet. Pumping the soap dispenser, she washed the pear. She'd slice it up for Ruby. She'd love it.

A wall of heat came up behind her, caging her in. His big body stood too close. What the hell did he want? He'd made himself clear that morning.

Maybe now wasn't the best time for a relationship, but for her…he was worth it. Worth the sacrifice. Obviously, he didn't think the same about her.

But this was his house. She was his guest. Glancing up, she expected to see an apology in his eyes for being so cold to her. Instead, she saw impatience.

"Can I wash my hands?"

"When I finish." She didn't know why she'd held her ground. It wasn't like she hadn't cleaned the pear enough. But she was pissed at him—no, herself. God, she didn't know. Nothing made sense. They'd been so close last night—she'd felt so comfortable with him, so free. And then he'd ruined everything with that kiss-off. *I have to stay on track.*

Okay, Will. Sorry for cutting in on your eight hours.

He stepped closer, reaching around her for the soap. His big, sweaty arms boxed her in, his thighs touching the backs of hers. He lathered his hands. "Let's not make things uncomfortable for Ruby, okay?"

He was right. "I won't." Of course, he was.

"I'm sorry if I hurt you, and we can talk about it later, but Ruby picks up on everything, and I don't want a strained, weird vibe in her home."

"I know." She didn't need to be bitchy. It wasn't like they'd made each other promises. They *had* gotten carried away, and it had been great. "It was just sex." She'd meant to lighten the mood, but the way he flinched—his arm grazing her bare skin—made her sizzle down to the soles of her feet. "Lackluster at that."

"Right." He held her gaze—hard, intense—but his words came out nonchalant. "Basic."

"Yep. I'm all about the extra."

"Never settle, Delilah Lua." He clamped down on what might've been an awesome grin. "Never settle."

She set the pear down and turned in his arms. "So, we're good?"

He gave her that burning, hungry look that made desire churn and a flash fire race across her skin. "We're good." And then he put a hand on Ruby's head. "I'm gonna hit the shower. You okay to stay down here with Wally?"

"Go wif you."

He lifted his sister and headed across the living room. When his foot hit the bottom stair, he turned to her. "For what it's worth?"

She waited.

"It was spectacular."

Thwack. An arrow struck a nearby tree trunk. "*Hey.*" Will stopped running, not taking any chances with Ruby on his back.

Her little legs kicked out. "Gee-yup, gee-yup."

"Lachlan?" He shouted so loudly, Ruby's little body jerked. "Sorry, Rubes. Your uncle's armed."

"Will?" Emerging from the trees with his compound bow and arrow case, his uncle stepped into a patch of sunlight. "What're you doing here?"

"Morning run." He hadn't intended on showing up here, but with his brothers gone and the weight of their sister's care bearing down on him, his body had taken him in the direction of his uncle's cabin deep in the woods.

Uncle Lachlan approached, his gaze fixed on Ruby. "She doing okay?"

No. "I guess." She'd been with them for three weeks, and she still wasn't sleeping through the night or eating regular meals. But what was normal for a two-year-old who'd just lost her mom?

Lachlan set the bow down. "You want to come in?" But he'd already turned back, tromping through the high brush. Will followed him to his cabin. Given how deep in the forest his uncle lived, Will always expected the place to be dark and moldy, so it never ceased to surprise him to find it sun-flooded with comfortable furniture and stainless steel appliances.

His uncle went right for the refrigerator. "I got tea. And Delilah made me some fresh-squeezed lemonade with the fruit I dropped off for her this morning." He glanced at Will. "But you probably want water."

Delilah. She hadn't smiled at him in four days. Hadn't touched him since that night in his bed. And he felt it. Every second of the day, he missed her. "Sure, yeah." He shrugged off the backpack and helped Ruby out of it. Checking around for anything harmful, he found a stack of survival books on the coffee table, fossils on every flat surface, and a basket of toys in the corner.

Holding Ruby's hand, he led her over to it. He recognized the old plastic music box record player with its brightly colored discs. "You kept our toys?" He crouched, setting the yellow disc on the player and lifting the arm to get it started. "Hey, Rubes, you want to dance?"

With an eye on Lachlan, she shook her head. But she peered into the toy box with interest. He rooted through it, making sure there were no small parts or broken bits, and thinking it was pretty damn sweet that his uncle had gone to this effort in anticipation of a visit from his niece.

It was nice. His uncle didn't socialize much—Will had never seen him with a girlfriend—but he was making a real effort with Ruby.

Seemed like all the Bowie men had some issues with their hearts. He thought about Delilah's perspective on why he hadn't had a girlfriend before and, while it rang true, she was wrong.

He hadn't had one because he hadn't met *her* yet.

He'd never felt this way about anyone before. And he didn't know what the hell to do with it, because it was fine to spout shit about her being a houseguest and Callie's friend, but he'd blown past all those excuses. He'd gone and fallen for her.

For a woman who'd never stay. The *only* reason he had her at all was because she needed to win the start-up capital for her restaurant in New York City. Jesus, why was he thinking about this shit?

She's leaving, so cut it out.

"You find a nanny yet?" His uncle came into the room with two glasses of water and a sippy cup.

He had a sippy cup? That touched the hell out of Will. Taking the glass, Will sat on the arm of the couch. "I found one, but I haven't hired her yet. She's coming out this Friday to spend the weekend with us. We'll see how it goes."

"You're careful. I like that."

"She's had enough loss. I can't have people coming and going." *Like Delilah.* "I have to know that whoever takes the job fits with our family and in this town. And I have to know that she's good with Ruby."

"You sure about this Freefest thing?" His uncle watched him, concern in his eyes.

Lachlan didn't like to get in people's business, but Will knew what he was thinking. "I don't have a choice. The next time I hit the starting gate, it's going to be free and clear. No innuendo, no shadow of doubt in anyone's mind." He watched Ruby play for a moment. "Besides, Dad doesn't deserve to have his reputation dragged through the mud."

"No, he doesn't." Lachlan dropped into a high-backed leather chair. "But he wouldn't want you trying to prove shit to the world. He didn't care about any of that. He just cared about you boys."

"He'd want that gold medal." He thought of the glass case his father had built for Brodie all those years ago. It stood empty. It was on Will to fill it.

"He didn't give a damn about medals."

"Right." His uncle had always revered his older brother.

"You think that trophy room was about him?" He waved a hand. "Your dad didn't care whether you won or lost. He just wanted you to work hard and stay focused. It was all about building your confidence."

"The room he built proves otherwise."

"He didn't build a *trophy* room."

Will eyed him skeptically.

"You don't remember how that got started?"

"No." It had always just been there.

"That used to be a laundry room. After every event, your dad marched you boys upstairs and made you strip out of your onesies and wash your own clothes."

Will smiled. When he was a kid, his dad had dressed them in one-piece snowsuits. He and his brothers hated them. Not only because they weren't cool, but because they were restricting. Will didn't always want to ski with a coat.

"One time, you left your medal on the dryer. Marcella found it and hung it off a hook, so it wouldn't get lost. Next time someone won a medal it went on the same hook. *You* guys put them there—not your dad. He figured it meant something to you boys, so he turned it into a trophy room."

Holy shit. "I didn't know that."

Lachlan shook his head. "Your mom sure did a number on you boys."

"My mom doesn't have anything to do with the trophy room. She was long gone by then."

"I'm not talking about the damn room. I'm talking about the ideas she put in your head. Sure, your dad was competitive. That's why he was so successful, but when it came to you boys? He wanted what was best for you." Lachlan stared into the cold fireplace. "But that's all you heard from her when you were little, that your dad was too competitive, too detached, too…heartless. He wasn't helping her with you boys. He worked too hard. Everything wrong in her life was your dad's fault. And if she didn't get her way, she lashed out. Made everyone else the bad guys. Always the damn victim." His shifted his gaze to Ruby. "Didn't like seeing her do it to Ruby. What two-year-old wants to try on dresses? But somehow it's the kid's fault for not cooperating."

Will glanced at his sister, but she was too absorbed in a board book to pay attention to their conversation.

"She did the same thing with you."

Will's body went on alert.

"Acted like you boys were out to get her." Lachlan leaned forward, elbows on his knees. "Sure, you kids ran around like wild animals, but where was she? What was she doing to tame you? Did she discipline you? Take you on a hike? To the damn park? Did she once take you to the lake?" He waited for Will to respond.

"Not that I remember."

"You don't recall because she didn't do anything. She just let you run wild and then told Mack to do something about it." His eyes narrowed. "And then blamed *you* when things went wrong."

Will's blood slowed, as he processed every word Lachlan said. "Well, I was the instigator."

"Yeah, that's what she kept telling you. But it's bull—" He shot a look to Ruby. "Crap."

Will's axis was tilting, and it *mattered.*

"Let me ask you this. If your dad had been retired at that point, what would have happened the night Brodie got hurt?"

Will didn't have to think about it. "He'd have gone with us. It would have been his idea."

"That's right. Or you'd have *asked* him. You only snuck around because your mom wouldn't let you do anything. Unless you played quietly with Legos or puzzles, she didn't approve of anything you did. She made you feel like you betrayed her very soul when you brought home a grass stain. If you broke a plate, you had it out for her. That's why your dad retired. Once she left, he knew he had to change the world for you boys."

He did change my world.

Every word hit the target. Missing pieces locked into place, making the picture of his childhood form into something that made sense for the first time.

Lachlan got up and went to the window, gazing out onto a perfect July day in the Tetons. "By the look on your face, I'm getting you didn't see any of this. Makes me wonder."

"Wonder what?"

He faced Will. "Who you'd be if you quit trying to get your mom to see you as a good man." His features softened along with his tone. "She's not going to get there, Will." He shook his head. "She's never going to be the mom you want her to be."

Chapter Fourteen

LAYING ON HIS BACK, STARING UP AT A MIDNIGHT ceiling, Will listened to the monitor.

Silence.

No rustle of sheets, no humming, nothing. Ruby had been quiet the last couple of nights, so did that mean she was sleeping? *Probably, right?* The therapist made her living off this kind of advice. She knew her stuff.

So, then, her technique had worked. He'd taught his sister to sleep through the night.

Turning onto his side, he punched the pillow to prop it up at just the right angle for sleep, but instead of feeling satisfaction at his victory, he felt uneasy.

What if she wasn't asleep? What if she'd found a way to climb over the double gate he'd installed in her doorway?

He cringed at the thought of his sister trapped behind a wall of gates. Locked in her room like an animal in a zoo.

It sickened him. *Forget it.* First thing in the morning,

he'd take them down. The therapist might be right about a lot of things, but the gates? *Nope.*

He drew up his knees. *Sleep.*

But all his senses were trained on the monitor, and the silence was edging him out. He couldn't sleep until he set eyes on her. Pushing off the covers, he got out of bed.

As he stepped into his athletic shorts, he imagined what the stacked gates looked like from Ruby's perspective. All alone in a room that hadn't become hers yet, peering through the diamond-shaped spaces…*trapped.*

That's how I'd feel. I'd freak the fuck out.

I'm taking them down right now. That made him feel better.

He had done *some* good things. Like…signing her up for preschool, so that she'd start making friends in the fall. And the nanny would come for a visit on Friday, the day after tomorrow. He hoped it worked out—but if it didn't, he'd keep looking until he found the right person.

All good stuff.

Of course, she still wasn't eating actual meals yet. But she was well-behaved. She didn't throw tantrums. She was a good kid.

Which meant she was adjusting. Getting with the program. So, gates aside, he'd done all right by her.

Had he followed Delilah's advice, Ruby would be wandering the hallways, climbing onto his bed whenever she felt like it. Baking cookies at midnight.

A small part of him liked the idea of her baking cookies with Delilah at midnight. *But that's messed up.* How was that healthy for a two-year-old?

In the glowing diamond-shaped puddles of moonlight outside her room, he stopped and listened. Not a single sound. If she wasn't there…no, come on. He had a monitor. He heard everything. Her silence meant she was fast asleep.

But he didn't even hear murmuring. Shifting. Nothing, for Christ's sake. Just dead silence.

Anxiety thrummed his nerves, as he leaned over the top gate and peered inside. She liked to sleep with her butt in the air—*cute as hell.* Squawk bunched under one arm.

So it took a moment to make sense of what he saw.

Because her face wasn't on the mattress, and her butt wasn't in the air. Ruby sat in the middle of the bed, not moving, eyes wide open. Watching him. She didn't reach for him. She didn't scramble to get to him.

Dread pierced his heart, leaking acid into his bloodstream.

Is she hurt?

What's going on?

Pushing on the pressure bar, he removed first the upper, then the lower gate. He wanted to hurl them but instead set them neatly against the wall. She didn't need any wild-ass drama.

Anxiety propelled him toward her. Where was that sparkle in her eyes, that joyful smile she always had when she saw him?

That she *used* to have. That he might have killed by constantly pushing her away. *Just like Delilah said.*

Pain ripped through him. *What've I done?*

He remembered the look of disgust in his mom's eyes when he'd approach her. The way she'd recoil when he'd climb onto her lap. He would never forget those bony hands pushing him away.

He'd never forget the hurt—the ugly, bottomless pain—of rejection.

He felt the clutch of pain like a heart attack. Delilah

was right. He'd done to Ruby what his mom had done to him. "Hey, sweetheart." He'd hurt her. Hurt this perfect little girl who only wanted him to love her.

And it all came crashing over him when he reached for her, and she didn't lift her arms.

"Wun wif you."

Fucking hell. She sat alone in her room, wide awake, because she thought if she made a sound she wouldn't get to run with him.

Because that's what you made her do.

"Yes, Ruby, you're going to run with me." Scooping her off the bed, he brought her to the rocking chair. Her arms remained at her sides, and he missed her hand on the back of his neck. Missed her knees latching onto his ribcage.

He sat down, adjusting her so her chest rested on his. She didn't nestle. Didn't set her head on his shoulder.

"Wun wif you."

"Yes. We're running together. Every morning." Shit, he shouldn't make promises he couldn't necessarily keep. Soon, Fin and Callie would be home, and they'd take over…*oh, shut the fuck up.* "Every day." *Enough about what might happen—give her what she needs right now.*

Rubbing her back, he started rocking. Pain leeched into his bones, breaking them down. "I'm sorry, Ruby. I'm going to do better." He touched her hair—so silky and soft—and then let his hand stroke down it. She shifted a little. "I'm trying. I'm trying so hard to do the right thing with you, but I'm not. I'm messing up."

He'd tried to erect a wall, a barrier, so that she didn't get too attached to him, and then he'd leave her. *What would that do to her?*

Bullshit.

You're a fucking liar.

For the first time, he saw the truth. Clear as day.

He'd kept his distance because *he* was getting attached to *her* and, when he passed her off to Fin, it would hurt like hell.

Selfish prick.

A fierce sense of affection swept through him. He should've gone all-in. "I hope you can forgive me." He hoped like hell he hadn't ruined her—the way his mom had ruined him.

She lowered her head to his shoulder, her breath warm against his skin.

"I'm sorry." His voice, a whisper, shushed like the rocker on the furry throw rug. "I hope you'll trust me again."

And then that little hand patted his arm, like she was trying to soothe him.

Tears burned, and he held his breath. *This kid.* His heart squeezed with affection for her. "I'm going to do it right from now on, okay, Rubes? I'm going to take care of you." All the way. Not just her physical needs. *I'm going to show you how special you are.*

Her head popped up and she looked at him with sleepy eyes. "Where momma?"

Oh, Jesus. That simple question yanked his heart out by the roots. He'd waited for it, knowing one day she'd ask. Dreaded it, frankly, not because he was afraid to answer but because he didn't have a replacement. He couldn't say that *he'd* be there for her, and she certainly couldn't understand that all four of her brothers would do their best to be her guardians in the absence of actual parents.

But he did have an answer. He'd thought about it

endlessly on his ten mile runs and had conferred with the therapist. "She's not here, Ruby, but we can go to your house tomorrow." *And I'll tell you what happened to her.* "Would you like that?"

"See momma?"

"No, we can't see her. But I'll go with you to your house, and you can show me pictures of her. You can show me the toys you played with and your bedroom. Would you like that?"

She nodded. "Go wif Wheel."

"Yes, Ruby. We'll go together."

Her eyelids fluttered closed, and she relaxed against his chest.

He'd been telling himself to hold back because he wasn't her dad. Because his brothers would take over, and he needed her to get used to the way her life would be.

But Ruby needed someone now. She needed *him.*

He would give her everything. *Starting right now.*

Give it all to her.

He rubbed a circle on her back, and she nestled against him, her head on his shoulder, her body letting go, giving him all her weight. "Ruby?"

The way she nestled into him let him know she was listening.

"I love you."

She let out a contented sigh.

On a quiet street in Hoback, Wyoming, Delilah stood on the lawn of Ruby's home. A shutter hung crookedly off an upstairs window, paint peeled off the green shingles, and the overgrown lawn had small patches of brown.

"Momma." Ruby curled her hand and slipped it out of Delilah's. She toddled across the lawn so quickly she tripped and landed face-down in the grass.

Delilah scooped her up. "You okay, sweetie?" She brushed a few blades of grass off her chin. "We're going to wait out here for Will, okay? Let's give him one more second." A neighbor had mentioned seeing a black bear hanging around the backyard but, also, Will wanted to do a quick scan to make sure nothing inside would upset Ruby.

Because he was sweet like that. *Sigh.*

"Lego, pease." A rod of steel bolstered those polite words, as Ruby squirmed in her arms.

Delilah stroked the sweaty hair off the toddler's forehead. "Hang on. In just a minute, he's going to come right out that front door. Hey, should we pick some flowers?" Bright yellow dandelions sprung out of the grass, so Delilah tipped her over like a watering can. The little girl giggled, her plump little hand wrapping around a stem and yanking.

With great drama, she swept Ruby back up. She brought the flower to Delilah's nose but, instead of sniffing it, Delilah plucked it out of her grip and brushed the petals all over the little girl's face.

"Hey." The sound of Ruby's laughter made her heart swell. "Dat tickle."

"You're a cutie pie, Ruby-bean."

She grabbed the stem and lifted it. "Give Momma fowers."

Oh, Ruby. "You're such a sweetheart." *And way too young to lose your mom.* It made her heartsick to think Christy Leigh would never get moments like these with her daughter. She'd never get a fistful of wildflowers. She wouldn't get to take her to her first day of kindergarten or console her after a breakup.

Ruby'd only had two years with her mom. Would she remember anything? Delilah didn't have any memories before she was six, when she'd bit into a cracker and lost a tooth.

Maybe her mom had a particular fragrance that would linger in Ruby's memory the rest of her life. Delilah would have to look around for those kinds of things—a piece of jewelry, perfume, a favorite sweater or blanket. A scarf. Evocative things.

With the hot sun burning the tops of their heads, the cool July breeze brought relief along with the scent of rich earth and clean mountain air. For the first time, instead of sorrow that she'd lost her mom, Delilah felt fiercely lucky to have had her for eighteen years. She'd gotten the soothing touch of her mom's hand sifting through her hair, advice when she'd had trouble with a friend, and companionship during all those long nights when she couldn't sleep.

Girls needed their moms so, so much.

Life just didn't make sense sometimes.

Ruby glanced at the house. "Go now. See momma." She rocked her hips, as if to get Delilah moving.

She didn't know how much more she could take, knowing the truth this little girl was about to face when she got inside her empty home. "I wish I'd known your mom, because she made the most wonderful little girl in the world." She swallowed past the hard knot in her throat. "Ruby, I swear, your momma loves you with all her heart." The force of her emotion caused her to squeeze Ruby a little too hard. "She *loves* you."

The front door creaked open, and they both looked

over to find Will taking up the doorway with his big, strapping frame.

"Wheel!" She squirmed, and the moment Delilah set her down she took off like a bottle rocket. When she hit the porch stairs, she lifted her knee and hoisted herself onto the next step.

Will's powerful arms lifted her easily, and the look in his eyes as he drew her to his chest made Delilah's heart flip over. Something had changed in him. Overnight, he'd become easier with her. More open.

Ruby had captured that man's heart in a way she suspected no one else ever had.

Her heart squeezed with longing. *I want to capture his heart.*

She really did. Now that a few days had passed, she had better perspective. She believed he had strong feelings for her—she wasn't blind; she saw the way he looked at her. She also understood that distraction had serious repercussions for him. And, like it or not, she was a distraction.

Why would he take time away from training and his sister to play with her when she was leaving in a matter of weeks? No, she got it. She did. And, seriously, she admired him so much. Look how hard he was trying with Ruby. He was pushing past the only way of life he'd ever known to help her. And that…that was freaking powerful.

He was such a good man, and she just knew whoever he wound up with would be so damn lucky. *He's going to love someone so hard.*

But it won't be me.

Because I'll be gone.

"You coming?" he called to her.

"Yes, of course." Delilah forged ahead, but then stopped. "Unless…do you two want some time alone?" He might want a private conversation, just between brother and sister. "It's so pretty here, I can take a walk." She gestured toward the woods at the end of the street.

"Delilah." That commanding voice held an element she hadn't heard before. Vulnerability. "What do you say, Rubes? Do we want Wally with us?"

The little girl's face lit up, and she flapped a hand. "Come, Wally."

Happiness breezed through her, fluttering the curtains of every room in her heart. She kicked into gear, heading up the walkway and following the siblings inside.

The house had been sealed up for several weeks, making the air stale and the rooms…forlorn. A staircase divided the small downstairs into a dining room to her left and living room to her right. Not a single personal item—photos, toys, clothes—to be found. At the top of the stairs she could see a bathroom, a hand towel hanging carelessly off the rod, as if someone had quickly dried their hands before dashing off.

"Momma!" The moment they hit the foyer, Ruby twisted in Will's arms so violently he nearly dropped her. He set her on the floor, and she took off toward the kitchen. "Momma?" The raw excitement—*relief*—made tears burn in Delilah's eyes.

Poor Will. He looked utterly stricken. "Ruby." He said it forcefully enough to get her attention, but the girl ignored him. "Your momma's not here." He went after her, but she ducked out of his reach and headed for the staircase.

"Momma, momma, momma." She leaned forward in what had to be a routine of scrambling up the stairs with both hands, but Will latched an arm around her stomach and pulled her to his chest. "Ruby, stop. Listen to me, sweetheart. Your momma's not home. She's not here."

"Here, Wheel. Momma here." She scraped a pudgy hand across her face, shoving the hair aside to look at him. Her chest pumped hard, and her forehead creased in frustration. "Lego."

"Not yet, okay? I want to talk to you."

"No, Wheel. No." Her cheeks bright red, Ruby looked wild-eyed. Perspiration gleamed on her forehead. She writhed in her brother's arms. "*Lego*."

"Hey, hey, listen to me." Will's hold tightened as he cupped his sister's chin and forced her to look into her eyes. "It's okay, Ruby. Everything's going to be all right, I promise."

Slowly, she stopped resisting.

He caressed the back of her head, holding her gaze. "I got you, sweetheart. I got you."

Her chest stopped pumping so rapidly.

"We're just going to sit down, and I'm going to talk to you, okay?" He gave her a soft, sweet smile. "You with me, Ruby-bean?"

Slowly, the wildness in her eyes settled.

"We're going to be okay, Ruby. We really are."

Delilah had never heard him use that voice. Gentle, but with an underlying confidence that would turn the harshest skeptic into a fervent believer. Soon, Ruby relaxed in his arms.

As they headed to the couch, Delilah looked around the living room. "Where are the photos? She'll want them when she's older."

"The babysitter brought over Ruby's clothes and books and toys, but she didn't want to touch anything else. She wasn't sure how we'd want to handle pictures and her mom's things, so she put them in the mom's room and shut the door." He glanced back to the stairs. "We'll let her choose a few things before we go, and then I'll have Lachlan come by and box everything else up. But I want her to have pictures of her mom in her room and in the hallway, alongside our family photos."

"That's…that's really nice." She wanted to reach for his hand and squeeze. She wanted to be close enough that she could tell him how she really felt. To touch him whenever she wanted.

She wanted him to be hers.

"Want Momma, Wheel." The little girl sounded like she'd just had enough.

"Yeah, Rubes. I know you do." Sitting down, he settled her on his lap. He patted the cushion beside him. "Sit with us, Wally."

Perched on his knee, Ruby gazed up at her, clutching her chicken. Delilah sat close to Will, their arms and legs touching, and she rested a hand on his thigh. *I'm here.* Will looked at it for a moment, before letting out a rough exhalation that let her know how hard this moment was for him.

Then, he turned his attention to his sister. "Rubes?"

The little girl looked up at him with big blue eyes brimming with innocence and trust.

"I know you miss your momma, but I have to tell you something. Your momma died, and she's not coming back."

The starkness of his words hit like a mallet to her funny bone, the sensation reverberating in the stunned silence.

Ruby swiveled to Delilah, her brow scrunched in concern. "Momma wuv Wooby."

Oh, shit. She'd thought she was reassuring the little girl…not betraying her trust. Crap, she never should have said anything. Speaking of her mom in the present tense had made Ruby believe her mom was alive. She looked helplessly to Will.

But he wasn't paying attention to her. He tipped Ruby's chin and brought her focus back to him. "Yes." He said it firmly, like planting a flagpole in the earth. "Your momma loved you more than anything in this world, but she died, and she's not here anymore. She can't come back." His Adam's apple jumped as he seemed to swallow an ocean of sadness. "I'm very sad, and we're all going to miss her. But, sweetheart, she's not coming home."

Delilah had faulted him for taking advice from books and a therapist, instead of acting on his instincts. And now she felt like a fool, because how did anyone know how to behave in such a horrible situation? That research had shown him how to handle a conversation no one should ever have to experience.

Up until this moment, no matter what had come Ruby's way, she'd maintained her irrepressible spirit. Now, though, it all seemed to leak out of her, and she slumped on Will's lap. Delilah had no idea what was going on in the little girl's mind—how she could begin to process such enormous news—but she looked lost. Her fingers curled in the stuffed chicken. "Momma come home. Come home to Wooby."

Through a wall of tears, Delilah looked down at her sandals.

"No, sweetheart." Will's voice was soft but firm. "She isn't coming home. But—" He tipped her chin and forced his sister to look him in the eye. "But I'm going to take care of you. You're my sister, and I'm always going to be here. You live with me and your other brothers now. You're our family."

Will's usually implacable features wavered with a sorrow he clearly struggled to rein in. He shifted her onto the cushion, got on his knees on the carpet, and cupped her cheeks in his big hands. "You're with me now, sweetheart, and I'm always going to be here for you." He let out a short, sharp breath. "I love you, Ruby."

Oh, my God. What had happened between yesterday and today that he was calling her sweetheart, promising to be there for her, and expressing his *love*?

Her heart swelled with affection as she watched Will hold his sister's gaze unrelentingly, until loss turned to peace, and confusion to trust.

Then he smiled, and it was like sunlight breaking through clouds. *So much beauty.* He got up, knees cracking, and picked her up. "Let's go to your momma's room and you can choose pictures to take home with us. Okay?"

Delilah sat there for a moment, watching the siblings head up the stairs, and that was when she knew, clear as day, what she felt for Will was real. Her heart, mind, and body, were completely connected to that man.

She wanted him in a way that went beyond fun or a crush or anything she'd ever experienced before.

But he didn't want her the same way, and there wasn't a damn thing she could do about it.

For the three-day judged art festival at Owl Hoot, the chefs had to create a brunch menu. Delilah had sourced all her ingredients from local slow food growers, the hydroponic farm, and ranchers. Not that it mattered to the judges—they only cared about taste, creativity, and presentation. But to her…this was the fun stuff.

"Girl, this was the best sangria I've ever had." The waiter breezed past her with a tray of tall, clear glasses filled with the remnants of oranges, lemons, limes, apples, and pears.

"Oh, thanks." She'd thought it had come out well. "I'm so glad you liked it." Using a Spanish rosé, ruby port, and Cointreau, she'd added cinnamon, cloves, anise, and allspice berries to the fruit slices. Over each glass, she'd balanced a kebob of Cointreau-soaked apple chunks.

"It's pretty much cleared out now, so you can head in there." He tipped his head in the direction of the dining room.

The chefs could only circulate after the judges had submitted their score sheets, which meant Delilah hadn't gotten to watch Harry's face as he'd sampled her dishes. And she'd *really* wanted to see what he thought tonight. Even though he'd declared last week's mason jar of tiramisu "so good you probably won't believe it unless you taste it," she'd still come in second place.

Which wasn't bad, of course. With the point-based judging system, coming in third and then second meant she was still very much in the running.

But she wanted a win. She wanted that first place ribbon stuck to her table. It'd get her that much closer to the hundred grand, and it would mean her family could trust her to make a success out of her franchise. She'd learned her lesson, and she would absolutely stick to Nonna Abelli's recipes, but she'd also have a specials board that would bring a whole new set of customers into her restaurant.

And she needed that validation more than she'd real

ized. Because now that some time had passed, a hard truth had wriggled to the surface. It wasn't so much that her siblings had let her down by not giving her the franchise. It was that she'd let *them* down. They'd trusted her with the family brand, and she'd failed them.

That was completely on her.

Heading out to the dining room to check her scores, she reminded herself of something it had taken years to learn: she couldn't please everybody. Food preferences were subjective. More specifically, you couldn't set out to please a food critic. They weren't trained chefs. They knew whether they liked a dish, but they didn't have the knowledge to articulate the reason. Which was why, in trying to put a finger on it, they chose standard foodie words like *complexity*.

It just wasn't their area of expertise.

Over time, she'd learned to rely on her own instincts. Which meant she'd had to put Harry's complexity comment out of her mind and just do what she did best: cook.

Most of the guests had left to check out the art festival, leaving the chefs time to chat with the board members and unwind with samplings from the local wineries. She found herself scanning the saloon for Will. The last several days, he'd distanced himself. Polite and reserved, he'd offered to give her rides, but she could tell he wanted to divide his time between Ruby and his training.

She was a fool for falling for a guy who, at twenty-eight, had never had a girlfriend. A guy whose mom had taught him that the vast well of love inside him was repulsive.

But since when did the heart listen to reason?

Wait staff whipped off tablecloths, and bartenders

wiped down the bar. At the exit, she spotted Will chatting with Lachlan. A zing of pleasure rocketed through her so powerfully her fingertips tingled.

Standing a head above any other man in the room, shoulders broad, chest powerful, he was a warrior. A clan ruler. In the zombie apocalypse, he'd be the guy everyone turned to when devising a plan. He had that air of competence, like nothing fazed him.

I want him all to myself.

She'd thought she liked the good-time guys, the reckless ones who didn't take anything seriously, but that was before she'd met Will Bowie. His confidence and inner strength made her feel rooted and calm.

And that's why Ruby chose him. Because her instincts recognized him as the one person she could count on.

As she headed toward them, she caught a snippet of their conversation.

"Chris says her food's good," Lachlan said. "But says she treats the line cooks like crap."

"Waitstaff, too," Will said. "But it doesn't matter since she's not interested in the job."

"Not with that Michelin star, no," Lachlan said. "Oh, and tell him they're disappointed in Chef Nazaar. Said they expected good things, but he's not delivering."

Will shook his head. "I saw him on the phone this afternoon. Looked like he got some bad news. I'll give him another chance in the next event before I mention anything to Brodie."

What a good guy. She turned to head back to the kitchen, when Lachlan said, "They're impressed with your houseguest. Said she's 'knocking it out of the park.' You try one of those fig things? Damn, that was good. Wish she'd make those for dinner some night."

Delilah couldn't keep from smiling. To give the effect of petals, she'd ribboned a thinly shaved strip of parma ham around a split, ripe fig. With the basil leaf tucked into each, they looked like pretty, pink flowers. She'd make some just for him.

"They don't want her, though," Lachlan said. "Want someone with a long-standing reputation. Said it'd give the restaurant the best chance for success."

"She has one," Will said. "She's Da Nonna's."

"Don't know what to tell you. Guess it's not at the same level as Chef Mathilda," his uncle said.

She knew she should go—she had to no business listening in—but she was dying to hear Will's response.

"That's stupidly shortsighted. She's kind to everyone. Even under pressure, she doesn't throw her anxiety onto other people. Her presentation's always creative and clever. She's confident. And she's the only one who's taken the time to meet local ranchers, farmers, and chefs. I like that. I like everything about her."

Warmth spread through her body in a slow, voluptuous roll. *I like everything about you, too, Will Bowie.*

"Not that you're biased or anything." She could hear the teasing smile in Lachlan's voice.

"I'm not biased at all. She's got no intention of staying in town. But I'm telling you I think they've got their heads up their asses if they're seeing her age and not everything else that makes her a total fucking rock star." He clapped his uncle on the arm. "I'm going to go see if she needs a ride home."

The moment he broke away from his uncle, he spotted her. It was almost comical the way he did a double-take, eyes wide like he'd just seen a movie star.

But once he recognized her, his features softened. She

watched as a swift infusion of joy spread through him, making his chest rise. *You.*

Hard as she tried, she couldn't tamp down her emotions. *Me.* That magnetic attraction pulled them toward each other, and he set forth like he was the arrow. The target, her heart.

"Ready to go home?" When he reached her, the energy between them shimmered and glowed. "Or did you need to do a little more eavesdropping?"

"I heard all I needed to hear."

She led the way, pushing open the kitchen door. Pots clanged, water rushed, and clusters of wait staff worked together, laughing and chatting. Every step toward the back door ramped her excitement. Because she'd get to be alone with him. Even just for the short drive home, she'd have him to herself.

And, even if it took her hours to come down off the rush of wanting him and not being able to have him, she wanted those precious moments with him. They fed her, enlivened her.

They made her yearn.

She stepped out into the fragrant night air and turned to wait for him. When the door banged shut behind him, he said, "Delilah."

The look in his eyes made his intentions clear, and it made her pulse flutter out of control.

He wants me.

He doesn't want to want me, but he does.

Desire started as a rumble, grew into a roar, until her whole body shook with it. The force of these feelings grew too great for her to keep inside, and she launched herself at him. Her body hit his, and she got up on her toes to feel the whole, hard length of him.

Burrowing her face into his neck, she breathed him in. His soap, that fresh mountain air scent he had about him, and that zing of *Will* that triggered a hunger so real and deep, she wanted to swallow him whole.

His big hands cupped her ass, hitching her up, and she lifted her mouth to his ear. "You like everything about me?"

"I do."

"I'm an excellent houseguest. I don't leave messes, and I'm helpful."

"You are."

"And a great cook."

"The best."

"I have really good hygiene."

"That, too." She could feel his grin.

"Know what else?" She lowered her mouth to his ear. "I'm really good in bed."

Chapter Fifteen

WILL HADN'T TOUCHED HER IN A WEEK, AND HE WAS done with that.

As soon as they got to the truck, they'd have a conversation. He'd spent so much of his life intent on doing the right thing, he'd completely lost sight of the fact that not everything was black and white. That sometimes you just had to grab what was right in front of you and fucking enjoy it while you had it.

"We should bring Ruby here." Delilah stopped to take in the festival. "She'd love this."

It was late afternoon, and the town was vibrant with visitors checking out the art in the various booths lined up on either side of the street. In front of the jail, vendors sold ice cream, cold drinks, tacos, churros, and barbecue.

"You want to look around now?" She'd cooked all day, so she hadn't had a chance to explore. He wanted to be alone with her, but he'd stay if that's what she wanted.

"I want to get in your truck." She looked down at the hands he'd squeezed into fists. "So you can put those where you want them." That pink tongue licked her bottom lip.

He flexed his hands because, yeah, he'd like nothing more than to grab a handful of her ass and haul her to him. "Let's go." Will knew he sounded stern and impatient, but for Christ's sake, Delilah had jumped into his arms and pressed her breasts into his chest, licked his earlobe...and it had been six days and eleven hours since he'd touched her. There was only so much a man could take. Snagging her hand, he led her toward the parking lot.

"You're looking pretty worked up over there."

"Yeah, well, here's the thing. I can say I need to stay on track, force myself to keep to my schedule, but nothing changes the fact that I think about you all the time. I want you. So, all this separation...it's not working."

"You don't know how happy I am to hear that." She squeezed his hand.

He cut her a sideways look. "If your brother showed up today and offered you a franchise, would you take it?"

As expected, she didn't answer right away. She gave it some thought, which made her answer more meaningful.

With his truck in sight, he pulled his keys out of his pocket and hit the remote unlock button. He let go of her hand, and they both got in. Still not speaking, he headed out of Owl Hoot.

Tires crunching over gravel, he waited.

She shifted toward him. "No. I don't think I would."

Four simple words. They electrified him. *She'll stay?*

The frustrated breath she released made him check his enthusiasm. "I've had so much fun cooking in my life, with apprenticeships in Tokyo, Hawaii, and Paris—and I obviously love working in my family's kitchen." She looked down at the fingers laced in her lap. "But, see, that's the thing. I love being in the kitchen, but I don't love churning out the same recipes every night. I think who I am here is so different. It's like I have this incredible sense of freedom to do whatever I want." She gazed out the window. "Like, in Tokyo I made sushi the way Chef told me to. I learned to make the world's best béchamel sauce in Paris and prepare fish in Hawaii. But here…I'm making up my own recipes. I feel like I'm my best self here."

He forced his expectations to fit into the shape of her reality. "And you'll take all that freedom back with you to New York and knock the hell out of your restaurant. Make it bigger and better than anything the Lua family's ever seen."

She gave him a bittersweet smile. "Yeah. So, no, I wouldn't take a franchise, but when I win this competition, I'll use the money to start my own version of Da Nonna's."

He clenched down on the tide of disappointment threatening to crash through. He'd known this all along. "Okay."

She gave him a grateful smile that didn't match the uncertainty in her eyes. Taking in the meadow on either side of them, she said, "Where are we going?"

"The back way."

The truck bounced on the rutted dirt road, and he didn't speak, didn't turn on the radio. His body ached for her, so he had to call on every ounce of restraint to keep from hauling her onto his lap.

"Is this the scenic route?" she asked.

"It's private."

"So, basically, no one can see your boner?"

He burst out laughing.

She reached for his knee and gave a firm stroke up to his thigh. “Exactly how private is this road?”

“No one uses it but me and my brothers, and they’re are out of town. So, real private.”

Her hand closed over his cock. “Perfect.” She gripped him firmly through his jeans.

Sparks exploded at the base of his spine. His hips punched up, and he gripped the steering wheel. “Jesus, Delilah.”

Slowly, she unbuttoned his jeans, the heel of her hand rubbing his hard length. His breath turned shaky.

“Eyes on the road, mister.” Unbuckling her seatbelt, she got up on her knees and stretched the waistband of his black boxer briefs. “Mm.” She licked that damn lower lip, and it sent a pulse of electric heat through him.

Her thumb gently stroked the ridge, as she lowered her mouth over the head of his dick. Slick heat surrounded him, and his fingers turned white on the steering wheel. Lowering the boxers, she shifted closer and sucked his cock deep into her mouth.

Sensation tore through his body. “Fuck, Delilah.” He pumped the brakes, jerking the gearshift into Park once he’d stopped. All that gorgeous hair spilled over his thighs, just as he’d imagined a hundred times. His palm came down on her back, and he caressed her in firm, urgent strokes. He needed to close his eyes, needed to thrust his hips, but he wanted to see his fantasy come to life, wanted to hold onto it as long as he could.

His other hand went into her hair, threading through the silky waves, as her tongue zig-zagged along his length. Fuck, she was hot. He gripped a handful and gently tugged. “It’s been six days. Almost seven.”

"Mmhm." But she just kept sucking, one hand jacking his root.

His blood was on fire. "That means I'm not gonna last."

Her fist tightened, and she took him to the back of her throat.

"Jesus." His hips jerked. "Stop. I want…fuck…I want all of you." Breasts in his face, thighs squeezing around his, her scent, her hair…all of her.

But she just moaned like sucking his dick was the most erotic experience of her life, and that was it. He couldn't take anymore. "My lap. Now."

She jerked up, her eyes half-lidded with desire, and fell back onto her seat. Peeling off her leggings and panties, she climbed onto his lap, surrounding him with the fragrance that drove him out of his mind.

Kissing her, he reached for the button on the door to push the seat back as far as it would go. Her hips did a provocative roll, and he bucked up, pressing his painfully hard cock to her bare core.

Her hands cupping his jaw as she kissed him, she pulled back enough to murmur, "You sure this is private?"

"I wouldn't get you naked here if it weren't." He lifted her blouse and pulled it over her head, tossing it in the back seat. He kissed the breasts mounding over the cups of her bra, while reaching behind for the clasp. She tilted her shoulders forward, and he tugged the straps off, tossing it aside. Finally, she was all his to take in. "You're so fucking sexy."

Her long, bright-blonde hair—messy from his hands—spilled down her back, tendrils dangling over her full, round breasts. Luscious hard nipples teased him from between the strands. Those pretty hazel eyes sparkled with desire and a hint of vulnerability.

He thought he might die with the beauty in his lap.

With his hands at his sides, heart pounding—aching—he said, "I have to focus on training."

"I know." Her shoulders pulled in, more hair tumbling forward to cover her breasts.

He didn't want to make her feel bad, but he had to put it out there. "It's life or death. I lose my focus, I die on that terrain."

"I know that." Her voice went thin, nearly transparent.

"And Ruby…she deserves a hundred percent of my focus."

"Of course."

He lifted a lock of hair, pushed it back over her shoulder so he could see more of her creamy skin. His fingers traced a path from her collarbone down to her elbow, leaving a trail of gooseflesh.

"But all I can think about is you, and I'd be a goddamn fool not to take my shot with you."

Right there on his lap, she blossomed. "And you're no fool."

"You make me happy." He smiled. "My life's so regimented. It's good—everything's good…I just didn't know it could be like *this*. I want you, but I know I can't have you. I know you're leaving. I know you have to concentrate on winning the competition, but I want to spend whatever time we have together."

"Yes." She leaned forward, her hands going behind his neck, her hair spilling around them like a curtain, her scent filling his senses. "That's what I want, too." She pressed that lush mouth over his, sliding her tongue inside, and cupping the back of his head.

She caressed him like his skin was cashmere, kissed him like he tasted of cherries and chocolate and all the foods that made her eyes roll back in her head. And she moaned the way she did when her chocolate chip cookies were just coming out of the oven.

Like he was her favorite treat, and she wanted to gorge herself on him.

And, still, it wasn't enough. He palmed her breasts, thumbing the nipples, making her gasp. Sucked one into his mouth, flicking his tongue over it. He wanted all her edges blurred, sensation taking over until she was nothing but desire and pleasure and *them*. Their scents, tastes, sounds, and reactions mingled. He wanted them to become one.

As she reached between them to grip his cock, he pulled back. "I don't have condoms."

"I like that about you. That you're not a horndog. You could get laid every day of the week, if you wanted, and yet you're more…discriminating than that." She nuzzled his ear. "And I'll bet you're pretty diligent about protection."

"Always." Where was she going with this? His body stilled. "I'm clean, and I've always used a condom."

She got up on her knees. "Same, and I'm on birth control. I want you inside me, Will. I don't want a single damn thing between us." Fingers in his hair, she rocked on his lap and waited for his acknowledgment.

"Fuck, yeah." One hand on his cock, the other on her hip, he rocked up into her, thrusting until she'd taken all of him. *Oh, holy hell.* He'd never gone bare inside a woman, and it was fucking hot.

Lust slackened her features, softened her mouth, and she gripped his shoulders as she rode him. Each thrust of his cock through her slick, tight channel sent shockwaves through him. "Jesus, you feel good." Static electricity tripped across his skin.

Reaching for the headrest, she moved faster, slamming down harder. He got his hands on her breasts, tweaking her nipples, feeling the weight of them as they bounced and shook.

"Oh, Will." Her sexy, desperate noises let him know she was getting close.

He could feel her getting wetter, slicker, and then he just lost it. Lost himself in her sounds and her scent, the rhythmic slap of her rump on his bare thighs. With his orgasm bearing down on him, he reached between them, fingers seeking her hard nub, and when he found it, she threw her head back and cried out. "*Will.*"

That was it. He was a goner. Clamping his hands on her hips, he took over, slamming her down on him in time with his thrusts. Her breath stuttered out of her, her arms went rigid, and then her body jerked and twisted. "Oh, *God.*"

Holding her hard against him, he came so hard a universe of stars exploded behind his eyelids. Euphoric, he spun through outer space, and he never wanted to come back down.

When his ass hit the seat again, she slumped against him, arms pulled in tight to her sides, head on his shoulder, and she rested against him while she caught her breath.

And right then he knew. His heart was a ticking time bomb, wired to go off the moment she walked out of his life.

. . .

Wanting her…he was swollen with it. Need, yearning. He couldn't get enough. Just couldn't. Wanted his hands on her. His mouth, his tongue. He wanted inside her. Harder, closer, more. Fuck, he had to have her.

Rolling over, his arm reached to yank her tight against him and found air. It landed on the mattress. Will startled awake, and reality crash over him.

He was doing it again. Getting all needy and attached.

Why couldn't he have normal feelings for a woman? Why did they have to inflate like this?

He'd probably driven her back to her own bed with his greedy hands.

A fresh wave of fear rolled through him. Unless…she'd gone to take care of Ruby? He jackknifed up, listening for the monitor. That was when he noticed the cool air rushing in from the balcony, the French doors wide open.

Stepping into his boxers, he headed toward the hourglass shaped body silhouetted against the night sky. The breeze riffled the tips of her long blonde hair. Arms folded on the bannister, she gazed out into the darkness. A full moon bathed the meadow in its milky glow.

"Can't sleep?"

She cast a glance over her shoulder. "I'm just too happy."

Happy? So, he hadn't run her off. "How can you be *too* happy?"

"It's bouncing all around inside me. I can hardly contain it all. I love it here, Will. I never even considered visiting Callie let alone falling in love with this place. I love the freedom and the mountains. I love this house and watching you find your way with Ruby. And…" She turned back to the meadow.

He really needed her to finish that sentence. Wrapping

his arms around her waist, he set his chin on her shoulder. "And?"

"And I really like you."

For a moment, he held his breath, as if he could stop time and just revel in this one perfect moment. And then he broke the quiet with something he'd never said before. "I'm crazy about you. You make me happy."

She turned in his arms, clasping the back of his neck, and standing up on her toes to kiss him.

The breeze cooled his flushed skin, and he held her loosely, just kissing and kissing and kissing and kissing, soft, gentle, a slow tangling of tongues. Nothing had ever felt so sweet, so tender, so perfect.

When she pulled back, she let out a happy sigh.

He wanted more than stolen moments with her. "I'd like to take you somewhere on Saturday. Just the two of us."

"And leave Ruby with Lachlan?"

"No, the nanny's coming this weekend. Remember?"

"Sure, but I figured you'd find *something* wrong with her. There're enough resumes in the garbage to wallpaper a small home."

"I tried, believe me. But she's pretty damn perfect." She'd been with the same family in Denver the last sixteen years. The youngest had just left for college, so she was free. *Good timing.*

"Super." She sounded grouchy.

He grinned into her hair. "I feel the same way."

"I know she needs a nanny. I just...I like being with her. I like us...forget it."

Yeah, me, too. "It's just a test-run. It has to be the right fit on both sides."

"I hongry."

They both spun around at the sweet, little voice.

Delilah smiled at the little girl. "We're not eating until breakfast, sweetheart."

He knew Delilah wanted nothing more than to take his sister to the kitchen and make pancakes until she fell asleep in her arms, but she was setting aside what she believed was right to go along with his plan. And, damn, he liked that about her.

He lifted his sister into his arms. "Come on. Let's get you back to bed."

She reached over his shoulder, beckoning Delilah. "Wally."

Delilah leaned forward and kissed her cheek, but Ruby caught her at the back of the neck and held her in place, the three of them locked together.

With Ruby's arm around his neck and Delilah's palm on his back…a tide of emotion rolled in so powerful it nearly knocked him off his feet.

His heart thundered at the beauty of this…family… and the terrifying reality that it was something they could never be.

This is dangerous. Perspiration dotted his upper lip.

Delilah had two events left in the competition. Will left for Freefest the week after next. Right after that, his season began. Fin and Callie and the nanny would take over.

By playing house, they were misleading his sister. And, when they went their separate ways, it would be Ruby who paid the price.

In her two years of life, she'd experience more loss than most people do over a lifetime…why would she ever open her heart again?

Will never panicked. Not when he dropped out of a

helicopter onto the summit of a mountain. Not when he stood at the starting gate and took his final run of a competition. Not when he rotated nine hundred degrees and knew he was going to miss his landing—which could result in a broken bone and the potential end to his career.

But the two warm bodies pressing against him—the rush of affection he felt for both of these humans who'd dropped into his life out of nowhere—it was tearing him apart. He wanted them. He liked playing happy family.

But it was wrong for Ruby.

"Let's get you to bed." But he didn't move, and a strange sensation flooded his body. It saturated him, swamped him. Fucking overwhelmed him.

Delilah's hand touched his shoulder, slid up to his neck. Her fingers scraped into his scalp, as she tipped her head to his arm. Their scents mingled—sweet baby shampoo and honey-vanilla. One inspired a profound tenderness and a fierce sense of protection. The other… made him want to put a ring on her finger and keep her forever.

Both made his heart ache.

"Wheel." Ruby's voice, light as a feather, sounded sleepy.

"Yeah, Rubes?"

"I wuv you."

It took a two-year-old to make it all snap into place.

He was crazy about them. He loved his sister with a ferociousness that scared him. And he wanted Delilah Lua in way that breached the boundaries of good sense.

He was only just coming to understand that sometimes there were no answers. That no matter how much effort he applied, he couldn't always control the way things worked out.

The situation was screwed up. Ruby would have people coming in and out of her life, but she'd never have parents, and there was nothing he could do about that. So, what choice did he have but to shower her in love? Now and always.

He tightened his hold on them and pressed a kiss to his sister's chubby, hot cheek. "I love you too, Ruby-bean."

"Look at us," Delilah said with a sweet smile. "Making a Ruby love sandwich."

Love. It was strange and wondrous.

He couldn't control his feelings through structure or discipline.

And, so, he had to accept that even though it would hurt like hell when he lost these two, he still had to give them everything he had.

It wasn't like he had a choice. He'd fallen for them, and there was no turning back.

On the amphitheater stage, a rockabilly band played a rollicking rendition of Stevie Ray Vaughan's *Pride and Joy.* Will held his sister in his arms as they danced on the grass.

Delilah's heart had never been so full.

This past month had been the happiest of her life. Now that Will had eased up with Ruby, she'd turned into a feisty, rebellious, dramatic toddler—everything a two-year-old should be. She finally felt safe enough to be herself—and she was dynamite.

The vans arrived, the doors opened, and the wait staff climbed out, ready to deliver the tasting dishes to the tables.

Tonight, for the fifth event, the chefs had prepared

entrées. Will had driven her out to Culliver's Ranch, where she'd bought various types of game meat, and she'd spent the week experimenting. She'd come up with some fantastic dishes.

But two of the judges came from New York, another from Chicago, one from London…and she didn't think they'd appreciate her boldly western menus, so she'd pulled back, incorporating more recognizable flavors.

"Miss Lua."

The male voice had her turning around so quickly, the wine sloshed out of her glass. *Harry Morgenstern*. "Oh. Hello." Quickly recovering, she held out a hand. "Mr. Morgenstern. It's nice to meet you."

"The ragù was sublime. The polenta was creamy and salty and rich." He kissed the tips of his fingers.

"You're not supposed to know those are my dishes." Her teasing tone belied the frantic beating of her heart. Would he give her a higher score this week?

"I've been a food critic for nearly three decades, and I've come to learn that chefs have a style, a voice, if you will. And the reason I know which, out of the six possibilities is yours, is because of your distinctive presentation."

"Oh, I…" She wanted to say thank you, but what if he meant he didn't like it?

"You're incredibly gifted, Miss Lua. Your presentation always stands out. It's fresh and delightful, but your dishes…don't quite make sense."

Heat ripped across her skin. *Oh, my God.*

"It's not my place, especially in the middle of a competition, but may I offer a bit of advice?"

"Yes, of course."

"There's so much passion in your cooking. The flavors are robust, your vision unique and exciting, but I can't help getting the impression you're holding back." He held her gaze with an intensity that put her on alert—like she was about to get the code to unlock a safe, and he'd only say it once. "Given the inventiveness of your cooking, I suspect if you don't follow your inclinations, you won't be happy. Yet, if you don't bridge your inclinations with the marketplace, you won't be successful. You see, when your customers have their hearts set on Nonna Abelli's tiramisu...they want Nonna Abelli's tiramisu." He gave her a gentle smile. "And when they come to Calamity, Wyoming, they want the spirit of the west. Everything it has to offer."

She didn't know why his words crushed her. Her brother had certainly repeated them a hundred times over the last several years. But hearing it from Harry Morgenstern slammed it home. If she hung a Da Nonna's sign over her restaurant, she had to adhere to the franchise's menu and décor.

While she'd grasped it intellectually, she'd stubbornly clung to the idea that she could have her cake and eat it, too.

The thing was...tonight's dish...originally, she'd made it with wild boar. So, really, if she'd gone with her instincts from the start, she'd have given him exactly what he'd expected.

Worse, wild boar *would* have made a better dish. It'd have given it a cleaner, sweeter—with notes of nuttiness—taste than beef.

Dammit.

"I believe the combination of following your intuition and knowing your market will bring all the success you deserve." He gave her a warm smile, but right before he headed into the dancing crowd, he turned back and said,

"I look forward to the day you receive your Michelin star."

Delilah stood there, two fingers holding the stem of her wine glass, caught between elation—*he believes in me*—and wild frustration. The top food critic in New York thought her food was good enough to earn a star, but not until she figured her shit out.

She'd come out here hellbent on proving to her siblings that her food was good enough to serve alongside Nonna Abelli's, but she'd been wrong. The patrons of Da Nonna's didn't want her creative cuisine and putting it on the menu wouldn't draw new customers—it would create a sloppy brand.

If she wanted to own a franchise, she needed to deliver Nonna Abelli's signature dishes. Period. No variation. But if she wanted to be happy, she needed to follow her inclinations.

How on earth did she reconcile the two? Not owning a Da Nonna's…the idea sent her emotions into a tail spin. To not be part of the family business…it just didn't make sense to her.

If she wanted to follow her inclinations, she'd need to open her own restaurant—free and clear of Da Nonna's. Which meant separating herself from her family.

A simple enough idea, except that Da Nonna's…it was her *parents*.

There wasn't a single night in the kitchen that she didn't get a whiff of her mom's perfume—a scent she'd created herself in a shop on Bleecker Street. Or feel the ghost of her dad as he raced past her to accept a delivery, riffling the hem of her chef's jacket.

You know, maybe experimentation's normal for chefs just starting out. Maybe in time she'd have other things in her life—a husband, children—so that cranking out the signature dishes would be a relief.

Yeah, that made sense. In any event, she didn't have to worry about it right now. The only thing she needed to focus on was the final competition. For that one, they had two weeks to turn in a menu and sample tasting dishes. And this time she'd do it right. She'd follow her inclinations *and* fit the marketplace. Just like she'd originally envisioned.

A hard body came up behind her, a strong arm wrapped around her stomach, and warm lips pressed a kiss just below her ear. "What was that about?"

She gave Will a smile and brushed the damp hair off Ruby's forehead. "You're a dancing queen."

"I thought judges weren't supposed to talk to the chefs until after the scores are announced?"

"They're not, but he was giving me advice. Good advice. Basically, he told me to figure out my customer base and then marry my inventiveness to it. If I do that, he thinks I'll have a Michelin star one day." Since Da Nonna's would never earn one, had he been trying to tell her something? To go out on her own? "So, I'm going to do just that in the last event. I'm going to put a menu together with everything I've been working on this summer. I'm going full-on outlaw."

"That sounds good. Why aren't you happy about it?"

How did he know that? She'd been nothing but positive and smiley. *Because he knows me.* And that made her smile for real. "Because it means I can't be inventive and run Da Nonna's."

I have to choose.

Where do I belong?

"For what it's worth," Will said. "I just heard Chris raving about your dish."

"Really? What'd he say?"

"He said you've got flair. Thinks you're a superstar in the making." Will smiled indulgently. "He called your entrée hearty, robust, and incredibly flipping flavorful."

"Now you're messing with me. Chris wouldn't say that."

"You're right, but I don't want to use the exact word in front of my sister."

"So, other than 'flipping,' he actually said that?"

Will nodded.

"Wouldn't it be hilarious if I lost the competition but got offered the job here?"

There it was, that rush of energy between them, that crackling connection. Intensity blazed in his eyes, and he swallowed so hard his Adam's apple jumped. "Would you take it?"

Staying here with Will. And Ruby. Her heart pounded so hard it hurt. Did he *want* her to stay? Not just now, in the moment, but really and truly? For all that it meant?

A future together.

But the whole idea was ridiculous. Will had his competition season coming up, so he'd be gone for the next seven months. They'd known each other all of four weeks—hardly enough time to withstand a separation like that. And Fin, Callie, and the nanny would take care of Ruby. Which left her running a kitchen in Calamity…two thousand miles from her family.

Her mind said it didn't make sense, but her heart…her heart told a whole other story. "I don't know, but my ragù was sublime, so there's a chance I could win tonight." Regret twisted through her. If she'd gone with the wild boar, she might've created an actual signature dish of the spa restaurant in Owl Hoot. Hearty, robust, and every ingredient was locally sourced.

But she hadn't. *Dammit.*

"You didn't answer my question."

She reached out for his hand. "I know. I'm... confused. I love it here more than I ever imagined. There's something about the spirit of this place." It struck her that she fit here. The fierce independence, the exploration and experimentation—it defined the wild west. "I've talked to so many farmers and ranchers and chefs, and I feel like I would love to work with them, but this is summer break for you. When September comes, you go back to your real life. Fin and Callie and the nanny take over with Ruby. Where does that leave me? If I stay, it'll be like getting to eat your favorite cake but without the frosting."

"I'm the frosting?"

"You're the flour and the sugar and eggs and butter... you're everything. And I'm not sure I want to be here if you're not."

He opened his mouth to respond—looking way more conflicted than she'd expected—but she shut him down. He couldn't make her any promises. "And my family's in New York. So...I guess the answer to your question's no. I can't take the job here. I just...can't."

He drew in a breath so deep it straightened his shoulders. "Should we get some dessert, Rubes?"

"Shock-let!"

"Chocolate it is." He pressed a kiss to Delilah's cheek, then started off.

She watched him, a little panicky, because she was pretty sure she'd given the wrong answer. The Delilah Lua who'd just arrived in Calamity would've said that line about her family being in New York.

Not the woman she'd become.

But then Will stopped and, with a troubled expression, turned back to her. "You know, I've done a lot in my life, but I've never done *this. Us.* So…Delilah, if you're here, I'm here."

Chapter Sixteen

BACK ARCHED, FINGERS TANGLED IN HIS SILKY HAIR, Delilah bit down on a scream. Will clamped his big hands on her twisting hips, as his tongue flicked her clit.

Passion peaked, twisted, tightening her skin, burning her blood, until she shattered in an ecstatic burst of raw pleasure. The moment she slammed back down onto the mattress, she grabbed his shoulders and pulled him up.

The most handsome man in the world hovered over her with a wicked, sexy grin before planting his mouth over hers and kissing her ravenously.

She'd barely caught her breath, when his knees urged her thighs open and his hand cupped her ass, lifting her against him. He watched, as he slid inside, filling her and activating every single pleasure point. A shiver rocked her body. "God, Will."

With powerful thrusts, he leaned down and licked her nipple.

"Oh."

Then sucked it into his mouth. As his pace turned frantic, he pulled his mouth off her breast, grasped her hands and held them over her head. His hard body brushed over hers with every stroke, abrading her sensitive nipples and sensitive clit.

"*Will*."

His hips snapped, eyes closed in utter rapture, and she had to get her hands on all that hard, hot skin. Yanking out of his grip, she skimmed his back, down to the firm, taut muscles of his ass. Grasping, she pulled him into her, harder, deeper, and it just unleashed him. Wild, uninhibited, he slammed into her, choking on the sounds she knew he'd make if they didn't have Ruby right down the hall.

He opened his eyes, watching her, and she loved that about him. How much he cared about her pleasure. Her happiness, her success, *her*.

She'd wanted this so much, him focusing all that intensity on her. *And I got it.*

Lifting a knee, she urged him onto his back. He clamped a hand on her hip before rolling them over, keeping their bodies joined. She sat up, spreading her palms across the hard planes of his chest, and rocked over him. His expression desperate, he gripped her hips and worked her over his cock.

"*Fuck*." His voice a growl, he sat up, stuffing pillows behind him, and dragged her with him until his back was against the headboard. Hands on her breasts, her cupped them and licked one nipple and then the other, while she rode him frantically, wildly, her release so close. "Harder. Fucking harder. Give it to me."

She reached behind him for the headboard to steady herself through a climax that seized her body, spun it in circles of bright, vivid light, and then shot her into a timeless, weightless space of pure ecstasy.

Her spirit soared and tumbled, and nothing had ever felt so good…no one so right.

He slammed up into her, coming hard, hips pumping in short, twisting thrusts, his features contorted in an explosive release.

His pumps slowed, and he leaned back into the pillows just watching the place where their bodies were joined like he'd never seen anything hotter. She leaned in and kissed him full on the mouth.

Collapsing half on top of him, she caressed his chest, more content than she'd ever been in her life.

On the nightstand, her phone vibrated.

"You want to get it?" he asked. "Or let it go to voicemail?"

She'd better get it, right? Something could be wrong in New York.

Hey—you just said New York. Not home.

Interesting.

But seeing her brother's name on the screen wiped the smile off her face. He wouldn't call this late unless something was wrong. She hit Accept and sat up. "Joe?"

"Hey." Her brother, normally so confident, sounded wary.

She braced for bad news. "What happened?"

"You got a second?"

"Of course. What's going on?"

"Jeannie's getting a divorce."

"What?" She got out of bed, reaching for the silk robe she'd left on the chair. "How is that possible?" Her cousin was several years older than her, but they'd always been close. Wouldn't she have known if there'd been trouble in her marriage?

"Her asshole husband's not only been cheating, but he's gone through their savings at the casinos."

"Are you serious?" She couldn't believe it. He'd always seemed like such a great family man. "Did she have any idea?"

"You'd have to ask her about the details. The point is that he's left her with nothing, and she needs an income."

"That's terrible. I know how much she loves staying home with her kids."

"Listen, I need you to hear this from me, okay? We just had a family meeting, and we made a decision."

"Go on."

"We're giving her the eighth franchise."

Delilah's world spun, and she couldn't get her bearings. "By the 'eighth,' you mean *mine*."

"It's not yours. We're not changing our minds about that, but it's still in the long-term trust plans to have an eighth franchise, so it makes sense to give it to her. She's got two kids to raise and no money." His tone turned sharper. "Look, it's not just about getting her kids through college, Delilah. She's got to get herself through her retirement years. He's left her in a real bind."

"I hate that he's done that to her, but I'm a part of this family, too. You can't have family meetings without me." God, her hands were shaking.

"You're not here, and we had to make a decision. You know as well as I do, it's what Dad would've done."

"I cannot believe this. You don't trust *me* to run a restaurant, but you trust Jeannie?" *I went to the Cordon Bleu. I trained with some of the great chefs of the world.* Jeannie had been an interior designer before she got married.

"No, we don't trust you to run Da Nonna's, and for

good reason. But it'll work for Jeannie because she can hire a *cook*, and she'll take care of front of house. It's perfect."

"Perfect? You've just shut me out of the family business."

"You're a *chef*. You're better than the family business, and you know it. But you're still our sister, the aunt to our children. You're still our family."

"It sure as hell doesn't feel like it when you're making major decisions without me." *And cutting me out of the business.* "I can't believe you're doing this."

"We've got something brewing for you, Delilah, I promise. If it comes together, it's going to be perfect for you. As soon as you come home, we'll tell you about it."

She had no idea when it had become the six of them against her, but they could forget it. *It's bullshit.* "Come home to what? Forget it. I'm just so glad I came out here and entered this competition, since it's my only shot at a future."

Ruby clung to him like they'd just jumped off the Titanic into icy waters. "Okay, Rubes, it's time for me to hit the road. Miss Kessler's going to hang out with you."

The nanny had spent the first half of her life raising her siblings after their parents died in a plane crash, and the second half raising other people's children. She knew her job the way Will knew halfpipe. "We're going to have lots of fun today, Ruby. I've packed us a picnic lunch for the beach."

Ruby sized up the woman with a look that said, *This is of no concern to me whatsoever.*

Delilah stroked the little girl's arm. "You have a good day, sweetheart, okay?"

With an efficient air, Miss Kessler got hold of Ruby's waist and pulled. "I know you have a long trip ahead of you, so if you'd like to get going, Ruby and I are going to put on our bathing suits and look for our sand pails. We're going to collect pebbles."

"Shist," Ruby said.

The woman faltered, shooting a look to Will.

"Ruby and her uncle have started a rock collection. She's got granite, schist, pegmatite, and gneiss so far." Will smiled at the woman's relief.

"Ah. Wonderful. Let's see if we can add to that collection." With Ruby struggling for freedom in her sturdy arms, the nanny started for the stairs. "Do you know which swimsuit you'd like to wear? I like that bright yellow one. It reminds me of the sun."

Will watched Ruby shake her head vigorously, insisting on the "poople" one. He smiled through the mild heartache of finding out he was perfectly replaceable.

But then, at the top of the stairs, just before they disappeared down the hall, Ruby grabbed the wall and twisted around to him. "Back, Wheel?"

Funny how he already knew exactly what she meant. "Probably after dinner."

And then she balled her hand into a fist, kissed it, and punched the air. Without even thinking, his arm shot up to catch the kiss, and he smacked it onto his cheek. Ruby's grin hit like a spray of bright fireworks against a black sky, and his heart got so full Will didn't know how much more it could take.

Without a word, he turned and followed Delilah out

the door. Emotion crowded every nook and cranny in his body, and he just needed to let it subside a little.

He got into the truck and turned the ignition, driving off in the complete silence Delilah gifted him with.

With Freefest just ten days away, he had no business taking off as much time as he had this summer. But for that moment with Ruby? No trophy, no medal, nothing could come close to the satisfaction, the joy, of having worked through issues with her and come out the other side.

Delilah's hand grasped his thigh and squeezed.

And the powerful connection he felt with this woman? No, he couldn't afford to take the day off, but he'd never once taken her on a date, and he wanted her to know how much she meant to him. He wanted time with her. Just her. Uninterrupted.

Because I can't get enough.

And he'd be damned if he let anything stop him from taking every second he could with her.

Just as he reached the gate at the end of the driveway, his manager's cherry red Ford F-150 pulled in. Will hit the remote, and the gate slowly swung open.

Getting out of the truck, he met Alex on the hot asphalt. "What's up?"

"Glad I caught you." He gave Delilah a nod.

She leaned out of her window to wave. "Hey."

"Listen, I'm heading out to LA this morning to meet with a new client, but I wanted to check in on my way to the airport, see how you feel about Damien's latest."

"Latest what?"

"His response to the footage we put up."

After reading some of the comments on Damien's YouTube page, Will had decided to break his silence by uploading the full footage of that last run of the World Games. He hadn't given any commentary, because he didn't need to—all of Damien's flaws of execution were right there for everyone to see.

"Haven't heard anything." It wasn't uncommon for Will to unplug during the off-season, but with Delilah and Ruby in his life, he'd been even more removed.

Skiing had been his sole focus for so long, he hadn't known what he'd been missing. Nothing much had tempted him, until he'd gotten to experience it with Delilah. Food, music, sex…everything became more…*necessary* with her.

"Does it bother you?" His manager's voice—annoyed—insistent—broke through the flurry of thoughts and images, thick as a snowstorm.

"Does what bother me?"

"That he entered Freefest?"

"Damien?"

"Yeah, that's what I just said." Alex let out an exasperated sigh. "Damien entered Freefest so he can prove to the world that he's better than you."

A slow smile spread across his face. "I'll have to think of a way to thank him for helping me clear my reputation."

"Funny thing," the jewelry store owner said. "These are the same stones my great-great-grandfather probably tossed back into the river during the gold rush days."

"They're gorgeous." Delilah pulled a deep green-blue sapphire ring in a rose gold setting out of the cushioned display box. "This one's my favorite."

"You don't wear jewelry," Will said.

"Not in the kitchen, but I like it for special occasions." But, really, she wanted it as a memory. Every time she wore it, she'd come back to this place, these feelings.

Of Will's hand clasping hers, and Ruby shaking her bottom as she danced around the kitchen. Will kissing her like the timer to the end of the world was about to run out, his mouth so soft and hot, his tongue so hungry for her…

A shiver ran down her spine.

"Is it untreated?" Will asked the owner.

"We mine everything ourselves, and everything you see's untreated."

Delilah pulled out her phone to snag a picture of the ring at the same moment Will reached for her hand. "Let's see if it fits."

She took it just as Will slid the ring onto her finger. It fit perfectly. Their gazes collided, sparking smiles so happy she felt giddy. *I'm crazy about you.*

Color splashed across his cheeks, as Will pulled out his wallet. "We'll take this one."

"You're not buying me a ring." She quickly tugged it off.

"Yeah, I am." He slid it right back on.

"*Will.* It's too much."

He brought her fingers to his mouth and kissed them. "Let me."

The way he looked at her made her heart jump into her throat. He rocked her world. Sometimes she thought…well, she was stupid. She shouldn't think about anything but winning the competition. She was on her own now, and she needed that prize money.

"I'll give you a moment to decide." The owner went back to the register, leaving them alone.

"I want you to have this memory," Will said. "Of us. Of this day."

As crazy as it sounded, it seemed unthinkable to leave Will and Ruby and this life she'd just discovered. "It's been the most perfect day." They'd driven up Highway 191, through the Tetons, and arrived in West Yellowstone just in time for lunch. Afterwards, they'd explored the Grizzly and Bear Reserve, caught an Imax movie, and hit up half the stores in the town that served as a gateway to Yellowstone National Park. "I promise I don't need a ring to remember it." She got up on her toes and pressed a kiss to his mouth. "I like you so much, Will. I don't think I've ever liked someone as much as you."

He looked pained. "I like you, too. And I want you to wear this ring, so I can be with you."

Be with me?

Five weeks ago, she couldn't imagine words like that coming out of this badass athlete's mouth. *I want you with me, too.* Should she just come out and ask?

Since when did she hold back? She'd always been a direct, wear-your-heart-on-your-sleeve kind of woman. Why not now?

Well, because her heart had never been on the line. And it just felt so scary, so…*screw it.* "What if this was just one memory out of many?"

"What do you mean?"

"What if we created more of them? Lots more."

"Are you saying you'd stay here?" All that energy he kept leashed so tightly strained to break free.

She wanted him to break all over her.

"Are you thinking about it?" His tone held an urgency

that excited her. "If the board offered you the spa restaurant, would you take it?"

"I might."

"But your family?"

"Well, that's the thing. They've cut me out, and I need to make something happen on my own." She waited for him to say something. Something like, *Please stay. Let's build something together.*

Instead he gave her that practiced smiled, took the ring out of her hand, and struck off to the cash register.

What was that? She watched him, but he didn't look back.

Why had he walked away so abruptly?

She replayed the conversation—remembering that expression—like she'd just told him she might like Brodie better. What had she said to piss him off—no, *disappoint* him?

She couldn't read his mind. She'd have to ask him about it on the ride home.

While he made the purchase, she uploaded the shot to her social media accounts.

Just discovered these Montana sapphires. Aren't they gorgeous?

She stared at the picture—her smaller hand resting on top of his bigger one, him sliding the ring on her finger, and her heart clutched with so much longing and hope.

In a million years, she couldn't have imagined falling for a guy from Calamity, Wyoming.

Her phone vibrated. *Bree.* She didn't want to talk to her sister, but...whatever. She wasn't going to be immature about it. "Hey. What's going on?"

Will swung around to look at her, and she pointed to the door. Quickly, she stepped out onto the boardwalk.

"You tell me." She sounded alarmed.

"What do you mean? Is everything all right?"

"I just saw your post."

"Which one?" She couldn't mean the one she'd uploaded five seconds ago, could she?

"*Delilah*. Do you have something to tell me?"

"I don't know what you're talking about." She could barely hear her sister over the pedestrian and motor traffic in town, so she hurried down the boardwalk, jumped off, and headed down the quieter side street.

"That man put a ring on your finger."

She laughed. "Oh, my God, Bree. It's not that kind of ring. I'm not *engaged*. Will took me to West Yellowstone for the day. We stopped in a jewelry store, and I was curious about Montana sapphires, that's all."

"Okay, but that's how a groom puts a ring on his bride's finger. Come on. It totally looks like an engagement shot."

"Well, it's not. The point was to show the sapphires, since they're unique to the area."

"Yeah, but it's not just that. You usually post about food and farmers markets. Lately, it's all pictures of you with Will and that little girl."

"That's because I'm spending a lot of time with them."

"You obviously have feelings for him. It's clear in every photo."

"I do." It felt good to finally tell someone. She turned her back on Main Street. "I'm crazy about him."

"Well, isn't that what you usually do? Every relationship you've ever had either started at work or school. I know it's fun for you, but this time there's a child involved. A girl who's lost her *parents*."

Reality crashed down on her, covering her in sludge. "I love that little girl."

"But you're leaving. You're letting her get attached to you, when you'll be gone in two weeks."

"I'm here now, though. Why wouldn't I give her all the love and attention I can? Besides, I'm just one of many babysitters she'll have over the years. Bree, you're acting like I'm some horribly selfish person. I'm in a relationship with Will. I—" She swallowed the word she was about to say. "Like him so much." But it got stuck in her throat, so she just spit it out. "I *love* him."

Her admission hung in the air, taking the form of heavy, beating wings.

"You can't be in love with a guy from *Wyoming*. Is he willing to move here?"

Will in New York City? "Of course not. He's a skier. He trains in the mountains, *and* he's got Ruby. He can't just leave her."

"Okay, but your life is here."

"Is it? Because I'm really not sure what I'm coming home to. You've just given my restaurant to Jeannie."

"God, Delilah, would you stop punishing us already? It was a hard choice for us to make but, in the end, we had to do what was right for the whole family—including you. As soon as you come home, we'll tell you what we're working on."

Stop punishing *us*, hard choice for *us*, *we, we, we*. Could they make her feel more of an outsider? "That's nice of you guys to brainstorm about my future." *Without me*. "But I'm taking care of it myself."

"By shopping for rings with that guy? Don't use him to get back at us."

"Use him?"

"You don't see it yet, and I get that. You had your whole life planned around that franchise, and it knocked you off balance to lose it. Just come home, okay? Let Callie's family get back on its feet."

"You act like I'm using them as pawns in some kind of game. I love them."

"That kid isn't yours. It's not Will's, either. From what you said, Fin and Callie will be taking over in just a few weeks."

She hated hearing the words.

"Look, I know you. You jump right in and give your heart away. But this time…" Her sister let out a huff of breath. "I mean, look ahead a few months. Will's gone, Fin and Callie are taking care of the little girl, and what will you be doing? Where will you live? Have you thought about any of this? Because I would hate to see my wildly talented sister working as a sous chef in some small town and babysitting when Fin and Callie want a date night. You'll have given everything up for nothing."

Chapter Seventeen

"Delilah."

Just the sound of his voice flipped her right out of her foul mood. She dropped her phone into her tote and turned towards Will, watching the play of his sculpted thigh muscles in jeans so worn they were almost white and the biceps that popped and flexed in his dark gray T-shirt.

All that athletic grace and swagger had heads turning to watch him.

His smile grew wider with every step that bridged the distance between them. If her sister could see him now, would it dispel all her doubts? Will didn't open his heart easily, but he'd done it for her. He'd let her in.

Or had he? The image of him walking away from her in the store popped into her head, dimming her smile. Why had he done that? It sure didn't fit with the way he was looking at her right now.

"Hey." He caught her around the waist, walked her back against the side of the jewelry store, and kissed her. Long, sensual sweeps of his tongue, hands squeezing the rise of her bottom. When he pulled back, he brushed the hair out of her eyes. "Everything okay?"

Sensation bloomed across her skin. She'd thought his mother had done such a number on him that he'd never give his love to anyone again. *Look at him now.*

Well, not that he *loved* her. *It's only been five weeks.* But he was so open to her, so sweet. She couldn't even imagine leaving him.

But what did *he* want? When she'd brought up the idea of staying, he'd just walked away.

He bent his knees to get eye-level. "You all right?"

"Yeah." She shrugged. "My sister. I put up a picture of the ring—which happened to have your hand in the frame—and she freaked out, thinking we were engaged or eloping or something crazy like that." *Is it crazy, though?* She looked into his eyes for an answer—anything that said he was in this with her—but got nothing. Her heart crashed.

Taking the royal blue box out of the bag, he cracked it open and pulled out the ring. He kissed her palm before sliding it onto her finger. "With this ring, I thee… remember fondly."

She couldn't cover the shock of hurt. "Jerk." *Here I am twisting myself inside out over whether to stay and he's making a big joke out of it?*

"You're so beautiful." He stroked a finger on her cheek. "All flushed and pretty. If we were in Vegas, I might marry you right now."

Oh, he didn't know. He had no idea what those words did to her. Her spirit rose, soared. Her feet left the ground and her fingers stirred the clouds.

The way he looked at her made it feel like he was floating, too.

I do.

Until he blinked, and they both came crashing back to earth. "Sapphires are pretty indestructible, so you can wear it in the kitchen."

Confused by his mixed messages, she looked away. *The ring.* Holding it out in front her, the green-blue as alive and vibrant as the lake, she took in its beauty. "I love it so much."

"So. What do you want to do next?"

"Is it awful to say I want to get back to Ruby? She's been without us for over five hours, and we've still got a two-and-a-half-hour drive back home." Even though they'd checked in regularly, it was still her first day alone with the nanny.

He looked at her with relief and admiration. "Right there with you. Let's go see our girl."

Her heart squeezed fiercely. *Our girl.* Why did that feel so right? But her sister's voice pierced the bubble of happiness. *That kid isn't yours. It's not Will's either.*

She didn't want to be one of the people passing through Ruby's life.

She wanted to stay.

Keeping his body straight, Will bounced off the trampoline and caught air. *Not high enough.*

Again.

Coming back down, his feet hit the bounce mat, and he pushed higher.

Come on, man. Higher.

Get it right this time.

He hit the surface and exploded.

Delilah popped into his mind. It struck him that when she came home from teaching at the Slow Food Grower school, she'd find an empty house. After what happened with his mom, she might worry. He should've left a note that Miss Kessler had taken her to the book store.

"*Will.* Where's your head at?"

His trainer's voice snapped him out of his thoughts. *Fuck. Focus.* Holding his arms to his sides, he bounced off the surface. Not nearly high enough to pull off a cork 720.

Again.

He shut down his mind and focused. The next jump, he soared, tilted his head back, pulled in his legs, and turned toward the side of the trampoline.

An image appeared in his head—Delilah's expression when they'd found out Ruby was missing—the abject fear.

Should've left a damn note.

Coming down, Will spotted his landing, but his timing was off by a second. *Oh, shit.* The covered metal bar of the trampoline came up fast. He corrected but not quickly enough. His heel clipped it, jolting his body sideways.

He twisted and landed with a shock of pain in his right knee.

"Whoa, dude, are you okay?" His trainer knelt by the side of the trampoline.

The same knee that had kept him out of the last winter Olympics.

Blood thundered in his ears, and he waited for the pain to subside.

"Hang on," the trainer said. "Let me get doc."

"No. Give me a minute."

More people gathered around, everyone talking. "Back off," his trainer said. "Give him some space."

The heat and humidity in the gym bore down on him as he took inventory of his body. A gentle rotation of his ankle told him it was good. *Thank Christ.* Trampoline bouncing lightly, he lifted his left leg—*fine.*

Dammit, if he'd blown it out his knee…*don't go there.*

What the hell happened? He could do tricks like this in his sleep.

But, of course, he knew exactly what had happened. *Delilah coming home to an empty house? That's what you're thinking about while training?*

Once the pain subsided, he tentatively lifted his right knee. *Feels fine.* He bent it.

"Whoa," the trainer said. "Not so fast."

"No, it's good. I'm good." Will got up, careful not to put all his weight on his right leg. Hopping to the ladder, he set his left foot on the bottom rung.

It's okay. He hadn't done any damage. *Screwing up your knee a week before Freefest?*

With Damien there?

Not a chance.

Nothing would stop him from shutting that asshole down once and for all.

Heading up the ladder, he let his right leg bear some weight. Still no pain. With his full weight on it, he felt a twinge, but that was it. Just a twinge.

"I'm going to call it a day." Will climbed out of the pit, favoring his left leg, and snatched the clean, white towel he'd left on the railing.

"You sure you're okay?" the trainer asked.

"Yeah." He scrubbed his face. "Fine."

"Never seen you mess up like that before."

"Oh, come on. I mess up all the time." He just needed

to get out of there. Too many people, too much noise. He headed toward the exit.

"Sure ya do." The guy laughed. "You're the one who talks about consistency. You've taken a few days off lately, so I'm thinking we better get you back on track. You leave next week."

"You're right about that." He had to get his head in the game.

Pushing on the metal release bar, he stepped out into the bright sunshine, a warm sage-scented wind cooled the perspiration on his skin.

Next week he flew to France, leaving Ruby with Miss Kessler. Marcella would be back, Lachlan would be around. Fin and Callie would be home soon.

She'll be fine.

Of course, Delilah would stay in town a week longer, but she'd be gone by the time he got back. Unless the board offered her the executive chef job. *Nah. She won't take it.*

For a moment there in the jewelry store, when he'd asked if she'd take the job, he'd thought she'd actually choose Calamity. *Me.* But then he understood she was just pissed at her siblings and using him to scare them into giving her what she wanted.

And they would. She had more power over them than she realized.

So, then, yeah, when he got back from Freefest, she'd be gone.

Which meant he'd go on with his life like this summer had never happened, except he'd get to see Ruby. Hang out with her from time to time.

Not Delilah, though. He'd never see her again.

No regrets. It'd been good. Fun. Definitely worth it.

A couple guys training in the freestyle pool climbed down off the scaffolding and jogged toward him. "Dude, did you hear?"

The other guy said, "Is there anything we can do? This isn't right."

What the hell now? "Hear what? I don't know what you're talking about." Jesus, if it was more shit from Damien, he didn't care. He'd prove everything on the course.

Other people joined them. "He's gone too far."

"Time to lawyer up."

A *lawyer*? "Hang on. What's going on?"

Someone pulled out his phone and swiped the screen a few times before handing it over.

"Damien posted it about an hour ago."

With bright sunlight obscuring the screen, Will headed for the overhang. Seemed to be an old photo, when his dad had a full head of dark hair. He stood beside some man Will didn't recognize.

The headline made Will's blood turn cold.

Looks like the Bowies might need a dump truck to get rid of all their ill-gotten medals. Turns out their father was one of the first investors in Sprocket, the biggest sponsor of the U. S. Freestyle Ski League's competitions.

"It's bullshit." He handed the phone back. "My dad didn't buy my wins." Fucking Damien. He was just making a fool of himself. Will carried on. He just wanted to get home.

"*Will.*"

Exasperated with all the drama, Will snapped. "What?"

"You've been banned, man. The League banned you."

A hawk's screech snapped him back to the moment and, when he looked up to check his surroundings, he found himself at the family cemetery. His grandparents, aunts, uncles, cousins—all the way back to eighteen ninety-seven, when the Bowies had first arrived in Calamity—had been laid to rest in this shaded patch of meadow.

How the hell had he wound up here? Instead of running home after training, he'd walked to give his knee a rest. But his head had been filled with so much white noise since finding out he'd been banned that he'd wandered way off course.

Under a grove of cottonwood trees, a breeze stirred the branches. He knelt at his father's grave. *Dammit, Dad. Why'd you have to die?* Will needed him now more than ever. He brushed the pine needles and dirt off the stone. "I just want to make you proud. I don't know why this is happening" —*banned, Jesus*—"And I don't know how to fix it." How had his dad gotten dragged into this mess anyhow? "But I will. There's not a chance Damien's going to ruin your reputation." His dad had sacrificed everything for him, had turned him into the man he'd become. He would clear his family's name.

The hawk circled overhead, and the bushes nearby rustled with wildlife.

He couldn't help thinking about what Lachlan had said. That what drove him was not his dad, but his mom. That he kept competing to prove he was a good man.

He shuffled through a lifetime of memories.

His birthday party—sixth? Seventh? Candles, cake, a bunch of kids. His mom had gone all-out—hired some company to put a racetrack in the backyard. Foot-pedaled cars. The kids had crashed—big pile-up. He'd hurt his neck pretty bad. He'd wanted to cry, but his mom had given him this look—hard, mean, like, *don't you dare ruin this party.* Made him fight hard to swallow his tears, his hurt, his pain.

When he was eleven, his back pressed to the wall as he'd eavesdropped on his parents the night before his mom had left the family.

His first competition—he must've been fifteen—looking at the scoreboard to discover he'd come in twelfth. Cursing himself for screwing up so badly.

He sank into that one, trying to remember his reaction. His first impulse had always been to scan the crowd for his dad. Why? Because he wanted that look of pride and love he got no matter where he placed.

So, no, his dad never made him feel like he had to do better, be better.

When he was seventeen, he'd placed second in a competition. His dad had hugged him so hard, his feet had left the snow. *Did you text Mom?* That had been the first question he'd asked.

So, yeah. Maybe Lachlan was right. Maybe winning his mom's respect had driven him all these years.

Respect? The word landed like a chair with one leg too short. *Come on.*

Love. A wave of heat swept over him, coaxing out beads of perspiration. He wanted his mom to love him.

Fuck. She never would, would she?

He thought about the way she'd looked at Ruby with

such disdain. His sister hadn't done what she'd wanted, so his mom had washed her hands of her.

All this time he'd thought his mom hated him, but…*it was never about me.* He picked up a dry twig and snapped it in half, then tossed the pieces into the tall grass.

He wished he'd talked to his dad about this stuff. They just never had. "When mom left…I was scared shitless."

Alone in his room, he'd stare up at the ceiling, awash in terror. But it hadn't been a fear he could name, which made it so much worse. If he'd been staring into a grizzly bear's beady eyes, it would've been manageable. He could've taken action to control it.

But not knowing had created this spinning, grinding, pulsating fear that ploughed through him, shredding his tissue, organs, and bones, leaving him pulverized.

He snagged another twig and tossed it. "But you threw me a lifeline. You quit your job and spent time with me, got me focused on skiing. And, even though I knew you did it because you felt bad for me, I loved you for it. You were my best friend, Dad, and I never got to thank you." A rush of wind through the leaves made his skin tingle. "So, I'll thank you now by getting to the bottom of that photograph."

Given the lack of gray in his hair, it had to have been taken twenty years ago.

"And by writing a letter to the League, letting them know the kind of man you were." Energy rolled in, and he sat up straighter. "I'll tell them you wouldn't have wanted us to win in any way other than through hard work, dedication, and focus."

He'd tell them stories about the way his dad had made them work for everything. Their first snowboard, their first

ATV, their first trucks. How he'd given them nothing freely other than his time, attention, and love.

"Damien's not going to get away with this." Will would talk to his lawyer, get him to do a deep dive into Mack Bowie's financials. He'd clear his dad's name.

His phone vibrated. Relief hit him when he saw Gray's name on the screen. "Hey."

"Ya fuckin' hooligan."

"Right?" He stood up.

"I called James."

Even better than their attorney, the trustee of his dad's estate would know the story behind the picture. "What'd he say?"

"He says Dad was an original investor of Sprocket in nineteen ninety-three. He sold his shares in 'ninety-five."

Knew it. "Good. Now we have to get the facts out there. Take Damien down."

"Already on it."

Emotion swept through him hard and fierce. He fucking loved his brothers. "Thanks, man." Gray liked to come off all nonchalant, like nothing mattered to him, but Will knew that was a cover. Shit sank into Gray way deeper than it did with the rest of them. Always had. "Appreciate it."

"Think I'm gonna meet you in Tignes."

This year, Freefest would be held on the Grand Motte glacier. For halfpipe, they needed a great terrain park. "Yeah? Cool."

"Send me photos of the course."

"Will do."

"And don't let this get inside your head," Gray said. "We're gonna clear your name."

"Damn right we will."

"I just don't want it fucking with your focus."

"Oh, shit." Will paced to the trail. "You think *that's* why Damien's doing this? To get me off my game?"

"That's exactly why he's doing it. Rattle you so you screw up on the course."

Determination sliced him wide open. "He has no idea who he's messing with."

In his deep, gravelly voice, Gray chuckled. "No, he doesn't. I've never seen anyone lock down under pressure the way you do. You're a fuckin' champion, and he's about to get his ass handed to him."

Sun bearing down on his head, Will made his way back home. With his plan in place—talking to the lawyer and the estate's trustee and writing the letter—the chaos in his mind settled.

For his first eight years of competing, he'd hardly won a single event. Not winning did something to a man. Put a fire in him to finally ring that elusive bell at the top rung. And once he'd gotten there? He'd worked even harder to hold onto his title.

So, no one—especially not some guy who wanted to win based on his own set of criteria—would mess with the reputation he'd worked his ass off to build. And the idea that Damien would attack a man who'd passed away, who couldn't defend himself—it got Will's blood boiling.

It struck him that, since finding out he'd been banned, not once had he panicked about the idea of never skiing competitively again.

Why didn't it bother him?

Easy. Because of Delilah. And Ruby. For the first time in seventeen years he'd focused on something other than training and competing, and he'd liked it. Now that he'd experienced another side of life—of himself—he couldn't go back to the old way.

It wasn't like he wanted to get drunk or shove fists full of cake into his mouth. He didn't want to take up sky diving or knitting.

He wanted to live an ordinary life.

Wrong. He broke into a smile at the truth. His life with Delilah was extraordinary, and he'd be a damned fool not to beg her to stay.

She made him happy. She made him feel alive. He wanted to watch her cook and eat and laugh and throw her head back in the throes of an orgasm.

Yeah, that. As the image hit of her hair spread out on his dark blue pillowcase, eyes closed in ecstasy, lips parted in abandon, desire hummed in his body.

Maybe he'd start a new career as Delilah's boyfriend, just so he could spend every free minute with her.

He'd been asking the wrong question. All summer, he'd asked what she'd do if her siblings gave her the restaurant, but he'd never asked her to stay.

He'd assumed her life would be better, happier, more fulfilled in New York with her family, but maybe it wouldn't be.

Hadn't she come here to find out who she was away from them?

Find it with me.

Nothing would make him happier than watching her become the woman she was meant to be.

I love her.

Oh, fuck. He stumbled, catching himself before he landed in a sprawl on the dirt path.

I love her. It was so true, so pure, that it didn't scare him. Not a bit. *I love her. I want her.*

I'm going to ask her to stay.

And, after Freefest, I might just retire.

Make loving Delilah my full-time job.

When he reached the house, a glint of sunlight on metal caught his attention. He cut around to the driveway but didn't recognize the tan Buick with its engine still ticking,

No one he knew drove a sedan like that.

Was this about Ruby? He leapt up the porch stairs and let himself into the house. The familiar scent of Delilah's cooking hit him at the same moment as the unfamiliar male voice.

"You're too talented to be stuck in some cow town working a chuck wagon for tourists."

Delilah burst out laughing, and he just loved her so fucking much. The fact that she didn't get hurt or insulted by that comment? She had the best spirit of anyone he'd ever met.

"It's not like that, I promise."

"Look, if maintaining the legacy means losing our baby sister, then I'm doing something wrong." Her brother let out a harsh exhalation. "I want to do right by Mom and Dad. You have to know, that's my sole focus. I was thirty-two when they died, and to find out they'd made me the executor of the estate? It was huge. And I can't mess up."

"I understand that," Delilah said. "Well, maybe I never really *got* it, you know? You're my big brother, and you've always just taken care of things."

"But even worse than losing customers is losing our

sister."

"You're never going to lose me, Joe. I love my family. Look, I've had a lot of time to think about things."

Planting his ass on the arm of the couch, Will listened to her tone as much as her words.

"And I'm so angry that you guys are making decisions about *my* life behind my back. Giving me that envelope on my birthday? That wasn't cool. You could've just shown me Harry's column and talked to me about it."

"You're right. I was angry. I work so hard to keep our business strong, and then to see the top food critic telling his followers to eat somewhere else? I was pissed."

"I get that. But I figured something out this summer. In spite of the way you guys went about it, you're right. I'm not going to be happy churning out the same dishes night after night."

What does that mean? Hope kicked his pulse into overdrive.

"And I'm really happy here. I like the *freedom* I have here."

Holy shit. Is she going to stay? He sprang off the couch.

"I've fallen in love with this place, with…everything."

Say it. Tell your brother.

Make it real.

"I love Will."

Yes. Fuck yes.

"I do. And I love his sister."

She's going to stay. Even without knowing the outcome of the competition, Delilah was making the choice to be with him. *Jesus.* He walked in a circle, hands clenched into fists, so damn elated he didn't know what to do with himself.

"What're you saying, Delilah?"

"I'm saying that I'm going to stay here."

I fucking love you, Delilah, and I'm going to spend my life making sure you never regret your decision.

"And there's nothing we can do to change your mind?"

Something about her brother's tone sent a spray of anxiety through him. He sounded pleased with himself.

"Nothing *you* can do." She laughed. "Now, *he* could tell me he doesn't want me. That would change my mind."

Never. He headed toward the kitchen. He'd tell her right now. In front of her brother. Will had never been more sure about anything.

"What if we found a way to give you everything you've ever wanted? To let you run Da Nonna's with your own creative flair. Would *that* would change your mind?"

Slam. It was like a car crash, the crunch of metal, the shattering of glass. Will froze, listening.

"What're you talking about? We both know that could never work."

"The same review that sent you to Calamity caught the interest of Dino Romano, the top restaurateur in the city. He called me up a few weeks ago, said Harry's review had sparked an idea. He wants to launch a new franchise off the back of Da Nonna's. It'd be a contemporary reimagining of Nonna Abelli's recipes."

"*What*?"

"Yep. He wants the classic old school Italian standards 'invigorated' by your creativity."

"When you say me…"

"I mean you. He wants you, specifically, as executive chef."

"Holy shit. I know Dino Romano. Anyone in the food business knows him. I'm twenty-six years old, and he wants *me*? I don't even know how to process this."

"It couldn't be more perfect. Dino Romano's given us a way to have it all. We can expand the business and bring you home. You belong with us, and now we've finally got a way to make it all work."

Will didn't know why he needed to hear her answer. He already knew she'd take it. She had to. They'd come up with the perfect situation for her.

"You okay?" her brother asked.

"I don't know what I am." Her voice sounded shaky. A chair scraped back. "Is this a done deal? I have carte blanche to run my own restaurant?"

"No. We've had several meetings, but there's no point in moving forward until you join the discussion. Which is why I came out here. I know you've got one more competition at the end of the week, but we're meeting with Dino on Tuesday, and he's only going to come if you're there. I've taken the ball this far, but you're the one who's got to score the touchdown."

"He said that? That he's not moving forward without me?"

Pure awe, that's what he heard. He tried to be happy for her—Delilah deserved the best of everything—but he couldn't help thinking it was a mistake. Even taking his own heart out of the equation, weren't they just putting her right back in the box? This one had more room, but hadn't she grown out of boxes altogether? Everything she'd talked about this summer had been about freedom, finding herself outside of her family. This job would rein her back in.

"That's right. I've talked to him about the business end of things." Another chair scraped back. "And now he needs to hear your plans for the menu."

"I don't have any plans."

"That's the thing, Delilah. He wants you to do exactly what you've been doing. Add andouille to the gravy. Use lemon curd in the tiramisu. He wants your spin on our standard dishes."

"Wow, I just…I'm blown away by this."

"In a good way?" For the first time, her brother's tone held uncertainty.

"In the best way." The rustle of clothing made him think she'd just thrown herself into her brother's arms.

"How quickly can you pack a bag?" he asked.

"If I go with you now, I have to come back for the last competition."

"What's the point? The moment we land in New York, you're going to hit the ground running with this new franchise. Why put off your future another day?"

It's done.

She's leaving.

Tick…tick…BOOM.

The explosion was cataclysmic. White-hot splinters of his heart rained down on him.

They'd given Delilah her dream. She'd get to run her family's restaurant with her own style.

Pain ripped through him like a flash fire.

Change the channel. Change the channel. Change the goddamn channel.

But it was stuck. Fire raged around him, blocking him in. He couldn't get out.

She's leaving. Taking her laughter and her hands and that smile that brought the first rays of light into his heart in twenty years.

Action. Move. His feet carried him to the stairs. He'd call the pilot. Take care of his travel plans. He'd gotten an email a while back, inviting him to share a cabin with a few other guys. Should've responded to it. *Hope it's not too late.*

Faltering on the step, he grabbed the banister. A little light-headed. Needed food. He'd get it later, after they left the kitchen. For now, he'd shower.

This is good for her. She's happy. He'd known her brother would cave. Who wanted to lose one of their siblings to another state? Another family? Another world?

How come he was only halfway up the stairs? Shouldn't he be in his room by now? His body felt sluggish, like walking through water. Probably from his fall on the trampoline. *Should take it easy the rest of the day. Read to Ruby in the hammock by the pool.*

Once in his room, he stripped off his damp T-shirt and walked into the bathroom.

Fingers under the spray of water, waiting for it to turn warm, it struck him what this overreaction to her leaving meant. He'd gotten so carried away, he might've given up the *Olympics* to be with her.

If she'd stayed, he might've ended his career without taking it over the finish line.

Big mistake. It wasn't just about him. His family's reputation had been challenged. It wasn't fair for Fin, Brodie, Gray…or even Ruby.

And it wasn't fair to his dad who'd rather his boys flip burgers than win by cheating.

Leaving it to his lawyer, writing a letter…winning Freefest? Not enough.

Play time was over. It was time to get back to training. With the heel of his palm, he shut off the faucet and went back out to his bedroom. He grabbed his phone and hit his pilot's speed dial. "Sarah? I need a ride to France."

Chapter Eighteen

DELILAH STOOD ON THE DRIVEWAY, SCANNING THE meadow.

Will should've been home from training by now. *Where is he?*

"You coming?" Her brother looked like a kid on Christmas morning as he climbed onto the bright red All-Terrain vehicle.

She shook her head. "No, you go." She had to talk to Will.

Once her brother was set, Lachlan boarded his ATV, and the two of them took off toward the mountain.

Why wasn't Will responding to her texts? Her calls went straight to voicemail. She headed back into the house. All her life she'd dreamed of owning a franchise—to sit at the table as an equal with her siblings. Her restaurant would be the final, missing piece in the family business. But executive chef of a spin-off franchise?

God. What an honor that Dino Romano believed in her ability. With one hand, she'd hold onto her family legacy, and with the other she'd create her own. *It's a dream come true.*

On the porch, she stopped to take in the wide-open Wyoming sky, the sage meadow, and the jutting mountain peaks capped with glistening snow. She'd fallen in love with Calamity. And the idea of leaving…

Her pulse fluttered in her throat, and her palms went clammy. She'd never see Will again. She'd miss out on Ruby growing up. She couldn't imagine leaving all this splendor behind.

Checking her phone and not seeing anything from Will, she opened the door and went inside. The large fan blades stirred the air, and it felt good on her sun-heated skin. As she headed for the kitchen, she caught the low murmur of Will's voice. *Oh. When did he get home?*

Anxious, she hit the stairs, not knowing what he'd think of her leaving. He'd never once asked her to stay, so maybe he'd be happy for her. *Baloney.* She knew him. Knew by the way he looked at her and touched her that he wanted so much more than he let on.

He's afraid to show his love. And she'd seen for herself why. His mom was horrible.

And she was about to do exactly what his mom had done—leave him. Yeah, this was going to hurt.

Both of us.

At the threshold to his room, she hesitated.

With his back to her, phone to his ear, legs braced in the stance of a highlander surveying the battle field, he said, "That'd be great. Appreciate that." He was all business. "I just got off the phone with the agency, and Miss Kessler will move in this weekend, so you guys coming home early will give me a chance to get you all on the same page." He paused, listening.

"She's a great kid. You'll like her." He paced to the balcony, the French doors already open. "Who told you that? It's fine." He leaned down and rubbed his right knee. "No pain at all."

Had something happened?

"I'm *fine*. But he's right, I have been distracted. I've been slacking off the past few weeks." He listened for a minute, then let out a laugh she didn't recognize. "You got that right. Being banned has a way of getting a man's attention."

Banned? Will had been *banned?*

"But don't worry. I got my focus back." He listened. "Yeah, you go. I'll see you in a few days. Thanks, man." He pitched his phone onto his mattress.

"Will?" She stepped into his room.

"Oh. Hey. Thought you'd be with your brother."

"How'd you know he was here?"

"I saw the car out front when I got back from training."

"You've been home all this time?" *Why didn't you come meet him?*

He gave a curt nod.

"What's this about you being banned?" She watched him carefully, as he stood there, a wall of muscle, locked down, and regarding her like she was some houseguest.

"Yeah, can you believe it? Damien unearthed an old photograph of my dad with the founder of Sprocket."

"What—"

He held up a hand. "We're taking care of it. My father was one of the original investors, but he sold out after two years. The management's turned over several times since then. There's no connection."

"That's insane."

He moved around her—keeping his distance, like she

had fleas. "I'm on it."

"Will, you're—"

"Where's your brother?"

"Lachlan's giving him a tour of the ranch."

"Great. He'll show him a good time." He gave her the fakest, most insincere smile she'd ever seen. "Heard your good news."

"You did?" This…this wasn't her Will. This was the Will she'd met that first night, the one who followed advice from books and not his heart.

"Yeah. Got home right when he was telling you about the opportunity." His smile looked like something he'd be forced to give with his balls in a vise. "Congratulations."

On her twenty-sixth birthday, she'd opened an envelope with a tear sheet that had killed the dream she'd had since she was a little girl. That sense of the ground giving way beneath her feet? That stinging sensation in her limbs?

It's happening all over again.

The man she'd fallen in love with was gone, replaced by the disciplined champion.

She understood. He'd been banned from the sport that should be erecting a statue in his honor. He needed Freefest more than ever. He needed to distance himself, so he could focus. *I get that.*

"When do you leave?" he asked.

"Will, I…" She lifted her arms and let them drop to her sides.

"Sounds like you'll skip the final competition?" He reached for his laptop on the tall dresser. "Makes sense. No point in wasting time creating a menu for a Calamity restaurant when you're starting a kitchen in New York."

"Will, stop it. What're you doing?"

"Well, right now I'm organizing my travel plans. I'm

printing out the pictures of the course, making arrangements with Miss Kessler. Marcella will be back tomorrow, Fin and Callie the day after."

"That's good. But why are you talking to me like I'm some houseguest you've been courteously passing in the hallway?"

He set the laptop on his desk and flipped it open, powering it up. Staring at it, like he wished it would break into a jig or breathe fire, anything to create a distraction, he drew in a breath. "Because you're leaving. And I'm…adjusting."

"Can you please stop adjusting and just be with me? Just sit and talk to me?"

"No, Delilah. I'm not going to do that."

"Why?"

"Because this isn't easy for me."

"It isn't easy for me, either. Will, I love you." It was like peeling away a layer of grime and seeing clearly for the very first time. "I love you so much. I—"

With a pained expression, he held up a hand. "Let's not do this."

She took in the pajama shorts he'd stripped off her last night and flung onto the chair, the mound of dirty laundry in the closet they hadn't gotten around to washing because they'd spent every free moment they could together, and the snow globes she'd barely begun to discover. "You have to know how much this is tearing me apart. If my brother had offered me my franchise, I would've turned it down." She hadn't known that until this moment, but it was absolutely true. "But this is Dino Romano. He believes in me enough to let me run with my own vision for Da Nonna's."

"I know. And I know what that means to you. I'm

genuinely happy for you. But, right now, you're going to have to give me some time to…adjust."

"I don't want to do that. I want to talk to you. Because I love you, and I…"

"You what, Delilah? I don't know what you want me to do with this information. You tell me you love me now, when you're leaving? What is it you're looking for? Do you want to have a dramatic scene where we confess our love for each other, reminisce on all the good times we've had, and have some long, drawn-out goodbye? Because I don't want that." He stalked towards her. "I want you to be happy, and there's nothing that'll make you happier than this amazing opportunity that's dropped into your lap. So, go. Go and live your dream."

She'd seen Will conflicted. Seen him angry, happy, and ecstatic. Defeated, sad, determined, and disgusted. She'd seen him filled with hope, and she'd watched him crash.

But she'd never seen him with a pain so intense it ravaged his features. "I don't have to decide anything right now. I'll be back for the final event, and we can talk then."

"I won't be here."

"I'll wait until you come back." Only, saying those words out loud drove it all home. If she stayed in Calamity, she'd be doing a lot of waiting. Will would be off chasing Olympic gold, and she'd be checking her phone every few minutes, hoping they could make a long distance relationship work.

Her sister's words flew up into her face like a swarm of gnats. *You'll have given everything up for nothing.*

Delilah didn't know what she'd do if she gave up the chance to run a franchise backed by Dino Romano, only to have Will's feelings for her change with time and distance.

He snapped his laptop closed and tossed it onto the bed. "What I feel for you…I've never felt it before, and I'm pretty damn sure I'm never going to feel it again. So, I'm going to ask you one last time, and if you can't give me the answer I need, then I want you to be kind enough to walk out that door without looking back." He drew in a shaky breath. "If you brother showed up today and offered you the chance to run your own Da Nonna's, just the way you want to do it, would you take it?"

Sorrow burned like a razor's slash across her chest. Her soul literally felt like it was being ripped in half. She truly, deeply wanted to stay. But how did she pass up a chance to grow her family's business, while doing what she loved?

If she didn't win the competition, she'd get a sous chef job in town, while Will went off on his competition season. Was she willing to give up an executive chef job with Dino Romano to find out if their relationship would last?

Her muscles wouldn't move. Her lungs wouldn't pull in oxygen. Nothing felt right. She wanted to stay with him as much as she wanted to run with this new opportunity. But her indecision was killing the man she loved, and she couldn't do that to him.

With her limbs barely functioning, she turned and walked out the door.

Asleep on her stomach, rump up in the air and face squished by the pillow, making her lips pucker, Ruby slept peacefully. Squawk's big yellow legs stuck out because of the arm wrapped tightly around its middle.

Her bedroom smelled of raspberry jam and crayons,

and images of their roughhousing earlier that evening echoed through him. With his back against the wall, Will stretched out alongside her, feet dangling off the edge of her mattress. He had a palm on her back just to feel her steady breathing.

The only thing missing was Delilah to close the Ruby sandwich. He missed the electric connection, missed seeing her smiling face—that *aren't we the luckiest bastards in the whole damn world* sense of togetherness. But she'd left with her brother yesterday morning, and his world had gone quiet and still. Colorless.

Thank God for Ruby.

Awareness hit like a shock of ice cold water. After he came back from Freefest, Ruby would be in Fin's care. Over time, she'd bond with his brothers, Marcella, Lachlan, and Miss Kessler. She'd barely remember him.

Strange how what mattered—what gripped his heart and squeezed—wasn't his career but his girls.

At least he saw a path back to skiing. If he won Freefest, the League might lift the ban against him. That would clear him to make the Olympic team. His attorney had set a lot in motion, and since he hadn't done anything wrong, he suspected he'd be vindicated.

And that meant his life would go back to what it had been before he'd met Delilah and Ruby. Only, he *had* met them, and his life would never feel the same again. He'd liked plenty of people in his twenty-eight years but, other than his brothers, they'd all come and gone, everyone on his own path in life. He might've only known Delilah for five weeks, but she'd imprinted. On a cellular level, she'd become part of him.

He'd tried to turn the channel. *That's what I do best.* But it hadn't worked. Maybe when he got on the plane, got his head in competition-mode, started hanging out with his buddies, maybe being busy would edge out the space she'd taken.

He visualized the papers still in the printer, the passport he needed to get out of the safe, the wool socks he'd forgotten to pack. *See?* Once he had other things to focus on, he'd stop hurting.

Gently, he lifted his hand off Ruby's back and hitched up on an elbow to take in her sleeping form. All that crazy hair and those bare baby toes…damn, she was adorable.

When he lifted all the way up, she blinked and sat up on her knees. "Stay wif me."

How could he resist that sleepy voice and those questioning eyes?

But, of course, he had to. His plane left at four AM. He was leaving the country, for Christ's sake. He still had to get that damn passport. He tested his knee—*no pain. Good.* "I have to go, Rubes. You sleep. Remember, when you wake up, Fin's going to make you his famous sweet potato pancakes."

"No, fanks." Ruby shoved hair out of her eyes. "Go Wheel."

His lungs compressed like sponges in big fists. "I'll be home in a week." *She doesn't even know what that means.* "And you're going to the lake with Miss Kessler."

She leaned in and wrapped her arms around his neck.

Christ. He patted her hands, before prying them off. "Hey, look at me. I'm going to miss you, but I'm coming back."

Her lower lip wobbled. "Go wif you."

"No, Ruby. Not on this trip. But you're going to have fun with Fin and Callie, Marcella and Miss Kessler. And then, before you know it, I'll be back."

He got off the bed. He didn't want to crush her spirit. He didn't want to hurt her. He didn't want…

He didn't want to leave her.

She got up on her feet, looking so fragile in her little cotton pajama set. "Go wif you, Wheel."

His heart pounded furiously. "Sweetheart, I have to go to work. I have to get on a plane and work for a week. But I'll be back after that."

"Pease, Wheel?" She stomped her feet, clearly agitated. "Pease?"

"No, I…" *Shit. Fuck.* He'd drawn that line in the beginning for this very reason, knowing if she got too attached, she'd be destroyed when he left.

She lifted her hands, turning her palms upward and hunching her shoulders. "I dus wike you, Wheel. I dus do."

Oh, Jesus. Oh, fucking hell. She was apologizing for being too needy. For wanting to be with him. Pain landed like a spike into the center of his heart.

It was the worst thing he could've done to her. He scooped her into his arms. "I like you, too Ruby." He forced words through the hard knot in his throat. "You're my best buddy, and I love spending time with you. I like it better than anything."

Then why aren't you staying with her?

Because I'm not her damn dad.

"But I have to go to work. And, this week, my work is far away. But when I'm done, I'll come home and hang out with you again. Okay?"

But he knew from her expression she didn't believe him.

And she was right. Her whole damn life was about to change, and she'd have to learn to trust someone else.

Chapter Nineteen

STANDING INSIDE THE TENT, READY FOR HIS FINAL run, Will felt the biting cold in a way he never had before. Maybe he'd just been used to the cold or maybe he'd always been so focused on visualizing his tricks, but he couldn't remember ever noticing it. Not like this.

It felt like a couple of layers of skin had been stripped off, leaving him exposed, vulnerable.

Gray clapped him on the shoulder. "Did you hear?"

"Hear what?"

"Damien got an eighty-nine. Dropping last run's score, he's got a ninety-one overall."

"Hope he got a nice selfie," one of the other competitors said. "Since he's never coming to Freefest again. What kind of jerk-off invites the press to an event like this?"

"He wouldn't come back anyway," Will said. "This isn't what he does. He's a showboater. He likes the attention."

His coach entered the tent, giving him a chin nod. "You're up." His phone vibrated, and he rolled his eyes. "Never should've brought the wife and kid with me, man." He turned away to take the call.

The wife and kid. Just the thought of Ruby crunched his heart like a tin can. Walking out that door five days ago had been the hardest thing he'd ever done.

She was fine, though. He checked in with his family every day, and his sister was surrounded by people who loved her and would look out for her.

I miss her. He'd left his heart behind, tucked under her pillow. Most times, when he closed his eyes, he saw those little shoulders hunched, that apologetic expression. *"I dus wike you, Wheel. I dus do."*

Another clap on the shoulder startled him out of his thoughts. "Hey." Gray held his poles. When Will reached for them, his brother yanked them away. "You're not going out there if your head's not in it."

"No, I'm good." He wiped thoughts of Ruby out of his head. He'd already scrubbed out Delilah. All it took was an image of her in a conference room with Romano. He knew her, knew she'd turn it into a lunch meeting. Wow him with her food. *She's right where she needs to be.* He shook it off and grabbed his poles.

"You sure?"

"Absolutely."

"Okay, then. Let's do this."

Tuning out his brother and shutting the door on the mess of his personal life, Will skied over to the starting block. He stood there for a moment, visualizing the take-off, and then scissored his skis in the fresh, crunchy snow.

I got this.

He pushed off and slid down toward the rails. Pulling in his arms, he picked up speed, gearing up for the first set. *One…two…three…*he popped the lip.

Don't hook an edge. Go, go, go.

He started rotating. *One-eighty. Go, go, perfect. Yes.*

Three-sixty. Right when he hit Cab 3, he spotted his landing. *Got it.*

And…fuck yes. He'd stomped it.

The wall came at him in a rush, and he soared up it. His body tensed, shoulder ready to pull back, knees ready to lift. *Wait. Wait. Wait—now.* Will caught air, his right hand grabbing the ski behind his leg, the left gripping near the binding in front. Pulling his knees in, he held on hard for *one…two…tighter, man, pull in tighter…three.*

Fuckin' A, man. Corkin' it hard.

He let go of the grab, and it couldn't have felt sweeter.

Sailing up the other wall, he pulled in his knees, threw his shoulder back and took off. *One-eighty…spot it, man, fucking spot it…spin tighter…three-sixty…spot it, spot it… one more…push, push…come on…keep it tight…there…*He came in backwards. *Perfect.*

Racing toward the ramp, Will ripped off the jump and pulled in tight…grabbed the ski…and shot into space. He let his muscles do what they'd trained seventeen years for and flipped and spun, pulling his skis in tight…and then —*spot it—spot it*—he fucking landed.

Nailed it.

Energy crashed through him, and he pumped his poles as he skied down the rest of the course. Couldn't keep the smile off his face. *Fuck, yeah.*

Sliding in close to the gathered crowd, he turned his thighs in, slowing to an easy stop.

"Dude, that was epic," someone called, laughing.

"You stomped it, man."

"Will, look over here," a man with a press pass said.

As his friends swarmed him, he ignored the reporter who had no business being there. Damien had fucked up big-time inviting the press to this event. The freestyle community would shut him out now.

Buzzing hard, Will just wanted to hear his scores. Cameras everywhere, questions flying at him, he popped off his skis and checked the scoreboard.

All of a sudden, the crowd went wild. His coach broke through the crowd. "Ninety-eight. You won."

"Dude, you just won Freefest."

"You're the undisputed halfpipe champion of the world."

And it would feel great—he'd be elated—if it weren't for the unbearable ache in his chest.

"You coming, man?" Gray stood in the doorway of Will's bedroom in the cabin he and a few of the other competitors had rented on the mountain.

Fixated on the laptop screen, he barely looked up. "I'll catch up with you."

"You sure?" Gray stood there, waiting for an answer.

Will knew his brother would drop his plans and hang out with him if that's what he needed. "Just checking in at home. I'll be right behind you." As he waited for the call to connect, he heard the guys in the living room pregaming for a night of debauchery. Might be a small town, but it had a lively bar scene.

When it connected, Fin's face took up the screen. "Saw your runs, man. Well done. Congratulations."

"Shame about that last rotation." Brodie pushed into the frame. "Guess you got a little tuckered out."

"Shut the f—"

"Wheel?" Ruby shrieked and little feet slapped on the kitchen floor. "Dat you, Wheel?" She slipped under Fin's arm and climbed onto his lap, forcing her way between his chest and the kitchen table. Fin was cracking up, and Ruby stared at the screen like Santa had just offered her a week-vacation at the North Pole.

"Wheel." Relief saturated her tone, as her hand touched the screen.

"Hi, sweetheart." His heart beat so thick and hard he thought it might explode. "Ruby." He just needed to say her name out loud.

"Come home, Wheel? Come home to Wooby?"

"I—" He looked into those earnest blue eyes, filled with hope and trust, and everything he'd believed about life—structure and focus, rules and restraint—fell away.

He'd clung to all of that when his mom had left him behind. It had helped. Replaced the fear with something constructive. But he didn't need—or want—it anymore.

After his win, dozens of athletes had gathered around to celebrate him, swearing they'd known all along he hadn't cheated, shouting that he was the best skier in the world—and it hadn't moved the meter.

Now that Ruby and Delilah had gifted him with a whole new dimension to life, all the accolades felt hollow.

He looked at his little girl, and he knew. No, he wasn't her dad. *But so what?*

So fucking what? It just didn't matter. He was all-in. "I have one stop to make before I come home, but I'll be back this weekend."

"You don't have to do that, it's my turn," Fin said.

"Thanks for watching her for me while I was out of town, but I'm coming home to my girl."

Fin's eyes widened, and Ruby's smile turned ebullient. He wouldn't get her hopes up, but he hoped the next time he saw her, he'd have a special gift for her. For *them*.

The last time he'd seen Delilah, she'd wanted to sit down and talk to him, and he hadn't let her. Instead, he'd asked her to go.

Ever since then, it had been grinding through him. What if they'd talked? What if he'd told her he loved her so much he'd do anything to be with her? They might've found a way to stay together, but he'd never gotten to find out because he'd pushed her out the door.

But, now, the answer seemed so simple. She shouldn't give up this amazing opportunity to run her own franchise, so he'd move to New York.

Whatever it took for them to be together, he'd make it happen, because he'd never love anyone the way he loved that woman. In his heart he knew—he fucking knew—they were a family. Delilah owned him heart and soul. Ruby, too.

"Home to Wooby?"

"That's right, sweet pea. I'm coming home to Ruby."

Will stowed his duffle bag in the luggage compartment before settling into his seat. When he pulled his phone out of his back pocket, it leaped out of his hands, and he had to squat to find it.

Funny how he could dub cork, ten blunt without a single frayed nerve, but going to New York to get his girl had his stomach in knots.

He only found it, because it started vibrating. He checked the screen but didn't recognize the number. "Hello?"

"Will? This is Coach Davis."

Awareness pierced through the anxiety, situating him

firmly in the moment. The U.S. Halfpipe ski coach would only be calling for one reason.

"Hey." He probably shouldn't have sounded so blasé.

The man laughed. "Hey. Listen, congratulations on your outstanding performance at Freefest. I know I never should have seen it, but I did, and I want you on the team."

Will kicked off his untied boots and stretched his legs out in front of him. "Well, I appreciate the offer, but I've been banned from the sport."

"You didn't hear?" He sounded surprised. "Your name's been cleared."

"No, I hadn't." He'd gone straight to the private airport and boarded his plane, only one thought on his mind: getting to Delilah.

"There's zero evidence supporting Damien's accusations. Besides, your performance in Freefest puts any doubts to rest. In any event, I've known you and your family a long time, and I never questioned your integrity. Look, I know you're probably celebrating, so I won't keep you on the phone. I'll have Cliff send you the competition schedule. We're going to start training at the Utah center in two weeks, so I'll talk to you more then."

His uncle was right. On some level, Will had thought winning a gold medal would be the sure-fire way to make his mom see him as a good man. That it would make her love him. But Will was done with that. He no longer gave two shits what she thought of him. He cared about being the best damn brother to Ruby and the best damn husband to Delilah he could be.

He remembered that morning when Delilah and Ruby had come running towards him with cookie dough on their fingers, their bright, clever eyes shining, as they burst out laughing. He felt it all the way down to the soles of his feet, his body alive, electrified. "No."

"Excuse me?"

If he wanted to honor his dad, he simply needed to be a good man. If he needed to prove something to himself, he'd already done it with his seven medals.

"Thank you for the offer, but I'm officially retired."

Delilah reached for her pen and crossed out *penne*. She really loved the ribbony look of the pappardelle noodle in the bowl, so she'd use that instead. Flipping to the next page in her notebook, she scanned the braised bison recipe. Her taste buds lit up at the thought of adding marjoram and hazelnuts, so she noted those additions. *Yes. Better.*

That one's a winner.

On the next page, she really loved the confit goose, peach, butter lettuce, and dried cranberry salad, but she crossed out peach and put in fig. Not only did she like fresh figs, but she'd like to give the owner of the hydroponic farm the business.

She turned to the kouneli stifado recipe; that was her favorite dish. *Not changing a thing about that one.* Well, she'd use quail instead of rabbit. *The Tale of Peter Rabbit* and all. Her mom used to read her those books.

"Hey." Her sister pushed open the door with a big box. Looking around the crowded office, she said, "Where can I put this?"

"What is it?"

Bree set it on the desk, on top of a pile of invoices. "You were talking about making those mixed media pieces using some of Mom and Dad's things, so I brought you some stuff from home."

"Really?" She got up to hug her sister. "Thank you so much." Peering into the box, she saw her parent's wedding picture. They'd gotten married at the city clerk's office on Worth Street in the late seventies. Her mom had tamed all her long blonde hair into a conservative bun, while her dad wore a short-sleeve button down, jeans, and flip flops.

The day after tomorrow, when she went back for the final event, she'd bring all this stuff with her. Give them to Callie to see what she could do with them. It would be nice décor for the new franchise, a mix of memorabilia from Nonna Abelli's era to the new generation. "This is amazing." When she looked up, she found her sister reading her notebook.

"What is this?" Her sister didn't look angry so much as worried.

"It's not for Da Nonna's, don't worry."

"Then what's it for?"

"My menu for the final competition." She suspected her family wanted her focused on the proposal she needed to put together for Dino Romano, but that would have to wait. Her top priority was the competition. "No matter what happens here, I still want to win." They were really good recipes, though. *Shame not to use them.*

"Sure, yeah. It'll be good promotion for the new franchise."

The meeting had gone well, and her family seemed excited about the potential to expand their brand. But Delilah hadn't given an answer. She suggested they talk more when she got back from Calamity.

Because it was hard to concentrate when the rhythm of her heart beat in synch with Will's.

"Bison?" Her sister flipped a few more pages. "Kouneli stifado?"

"Yeah, well, it's pretty much anything goes out there. Well, as long as it involves meat."

Her sister didn't return her smile. "These look really good, keiki."

"Honestly, I think I have a real chance of winning." She reached for the document she'd printed out. "I finished the proposal. Not that the judges care—it's only for the chefs who want to be considered for the spa restaurant—but I'm turning mine in anyway." *It's that good.*

Her sister set the notebook down. "Why would you do that? You're not taking the job, so wouldn't it be unfair to mislead them?"

"They might not choose any of us, but at least I can give them my ideas." *And let someone else run with them?* "All of my products are locally sourced and sustainably grown, and I'm using the names of local outlaws for the dishes..." Each word that came out of her mouth tugged the string that tightened her sister's features. "Never mind."

"No, that sounds great, Delilah."

"Yeah, it's pretty cool. I invited a group of local chefs, farmers, and ranchers over to the house for a tasting party Wednesday night." She really didn't want to miss that. "Just to try out all the dishes so I could tweak them before the competition."

Her sister couldn't hide the pain in her eyes.

"Delilah?" One of the waiters leaned into the room. "The Sullivans want to say hey."

Stepping around her sister, she smoothed her chef's jacket. "Sure. I'll do that now." She turned to Bree. "You going to hang around?"

Her sister nodded but looked defeated.

On her way out of the kitchen, she stopped to taste the sauce from the line cook she'd hired last spring. He insisted on adding chopped fresh basil and pepper. She'd give him one more chance, and then he'd have to go.

No, the irony was not lost on her. She'd become her brother.

As she entered the dining room, several patrons looked up with welcoming smiles. They loved private visits from the chef, and her dad had made sure they all respected that tradition. She stopped at the table of an elderly couple who'd been regulars for as long as Delilah had been old enough to remember.

"Mrs. Sullivan, Mr. Sullivan, so nice to see you." She shook both of their bony hands, the skin like parchment paper. "How is everything tonight?"

"Oh, we're just in heaven. The alfredo's out of this world. We're thrilled that we happened to come in the night you're back in the kitchen. The food's just not the same without you."

Delilah's smile faltered. Actually, it was. It was exactly the same. Against her brother's wishes, she'd been adding special touches to the old standards for years. The new franchise would only sanction what she'd been doing all along.

But she didn't want to put Jicama in the house salad. She wanted to make kouneli stifado and wild boar ragù.

She loved her family—of course she did, but she missed Calamity, the town, the people, the mountain lifestyle.

Ruby.

And being away from Will was killing her. She craved him. Every minute of every day.

"I'm so glad you're enjoying it." She couldn't keep ignoring the insistent voice, the one that told her exactly where she belonged. The potential for success with Dino Romano was enormous, but it wouldn't satisfy her soul. And what did success matter if she didn't have the man she loved? "Can I tempt you with a creamy rose panna cotta tonight?"

"Oh, that sounds divine."

"My gift to you for being so devoted to us all these years." Heart pounding, she excused herself and hurried back into the kitchen.

She would always be close with her family. They'd be with her anywhere she went.

But her heart lived somewhere else.

She made a bee-line across the busy kitchen, desperate to get back to her office and change her flight. She'd started something good, *special*, in Calamity. Something that was uniquely hers. And she wanted it.

She hoped to God her family would understand.

As she entered the office, her sister looked up from Delilah's notebook. "I told them."

"You told them what?"

"This isn't right for you." Bree gestured around the room. "But they'd already given the franchise to Jeannie, and they couldn't take it back. They didn't know how else to get you home, so when Mr. Romano called, it seemed like the perfect solution. But it's not right for you." She waved the notebook. "You're so creative. You have a gift. And I'm not sure swapping out mascarpone for lemon curd in the tiramisu is going to be enough for you." She set the notebook down and cupped Delilah's elbows. "I don't want to lose you, but even more, I want you to be happy."

"He makes me happy."

"I can tell."

"And it's only a plane ride away. There's plenty of room for you to visit. Any time you want. You can bring Sam and the kids. They'll love it."

"I'm going to miss you so much." Her sister pulled her into her arms. "I know you're a grown woman but, in a way, you're also my little girl." She let her go. "Even when Mom was alive, I helped her look after you. I'd take you to classes and play dates. I helped you with your homework and made sure you brushed your teeth." Tears glittered in her eyes. "I don't want to lose you, but I need you to be as happy as that place makes you."

"But what about the new franchise? I don't want to disappoint everyone. This is a real opportunity for growth for our family, and it all hinges on me. Is everyone going to be angry that I'm bailing on it?"

Her sister drew in a deep breath. "When Mom and Dad died, you were just heading off for college. We didn't want you to be alone, so we all committed to keeping things as close to normal as possible. But I think we took it too far. I think, in trying to make sure you got everything Mom and Dad would've given you, we stole your ability to find your own way. You're so much more than our youngest sister. And, as hard as it for me to let you go, I think I'd really love to see you become the magnificent woman you're meant to be."

Hot tears spilled down her cheeks, and she'd never felt closer to her sister. "I love you, Bree. Thank you for giving me a home and traditions and so much of your time and attention. It didn't hold me back. It made me feel loved."

Her sister pulled back. "Don't worry about the business. You just go and win that competition."

Delilah peeled off her chef's jacket and tossed it on the desk. Grabbing her notebook, she dropped it into her tote.

Her sister watched with wide eyes. "I didn't mean right now."

"I've got people coming over tomorrow night to taste my dishes." She hitched the bag onto her shoulder. "I'm ready for that competition and…dammit, Bree, I'm going to win."

Peering out the window, Will took in Delilah's world. A melee of cars, buses, vans, and bike messengers, and a steady stream of pedestrians streaked past as the yellow cab turned off Bowery onto Broome Street.

He hadn't slept in eighteen hours. Couldn't stomach the idea of food.

What had he been thinking, telling her to walk away? *Well, that's the thing.* He hadn't been thinking. He'd been reacting. A childhood of rejection did that to a guy.

But he was done protecting his heart. He'd found the one woman in the world made for him—and he wasn't letting her go.

The cab slowed in dense traffic. *Fuck.* He couldn't wait to see her. Couldn't wait to tell her he loved her, that he'd move to New York—or China or Brazil. *Wherever she is, that's where I'll be.*

If only she'd answer her damn phone. *No, it's better this way.* What he needed to say had to be done in person.

What if she told him to fuck off? That it was too late? Fear sliced through him, and he sat up straighter in his seat.

If she said no, he'd woo the fuck out of her. He wouldn't give up.

Because Delilah Lua was a force of nature. Her pull so powerful, she'd caused a seismic shift in the landscape of his heart.

Catching his reflection in the window, he saw a desperate man. A frantic man. Neither of which he'd ever been before. And he smiled because this was what love felt like. Like you couldn't live without your person. Like you'd lose the very best part of yourself without her.

And it felt so damn good—like he'd punched through a wall. On the other side was fresh air, wide open spaces. Love.

Love. He loved her. And he'd fight like hell for her.

In thick gold lettering, a huge black sign heralding Da Nonna's took up the entire length of an old stone building. The bright yellow awning, umbrellas, and tablecloths gave the outdoor seating area a festive and welcoming feel.

The cab double-parked out front, and Will handed the driver two twenties. "Thank you."

Scraping a hand through his hair, he headed inside. His body trembled. Anticipation, need—

Yeah, need. I need her.

I can't live without her. And it was all right to love her that way. In fact, it was fucking great to love with his whole heart and soul. He didn't want to be stingy and shut off anymore. He wanted to shout it from the top of her building: *I love Delilah Lua.*

"Are you waiting for the rest of your party?" the hostess asked.

"No. I'm not eating. I'm looking for Delilah, actually." Emotion pushed hard on his skin, like it was about to bust free. "I love her. I want to marry her." He felt giddy with relief. "I want to spend the rest of my life with her." He stood there, making a fool of himself and not even caring.

The hostess smiled, glancing behind her. The wait staff had stopped mid-motion to stare at him. "That's awesome. But...she's not here."

Disappointment sped through him like a fireball. He'd learned, though, that chefs took their breaks around three, so maybe she'd taken hers a little early. "That's fine. I'll wait." He'd wait as long as it took.

"No. I mean, she doesn't work here anymore. She's gone."

"Delilah, can we talk to you?"

She turned to find Chris and a few other board members approaching her. "Yeah, sure. What's up?" She'd lost the competition, and she didn't want to talk to anyone. She'd been so sure she'd knocked it out of the park.

She loved her menu. Loved her dishes. Her guests the other night had eaten every bite and raved about her food.

Dammit, Harry. His was the only low score. Low enough to bring her down to second place in the overall competition.

Her only consolation? A Michelin-rated chef had lost, too.

The group surrounded her, but she couldn't read their expression. They seemed...nervous? She hoped they understood how grateful she was for the opportunity they'd given her. "You guys were so great to let me in at the last minute. I had more fun with this competition than anything I've ever done. I got to meet amazing people and learn about hydroponic farming and sustainable ranching. Honestly, I've loved everything about it."

"That's one of the things we like best about you," Chris said. "That you talked to so many local producers. That, and your attitude."

"Hey, we're not all temperamental." She smiled through her hurt. She wished the judges had appreciated her this much. "Only two of the chefs stomped off in a huff."

Chris glanced at the others before continuing. "So, we're wondering what's next for you. Are you going back to New York to run your family restaurant?"

No one knew about Dino Romano's offer. And, if they did, they'd think she was nuts for turning it down. But she was staying in Calamity no matter what. "Actually, no, I'm not." But she didn't want to make them uncomfortable. "Believe it or not, Chef Alonso was talking about me joining his kitchen in London."

"You give him an answer yet?" Chris asked.

"No. I think I'd like to stay in town a while. I like it here. Why? What's going on?"

"We had a very clear idea in mind for the chef of the spa restaurant, and you didn't meet our criteria," the older gentleman said.

Horrified, Delilah went perfectly still. He didn't need to tell her that. *God.*

"And yet…" He shrugged. "It turns out you're exactly what we want."

"Whatever we thought we wanted on paper," Chris said. "Went out the window when we saw all the chefs in action. You're perfect for the job."

Perfect? *Me?* "But my menu came in second place."

"With us, you came in first," the older man said. "Your

style is exactly what we want. Fresh, exciting, interesting—"

"Honestly, there was only one proposal that moved the meter for us," Chris said. "Yours."

"It fits the spirit of the West," the older man said.

She couldn't believe it. Was this actually happening? "You're choosing *me* to run the restaurant?"

Chris grinned. "Yes. You."

The moment felt surreal. Just a moment ago, she'd given up on all her dreams, assuming she'd have to start fresh. "I'm completely floored." And now...*this.*

The older man's forehead creased. "So, is that a yes?"

Just over his shoulder, a man came into the saloon. With his swagger and size, he immediately drew her attention.

Will.

It took about three seconds for his gaze to connect with hers, and the relief in his expression was palpable.

"It's a hell yes." She started for her man, then remembered that these people had just offered her a job. "Thank you so much. I would love to run the spa restaurant. I, um, I just need to..."

Chris laughed. "Go."

Delilah took off with only one thought on repeat. *I love him, I love him, I love him.*

And then, the most miraculous thing happened, restrained, stoic Will Bowie broke into a run.

In front of all those people—Fin, Callie, board members, the other chefs and remaining guests—he raced through the crowd with a look of such intense yearning it made her burst into tears.

Their bodies slammed into each other right in the middle of the saloon. His muscular arms wrapped around her, his mouth closed over hers, and he kissed her with all the intensity she craved.

"I love you." He tore his mouth off hers, breathing hard. "I know you only came back to finish the competition, and I know how much your family means to you—"

"It's not a choice."

He looked perplexed.

"I'm not choosing between you and my family. I'm in love with you, Will. And I'm staying in Calamity. With or without a job. I've already packed up most of my stuff. I live here."

Relief swept across his features, making him look about ten years younger. "With me?"

"Yeah, with you. It turns out that, all this time, I haven't been looking for new and different. I've been looking for myself. And I found it here. With you. And Ruby."

"We're a family."

"We totally are."

"I love you."

"I love you, too. Also..." She glanced behind her at the board members watching her with happy expressions. "I just got a job."

"Here?"

"The board just offered me the executive chef job at the spa. And I took it."

"Wheel?"

The shriek of joy had both of them whipping around to find Ruby toddling over to them. Will dropped to his knees to catch her in his arms. Wrapping both arms around his sister, he held her tightly, emotion squeezing his eyes closed.

"Back, Wheel?"

"I'm back." He stood up with her. "And I'm staying."

Delilah laughed at the chocolate smeared around the little girl's mouth. "What have you been eating?"

Ruby flashed a giant smile at Delilah and Will. "I gots shock-let."

"Did you save any for me?" Delilah asked.

Ruby reached for her, and Delilah leaned in. Flinging an arm around both their necks, Ruby drew them in close, so all three heads touched. She smelled like chocolate and baby shampoo, and, for the first time in her life, Delilah knew the true taste of happiness.

"Ruby?" Will said.

She pulled back to look at him.

"Will you be mine?"

"My Wheel."

"Yeah. I want that. To be your Will forever." He looked at Delilah. "Wally, too. Will you be mine forever?"

She drew in a sharp breath. "There's nothing I want more in the world. The two of you, forever."

Chapter Twenty

WILL PULLED THE SUV OVER AND KILLED THE ignition. He didn't know how many people would want a ride home, so he made a quick sweep of the debris lying on the floor and seats and stuffed it all in one of Delilah's reusable grocery totes. On the seat beside him, he picked up the box that had just arrived in the mail.

Now. He wanted to do it right now. Didn't want to wait a second longer. Tearing open the box, he removed the gift and headed into the empty restaurant space.

With a hand behind his back, he stood in the doorway and watched Callie spread her arms wide, as if to encompass the picture window overlooking Ballard's Pond. "I wouldn't even want window treatments here. The view's spectacular."

"I agree," Delilah said.

With the toe of his boot pressed on the tape measure, Brodie reached to the middle of the wall. "Seventy-two inches." He glanced over his shoulder to find Fin with his arms around Callie's waist, nuzzling her neck instead of writing down the measurements. "*Fin.* You think you can keep your hands to yourself for five minutes so we can get this done?"

Without turning around, Fin brought his hand to the small of his back and hoisted his middle finger. Brodie sighed. "Come on, man. I don't have all day."

"We're talking about..." Fin murmured in his fiancée's ear. Callie whispered, and he smiled. "Paint chips. Hang on."

"Lachlan?" Brodie sound exasperated. "Can you give me a hand?"

But their uncle had Ruby on his shoulders as he swayed and swooped around the empty room. Their sister, hands fisted in his white pompadour, giggled adorably.

"You gonna help or just stand there?" Brodie asked Will.

"I'm thinking." About what Delilah would look like when she said, *I do*. He imagined her eyes sparkling with love, mischief, and all the promise of the adventure their life together would be. "About décor."

Fin snickered, and Brodie shot him a look. "What's to think about? She wants it to fit in with the region, use locally farmed, environmentally sustainable blah blah blah, so why don't we just do antler chandeliers and be done with it?"

"He's right about that." Fin let go of Callie and turned to face the room. With both hands, he made L-shapes, like a painter eyeing his landscape. "Red leather booths, black and white cowhide rugs."

"You guys." Delilah had a smile in her voice. "I'm not doing *antlers*. I want Wally's to be elegant, but earthy and soulful."

"When she says she wants to fit in with the region,"

Callie said. "She's thinking white-washed wood, like Quaking Aspens, with sage green accents."

Switching his gift from one hand to the other behind his back, Will said, "You know what fits right in with sage meadows? Elk. And I've got a guy who can outfit this whole place with some nicely mounted heads."

"That guy out in Elgin?" Fin smiled. "He's got a great moose one, too. And a grizzly about…oh, twelve feet tall. That'd look real nice in that corner over there."

"I'm literally not listening to anything you clowns have to say." Callie stepped back from the window to pick up some paint samples. "We'll figure it out ourselves."

Will couldn't wait a second longer. "I've got an idea."

"Yeah?" Delilah looked up from her notebook and gave him a sweet smile.

"Let's do snow globes."

Lachlan stopped dive-bombing. "What?"

"You heard me. Snow globes."

"Can't tell if he's serious or not," Fin said.

"He's not." Callie reached for the tape and peeled off a strip. She tacked a paint chip to the wall.

"I'm not sure I get what you mean." Delilah came closer.

"We could have shelves all around the room and, over time, we'd fill them with snow globes. It'd become a thing. Our patrons will bring them in from all over the world. We'd have a whole collection."

"Weird," Brodie said. "But I like it."

"It has nothing to do with our theme," Callie said. "But it's really cute."

As she reached for his hand, Delilah had a gleam in her eye. "I like it. A lot." She mouthed, *It's us.*

"Good." He brought the snow globe from behind his back. "This can be our first."

Everyone stopped working. Some started walking over, but he only had eyes for Delilah.

"What's going on?" Fin asked.

"No idea," Brodie said.

"Shh," Callie said.

Will held his gift out to her.

"Oh, my God." She grasped it in her hands, eyes going wide as she took in the custom-made snow globe. Tipping it over and back, she watched glitter rain down over the kitchen scene, complete with a man, a woman, and a little girl. "This is amazing." She looked up at him with pure delight.

"Look more closely."

She blinked a few times and wiped her eyes, before staring at the man on one knee, presenting a ring to the woman, who held a hand over her heart.

"Delilah Lua?" Will got down on his knee.

Delilah gasped, wiping tears off her cheeks.

"Wally?" Ruby rocked her hips, signaling Lachlan to let her down. The moment she hit the floor, she toddled over.

Delilah got on her knees, too, and held her arms out for the little girl.

"Okay, Wally?" Ruby patted her shoulder.

"Yeah, sweetheart, I'm good." She turned to Will. "Just waiting for your brother to finish what he was saying."

Will had been noodling on these words for the last six weeks, so he was ready. "I don't know how it happened, how my life changed so suddenly and completely, but I've never been happier. And it's because I get to hear your laughter every single day. I get to watch you lick ice cream cones and interview ranchers and read books to our girl. Every day, I get to hold your hand and see your hair spread out on our pillowcase, and I'm just the luckiest damn man in the world. You're all I want, Delilah. You're it for me. There's nothing more I want to do the rest of my life other than love you. Will you marry me?"

"So soon?" Brodie asked. "Didn't they just meet?"

"Shut up," Callie said.

"Yes. Oh, my God, yes." Delilah hurled herself into his arms, knocking him onto his ass. Ruby climbed on, and the three of them hugged and laughed on the floor.

He kissed his fiancée and let the joy of his family wash over him. Nothing had ever felt so good, so right, so perfectly—

"Will." His uncle's voice broke through.

"What?" He shot him a look that said, *What could you possibly need from me right now?*

His uncle was watching the screen of his phone and shaking his head. "Well, guess the timing's good."

"What're you talking about?" Will headed over to his uncle and reached for the phone.

"You both going to need wedding dresses sometime soon?" With a smile in his eyes, Lachlan looked at the women.

"Yes, why?" Callie said.

On the screen, it looked like a car had crashed into the bay window of someone's ocean front home. And mowed down what had to be a dozen wedding gowns.

"What is this?" Will asked his uncle.

"Guess Gray had a little accident."

"Is he okay?" Fin asked.

Lachlan pulled the phone back. "He's the one who sent the picture."

"What'd he say?" Will asked.

Lachlan read the screen. "'Got a good deal on some wedding gowns, if Callie wants one. Also, I might need some bail money.'"

Thank you for reading WE BELONG TOGETHER! Up next is THE VERY THOUGHT OF YOU. Gray Bowie's been in love with Knox his whole life. The only problem? She's his best friend's girlfriend.

Do you subscribe to my newsletter? Get on that right now because I've got an EXCLUSIVE novella for my readers in 2022! You'll get 2 chapters a month of this super sexy, fun romance! #rockstarromance #whenyourcelebritycrushbecomesyourboyfriend #teenidol

Need more Calamity Falls, where the people are wild at heart?

KEEP ON LOVING YOU
WE BELONG TOGETHER
THE VERY THOUGHT OF YOU
JUST THE WAY YOU ARE
IT WAS ALWAYS YOU
CAN'T HELP FALLING IN LOVE
COME AWAY WITH ME
WHOLE LOTTA LOVE
YOU'RE STILL THE ONE

THE DEEPER I FALL
LOVE ME LIKE YOU DO

Have you read the Rock Star Romance series? Come meet the sexy rockers of Blue Fire:

YOU REALLY GOT ME
I WANT YOU TO WANT ME
TAKE ME HOME TONIGHT
MORE THAN A FEELING

Look for LOVE ME LIKE YOU DO in September 2022! Grab a FREE copy of PLANES, TRAINS, AND HEAD OVER HEELS. And come hang out with me on Facebook, Twitter, Instagram, Goodreads, and Pinterest or in my private reader group.

Excerpt of The Very Thought of You

Hurry up, hurry up, hurry up.

As the ocean roared through the open bathroom window, Knox Holliday snatched the towel off the rack and quickly rubbed her body dry. Wrapping it around her head turban-style, she eyed the line of surfers waiting for the next set.

She could feel it—the grip of her toes on her waxed board, the churning of the sea under her feet, and the slap of salty water on her skin. Her body yearned to be out there.

A storm somewhere in the Pacific had delivered massive waves to the island—rare for September—and she hated having to miss it. Her cell phone trilled from her nightstand. *Crap.*

Hurry.

Padding into the bedroom on bare, damp feet, she picked it up and accepted the FaceTime call. Setting the screen so it faced the ceiling, she said, "Hey, Luc. Just give me one second." She bent over, unwinding the towel and shaking out her hair.

"Are you all right?" he asked in his thick, French accent. "What is going on?"

She reached for the red satin underwear in the top drawer of her dresser and stepped into them. "Just running a little late."

"Why? Is there a problem?"

She could hear the panic in his voice. *Such a diva.* "Everything's perfect." Hitching up her panties, she eyed the line of dresses and blouses in her closet and yanked off a crepe mini dress with spaghetti straps. She stepped into it at the same time she shoved her feet into high heeled sandals.

"Why am I looking at your ceiling and not you?"

Her boss checked in every day at the same time. Normally, she'd be ready to show him the progress she'd made, but she'd had to make an alteration to one of the gowns, which had her running late.

"What is that…why is your ceiling bumpy?" He gasped. "Is it warped?"

She'd rented the cheapest house she could find on this stretch of beach in Maui. Of course, Luc had offered her his homes in the Maldives and Portofino and his flat in London, but she still hadn't gotten over what he'd done to her, so she needed boundaries.

Mostly, though, she wanted to keep him from feeling any sort of ownership in her collection. "It's called a popcorn ceiling, and what do I care what it looks like when I'm getting the place for a steal?" As if she hadn't lived in much worse conditions. She'd learned as a child to create beauty in her mind and with her own hands.

She slicked her hair back into a high ponytail and grabbed the phone. His handsome face came into view from his bright and airy Paris office, seventy-five hundred miles away. "Well, hello, there. Nice to see you."

"Bonjour, ma chère." His features pinched. "Why is your hair wet? You showered when you knew I'd be calling?"

Maybe she couldn't get over what he'd done to her, but she still hated to let him down. "Yeah, sorry about that. I'm a little late this morning." She had a show in six weeks, so she'd barely been getting five hours of sleep a night as it was. Last night, she'd gotten even less.

"Hmph. Every day for one year I have called you at ten o'clock in the morning."

That was because he didn't finish his day until nine or ten at night. His assistant brought him a baguette, some smelly cheese, and a bottle of wine, and he caught up on all his phone calls.

"And for three hundred and sixty-four of them, I've made it right on time," she said. "Ready to get started?"

She turned the phone around and headed into the living room, panning the sea of taffeta, silk, organza, chiffon, and tulle. Even after all this time, she still got a rush of happiness from seeing all that frothy gorgeousness.

"Stop, stop. Oh, dear God, what is that?"

Of course, of all the beauty in the room, he'd notice the one problem. A low beat of anxiety pulsed through her. *Please don't freak out.* "What's what?"

But he ignored her teasing tone. "On the floor. What is that?"

"It's nothing to worry about." She lifted the puddle of charmeuse and lace. "I made a slight alteration."

"To La Danseur? There was nothing wrong with La Danseur."

"Luc, I promise, it's all right. I tried it on my neighbor, and I didn't like the drape, so I'm redoing it."

"No, no, no. Does your neighbor have a portfolio with Elite? Is she a Ford model?"

Her sixty-two-year-old neighbor was fit and tall but not what Luc would consider a model. "Trust me, it wasn't working. It's going to be much better."

"It's in pieces on the floor. And Martine is coming on Monday to pack up the gowns. Ach, I'm growing a migraine. Stop this nonsense right now. We'll do all the tweaks when you arrive in the city."

A thrill shot through her. Thanks to Luc's support, she'd debut her haute couture wedding gown collection at October's Bridal Fashion Week in New York City. A big deal for a twenty-five-year-old, just four years out of college. In return, she'd had to create a year's worth of collections for him.

"I'll have everything ready by the time Martine gets here, I promise. When have I ever let you down?"

"When you left me." For a fifty-eight-year-old man, he had the pout of a two-year-old.

"I guess you shouldn't have *stolen* from me."

His eyebrows shot up into his thick, gray hair. "Take that back. I did not steal from you. Everyone who works for me signs the same contract. I own everything you create while under my employment."

Technically that might be true, but he'd devastated her. He'd swiped her sketchbook out of her apartment, designs she'd done on her own time. "Luc, you broke my heart." Since she didn't give her heart to many people, that was an even rarer occurrence than a storm in September. It had been scary to quit her job, but she'd believed if she was good enough for Luc Bellerose to steal from her, then she was good enough to go out on her own.

"And now I have healed it. Trust me, ma chère, you will take the world by storm with this show." He gave her a smile heavy with pride. "In my four decades in this business, I have never fallen so in love with someone's style. You are magic, Knox Holliday, and I'm going to make you a star. Ah. That's it." He reached for his laptop and his fingers went to town all over the keyboard.

"What's it? What're you doing?"

"Emailing Victoire."

"Why?" What did his publicist have to do with this conversation?

"I've been looking for just the right tagline." He tapped the final letter with a flourish, then shoved the laptop back. "You are the white-hot wedding gown designer." He grinned, obviously pleased with himself. "The hottest star in the bridal galaxy." His smile faded. "I mean that sincerely, you know. They're not just empty words."

Often, he drove her crazy—like when he stole from her—but sometimes she loved him. "Thank you, Luc. Your opinion means the world to me."

Tires squealed on asphalt. A shout pierced the air. Knox spun around to look out the bay window of her living room but couldn't make sense of what she was seeing. Her house, situated on a sharp bend in the road, saw a lot of traffic. It sat close enough that she could catch a glimpse of the drivers' faces as they whizzed by. But this car…this dark green Jeep…it was driving *across her front yard*.

Holy shit, it was careening toward the house.

Toward *her*. "Oh, my God." She dropped the phone and bolted into the kitchen, seconds before the car crashed into her living room. Glass shattered. Wood splintered. The Jeep sheared off wallboard.

The engine idled, and an Eddie Van Halen guitar riff screeched in the air.

"Knox? *Knox?*" Her boss's tinny voice got her moving toward the phone. She had to call nine-one-one. Brushing debris off her phone, she picked it up. "Luc? I have to call you back." She didn't give him a chance to respond, just hit End. Seeing no movement through the tinted windows, she called, "Hello? Are you all right?"

Swirls of dust filled the room. In her sandals, she made her way across glittering glass and chips of wood to the driver's side, focusing on her keypad as she dialed.

Someone answered right away. "Nine-one-one, what's your emergency?"

She had to shout over the music. "A car just crashed into my living room." As she gave her address and answered questions, her heart squeezed at the sight of crystals and beads and strips of delicate—filthy—lace under the big black tires. That lace…it was handmade. Literally irreplaceable. She tried the passenger side door, but it was locked. "Are you okay?" Peering into the tinted window, she made out several bodies.

The radio snapped off. The driver's door opened, and a woman got out. Wearing a bikini top and jean shorts, she looked dazed.

"Hey, are you all right?" Knox lifted the phone. "I just called nine-one-one. They'll be here in ten minutes."

"I'm fine. I just…" The young woman covered her mouth with a hand and took in the scene. "Oh, my God." She turned back to the car, pumping on the back door handle. "Guys? Open up." When it popped open, she stepped aside to let several large men out.

Knox moved toward them, her ankle twisting in her stupid heels. "Is anyone hurt?" Three of the men were shirtless, one wore a thin white tank top, all wore board shorts. Five surfboards were strapped to the roof of the car, the front edges snapped off by the wallboard that covered the windshield.

"What the hell?" one of them said.

"Whoa, man," another one said.

Her phone chimed, and she glanced quickly at the screen. Luc. *Not now.* She silenced the ringer. "What do you guys need?" She could grab some kitchen towels if anyone was bleeding.

"Knox?"

She'd know that deep, gravelly voice anywhere, even after all these years. A shock of recognition had her looking over to see—"*Gray*?"

What the hell was Gray Bowie doing in her living room?

"This is *your* house?" He scraped his fingers through his hair. "Jesus. Of all the people..." Fear twisted his features. "Did we *hurt* you?"

"No." *At least not in the way you're thinking.* "I'm fine." She deliberately didn't look at her gowns. It was the only way to keep her panic at bay. That...and she'd need her full attention to assess the damage. "What about you guys?" She gestured to his friends.

His gaze lingered for a moment, as if he couldn't believe he was seeing her. *Believe me, I feel the same way.* It had been seven years since she'd last seen or talked to him.

His choice.

With a slight shake of his head, he turned to the driver. "You okay, Amelia?"

"Yeah." The woman wrapped a hand around the back of her neck. "Shaken up, but I'm okay."

She looked disoriented, so Knox wasn't sure about that. Grabbing a kitchen chair, she said, "Maybe you should sit down."

For a moment, the woman looked confused. Then she pulled her hand off her neck. "No, it doesn't hurt. I guess I'm just expecting it to." She tipped a chin to the others. "You guys?"

The passengers all spoke at once, clearly stunned.

"I'm good."

"Fine."

"Jesus, man."

Hands cupping the sides of her head, Amelia turned to survey the damage. "Oh, my God. How did this even happen?" She blew out a breath, glancing at Knox. "We were just so stoked, you know? He"—she pointed to Gray—"literally got the call ten minutes ago. And we've got to head to the airport right now." She scanned the room, her attention zeroing in on the white tulle. "What *is* all this?"

With everything in her, Knox did *not* want to look at her beautiful, perfect gowns, wasn't ready to see their condition, dreaded that feeling of total devastation…but she had no choice, did she? Slowly, she turned to take it all in.

The three dress forms she'd placed in front of the living room window lay trampled under the wheels. Terror sliced a vein, and she bled pure adrenaline. She went light-headed, her vision narrowing.

Her showstopper gowns were destroyed. They couldn't be salvaged. Not a chance.

She drew in short, shallow breaths.

You don't have time for a panic attack. She forced

herself to rally. *It's only three dresses.* The others might be okay. She could still show twenty-two dresses. She dropped to a crouch, and the world spun and teetered. She blinked away the wall of tears, fingering the sheer organza with handmade petals that overlaid her favorite gown.

A hand came down on her shoulder with a firm grip. "Knox?" Gray knelt beside her, wearing nothing but bright blue board shorts. He smelled of coconut oil and ocean breeze. She could even see a trace of dried salt on his skin.

It was enough—the destruction of one year of her work—she didn't need *him*, of all people, compounding it. "Just…give me a second." Some of these could be salvaged. *Right?* She could fix anything. But no matter how hard she blinked, the room was still a blur. It made her frantic, so she swiped at her eyes. She needed to see, to assess, but the damn tears wouldn't go away.

There's still some fabric left. Plenty of embellishments.

I can fix anything.

The fist gripping her throat eased. She drew in a deep, calming breath. First, she had to get these people out of here. She couldn't think with them in her living room. She'd assess the damage the minute they left.

It'll be fine. Promise.

Everything felt surreal. The Jeep in the middle of her living room, the glorious dresses she'd hand-sewn lying beneath it, and…Gray Bowie right here talking to her. Especially since he looked so much bigger, broader, more masculine than the eighteen-year-old boy she remembered. The only thing that remained the same were his startlingly blue eyes.

But, holy cow, with his thick, powerful muscles, bronze skin covered in ink, shoulder-length dark hair that curled at his neck, and a strong jaw covered in scruff, he'd turned into every woman's bad boy fantasy come to life.

"What is all this?" Gray jerked his chin toward the mass of white, blush, lavender and a blue so pale it looked gossamer.

She tried to hide the panic from her voice. "Wedding gowns." Assaulted by a tumult of unwelcome emotions, she stood up in a rush. She needed him—all of them—gone. "You—"

"Wait, we ran over your wedding dress?" Amelia sounded horrified.

"Not mine. I'm a designer. I've got a show in six weeks." *Six weeks.*

But Martine is coming on Monday.

Oh, God. She couldn't fix this much destruction in three days.

Wrong. She would, because the alternative was unthinkable.

"Fuck," one of the guys drew out the word like a balloon leaking air.

"Well," Gray said. "Let's get this Jeep out of here and see what we've got."

A rush of energy had her practically tackling him. "Absolutely not. Don't move anything. I have to see what I can salvage before we back over the dresses."

"Good point." He turned to his friends. "Guys, let's pick up whatever—"

"No." They all froze at her sharp tone. "I need you to go outside and wait for the paramedics." At their perplexed expression, she explained, "There are beads and crystals and panels of lace…fine details that I need to handle on my own." Material created from Luc's heritage atelier and fabric mill. Nothing she could ever recreate.

Okay, that's enough. She had to stop catastrophizing. *You can't fix anything if you're freaking out.*

"We can at least pick up the dresses," Gray said. "Get them out of the dust."

The careless son of a billionaire, who spent his life chasing waves and snowstorms, Gray couldn't begin to understand that he'd destroyed not only a year's worth of work but the launch of her career.

"No. Please…just leave." No matter how in control she needed to be, nothing could stop the trembling from deep within. "I have until Monday to make it look like your Jeep didn't mow down my gowns." At their stunned expressions, she eased back. "I'm sorry, but this is my first show, and I've got the backing of the biggest bridal designer in the world. I swear to God, I don't want to lose it in front of you guys, but this is my life's work, so please, please, just go. I have to figure things out."

"Yeah, sure," one of the guys said. "Come on." Two of them headed out across the wreckage.

Amelia stood there, slack-jawed, looking destroyed. "I'm so sorry. I…" Her jaw snapped shut. She reached into the Jeep and dragged out a slate gray leather messenger bag.

A five-hundred-dollar Longchamp. It looked totally out of place with these laid-back surfers.

The woman pulled out a crumpled receipt and wrote something on it. "I'm Amelia Webber. This is my contact information. I'll pay for all the repairs. That includes your house, supplies, and whatever your dresses need." With a plea in her eyes, she said. "Anything I can do to help, I'll do it. I'm so sorry." She stood there a moment, looking helpless, and then turned and moved carefully out into the bright sunshine.

Only Gray remained. Stroking his scruff, he examined the tires. "I'm sure the car's got a jack. Instead of backing out over them, we can jack it up and let you get the dresses out." He turned those bright blue eyes on her, and a shudder of recognition traveled through her. "That sound good?"

God, she couldn't stop shaking. This time, when her phone vibrated, she glanced at the screen. How many times had Luc called? She knew he was going out of his mind with worry, but she couldn't talk to him until she had a handle on the situation.

With the others in the front yard, huddled together and talking quietly, and Gray opening the back of the Jeep and leaning inside, she had a moment to really take in the damage.

Destruction.

Dust swirled in the slanted morning sunlight, and sparkling glass, beads, and crystals lay scattered across the wood floor. A fine layer of debris covered the dresses heaped on the kitchen table--dresses far too fragile to clean. The dresses under the Jeep were a total loss. The tires had shredded the delicate fabric. Luckily, the fender stopped right before the couch, saving the dresses draped over it. They were covered in particles from sheet rock, though. Picking it out would tear the delicate material. Still, she'd try. She had to try.

Gray slammed the trunk, wielding the tire iron like a trident. "Called for a tow. Better to have a professional lift it. He'll be here in twenty minutes."

She gave him a skeptical look. Nothing on the island moved that quickly.

He shrugged. "I know a guy."

Of course he did. Everyone loved the Bowie family. All

four brothers were elite athletes blessed with good looks, ridiculously cut bodies, and the kind of confidence that silenced conversations when they entered a room.

He looked at her a little too long—his expression revealing nothing—until a smile softened his features. "I can't believe you've been here a year, and I never ran into you."

Choosing a house to rent on this beach for her year-long seclusion hadn't been random. Both her ex-boyfriend and Gray's families had houses here, and she'd come with them on vacations for many years. She might have godawful memories of her hometown of Calamity Falls, Wyoming, but she had the best ones in this place. "I've been working."

"Right." A hand on his hip, like a marauding invader, Gray surveyed the living room. "I'm going to send the others back to the house. While we wait for the tow truck, we can take all these dresses"—he gestured to the kitchen table—"to the bedroom."

"Gray, I'm going to be dead honest with you. I'm about two seconds away from losing my shit. Literally. the only thing between me and a total meltdown is the absolute false hope that I can still somehow make my Monday deadline. So, I'd be really grateful if you'd leave right now and let me get a handle on this disaster. Can you do that for me, please?"

He stood there, this mountain of a man, with his potently masculine features and that same aura of confidence that had always allowed her to lean on him at the lowest points of her childhood. She knew what he wanted. To be her hero. To fix her problems. *That's our pattern.* He'd been the one—not the school, not her mom, not her ex—to knock her bullies into next week.

That pattern had ended the night of the prom, when he'd walked away from her. She'd vowed to never be anyone's pity project again.

Her phone's screen lit up again, and then, just to make him leave, she held it up. "This is my backer. I was talking to him when your friend drove into my living room, so he's going to want to know what happened. He's a total drama queen, and when I tell him, it's a very big possibility he'll cancel my show."

"Don't tell him."

"He hired me out of fashion school, included me with his family over the holidays, and backed my show even after I quit on him. I have to tell him." The adrenaline rush was subsiding, allowing the slow tide of fear to roll in. "He's sending someone on Monday to pack up the dresses and ship them. And, unless you have a superpower beyond being unnaturally good at everything you do, there's not a chance in hell I'm going to have…" She glanced around the room, making a quick count of the unaffected dresses. "More than ten dresses ready to go. And that's not enough for a show."

He stalked right up to her. "Trust me?"

She'd never known her father. Her mom was a good person whose lust for life meant a lot of lonely days and nights for Knox. Other than her ex and Gray, she'd had no friends growing up. And she still had few…okay, fine, no friends. So, it was safe to say, trust didn't come easily to her.

But she *had* trusted this man. "Not since the day you walked out and never looked back. Goodbye, Gray."

About the Author

Award-winning author Erika Kelly writes sexy and emotional small town romance. Married to the love of her life and raising four children, she lives in the southwest, drinks a lot of tea, and is always waiting for her cats to get off her keyboard.

https://www.erikakellybooks.com/

facebook.com/erikakellybooks
twitter.com/ErikaKellyBooks
instagram.com/erikakellyauthor
goodreads.com/Erika_Kelly
pinterest.com/erikakellybooks
amazon.com/Erika-Kelly
bookbub.com/authors/erika-kelly

Printed in Great Britain
by Amazon